A Story of Gylranor:

The Argom's Influence

J. G. Velez II

Illustrated by Ana Ristovska

www.gylranor.com

The Argom's Influence is a matter of fiction, and fiction only. To that end, the story, the characters, names of locations within the work's world, and everything in between are purely from the author's imagination.

GYLRANORIAN CALENDAR

SPRING

Sun's Light

Sun's Rain

Sun's Blessing

SUMMER

Aura's Centrum

Aura's Bounty

Aura's Gaze

AUTUMN

Star's Crossing

Star's Swelter

Star's Harvest

WINTER

Moon's Hailstone

Moon's Favoring

Moon's Slumber

CONTENTS

Barbatius
Sauron
Argoth
Darkwood
Oswacath
Zal'man
Tinith
Breia
Deserted Lands
Chel Emon
Slii Eslan
Ranoram
Masegene
Ni'shorus
Erade
Nell
Eleimor

Naros
Naros Archipelago
Hilrayn
Edelag
Edea
Uln Alzor
Insetia

CHAPTER ONE

THE SOLEMN HAND

Aura's Bounty

The Argom War, a conflict between the nation of Argoth and the many port cities situated along the western coasts of Eradell, has ravaged the continent far more than any who dwell in it realized, causing disruption to trade and their import and export services. Much damage fills these coastal cities, especially the great port capitol of Nell, Elbynshire.

Argoth, nestled on the continent of Saluron, is home to the Argoms, proficient magic users that are commonly referenced as having saber-tooth fangs that rest over their mouths when closed and large tails they also use in combat. Those who engage the Argoms in this war consists primarily of Neledar and Elves. Neledar are similar in appearance to that of Elves but are distinguished by their ears. Where Elves have pointed, long ears, Neledar have no point to speak of. The rounded earlobes commonly found in Dwarves or Barbs are not found in Neledar. Their lobes are pointed and curve upward; almost like a reciprocated Elvic ear.

For three years the Argom War has endured with no end in sight. Recently, things changed…After the mysterious murder of Neledarian Landseer Eloran Pinshot, a newly appointed Landseer succeeded him. She goes by Estith Elwerth, and drew the Violet Veil Accord, a ceasefire agreement with barely enough support from the Diet of Nell, Nell's governing body. Nell is home to the Neledar.

The details of the Accord decree the Argom War to continue no longer and allows the integration of Argoms into Neledarian society. Argoms haven't been allowed in Nell since the end of the War of the

Netherid in the Third Dawn of time. Netherids are beings similar in appearance to Argoms and do not dwell on Gylranor; they inhabit Nethermire, an underworld of Gylranor. The Nethermire is ruled by Orma, the Dark Primal, once part of the Pantheon of Gylranor, and cast out for his treachery in the Beginning, a time when Gylranor was in its infancy.

With the Argoms' unfair return, they have started a period known as the Argom Influence. Many Nellians have voiced their protest with many more being forcefully silenced.

This Argom intimidation caused large numbers of Nellians to greatly diminish their want to be heard, and far fewer acting upon it until now…

Far in the corners of the Greater Anloth region in Nell sat a little town. Those who dwell in this little town can easily tell you that Frodrir doesn't experience much mayhem. Although in times past, it's known a battle or two. Aside from the bustling market square, Frodrir experiences calm days.

Following one of the walkways out of the market square will take you to a grassy road connecting the outer properties of Frodrir. One of these properties was Ogthorne Cottage: a modest cottage of two stories clothed in vines along one wall with a walkway to the front door neatly lined with flora. This cottage, and its neighbor across the grassy road, were built with their backs against natural earthen mounds.

Up the walkway two Neledar, one with a shaved head and a black beard resembling that of a Dwarf's, and the other taller with short black hair, slowly made their way to the cottage's front door.

"I like that one," said the taller Neledar.

"Dunn gave it to me," said the other, moving the ring on his eyebrow that the taller of the two complimented. "Sirien, do you think the others will come?"

"I don't see why not, Nerod," said Sirien Ogthorne. "By the way, I am eternally grateful that you've chosen to do this."

"How could I not?" said Nerod, placing his hand on Sirien's shoulder. "You're my best friend, and I could not be more honored than now. Besides, Astronitus, really does know how to lay it on thick."

Sirien chortled.

"Yes, my dad really does, doesn't he?"

"Cornered me in the Felefor Depository to give a speech about how several groups like this one have come and failed trying to thwart various enemies," said Nerod. "Talked about the Hilt, the Defenders Guild, the Society of Rosnios, and vagrant cults like the Exeri and Hunger Cult. Then those who simply disappeared overnight without a single trace like the Order of the Two Branches or the Guild of Guardians. Not sure if their ends were supposed to resonate well in me, but it did. Gave me hope for a new success."

Inside the little cottage, they were met by a wooden spiral staircase that led to the top floor. They could hear thumping coming from up there, which they assumed to be Astronitus Ogthorne, Sirien's father.

"This way," called Sirien.

"Again, I cannot begin to express how sorry I am for her death," said Nerod, as he entered the room connected to the kitchen.

"I know you are," said Sirien kindly, taking a seat at the only long table in the hall. "I am truly appreciative of it. Therefore, we continue the fight started two years ago. To help and avenge those we have lost by their touch. I nearly disbanded the Solemn Hand after my mum's death—"

After the mixture of Argoms into Neledarian society following the Violet Veil Accord, more and more citizens of Nell, especially those not of Argom blood, have been exposed to intimidation tactics both verbally and physically. Many found themselves being the victim in cruel and senseless pranks bestowed upon them by the Argoms. Thus, the Solemn Hand came to be—to repel the nastiness of the Argoms.

The Solemn Hand operates mainly in Nell from this little town but don't close their ranks to any who are not Neledar, as the Argoms harming Nell is part of a larger scale that will eventually affect all. To avoid being discovered or talked about, Sirien limited the amount of people who were willing to join. He needed to be sure he could trust those who enter his organization.

"—but it was by my dad's push and the memories I have of my mother's that I did not."

"Boys!"

A lanky man with snowy grey hair, a mustache, and dressed in green robes had entered the hall. He looked very excited at the sight of them and proceeded to sit next to his son.

"Astronitus," said Nerod, rather surprised, "how did you make it back from the Depository before I did?"

"Frodrir is a tiny town, isn't it?" said Astronitus. "Where are the others?"

"On their way…hopefully," said Sirien. "Still no word from them, I assume?"

"Afraid not," said Astronitus, looking sullen now, as if the very question coming from Sirien's mouth spelled doom for them all. "I've tried endlessly to convince Rufious and Elnius to make a return, but they outright refuse. Keep giving excuses about their careers and what not. I know that's not it. Your mother's death really took a toll on them. They were close and I don't blame them for wanting no part in the continuation of this order."

"Elnius just lives across the road," said Sirien. "Why can't we—?"

"Don't even think it," cautioned Astronitus. The faint sound of a knock coming at the door saved Astronitus from having to reiterate his stance to Sirien. Before he opened the door, he said, "We've spoken of this already."

Astronitus welcomed whoever was at the door joyfully. The tallest of the two at the door, a woman with golden skin and cream-colored vestments, and about three feet taller than Astronitus, extended her arm out. The man beside the woman, clothed in leathery, thick armor, similar in height, though slightly shorter, also extended a greeting.

"I'm sorry, but I have forgotten your names," said Astronitus.

"Yliki Dranicc," said the woman. "At your service. I'm a shaman, hailing from Edea."

"Goodness gracious, really? Splendid! One of my dearest and oldest friends too hails from Edea. You'll meet her, as she will be in attendance."

"If you refer to Cosmera Rodriys, then we have met."

"Marvelous!"

"Joric Hasmius, sir," said the pink-skinned man next to Yliki.

"Ah, yes, Sirien has told me about your exploits. Quite an impressive number of Argom deaths you have beneath that girdle of yours."

Joric gave off a little smile, as though embarrassed, and nodded.

"Good to see you both," said Sirien, inviting them to sit wherever they would like. "And happy you made it out here. I hope your journeys were uneventful."

"Not bad," said Yliki. "Can't really speak about his travels from Barbatius."

"Just fine," said Joric.

Before long, Sirien introduced them both to his best friend Nerod Nilius, and not long after that the remaining members of the Solemn Hand were also present. Astronitus and the Edeic woman, who was as old as he was, embraced tightly. Behind them patiently waited a Dwarf with a long yellow beard and thick rings hanging from his ears for his turn to greet Astronitus. The last two behind them were Neledar of brown skin just like Sirien. One had a brown cape with a cowl and walnut hair while the other had light black hair and held a staff in his left hand.

"Sirien, we've arrived!" said the golden-skinned woman.

"Hullo, Cosmera," said Sirien, jumping to his feet.

Once introductions were out of the way and everyone pleasantly seated, Sirien and Astronitus addressed the group.

"If I could have your attention everyone," said Astronitus, moving his hands down in a flat motion. "Before we get this little gathering underway, I would just like to thank each and everyone of you from Sirien and I. Though, there is much work to be done, with our growing ranks, we will achieve it!"

"Here. Here," said the Dwarf, thumping the table in agreement.

"Thank you, Thiurwold, said Sirien. "As I mentioned previously, there is no business today. Take the time to get to know those new faces among us."

With a motion of Astronitus's hand, as if he were grabbing the air, several bottles of wine and goblets floated their way onto the table. No food could be seen, but no one of them complained regarding that matter. They were far too happy only having the wine.

"Thought I wasn't going to make it," said the Neledar with the brown cape and cowl, as he approached Sirien and Nerod.

"Marandir Dibble!" said Sirien. "I'll admit I thought the same."

"Don't see your brother around? Is he coming?"

"You know Percivine isn't ready to know just yet," replied Sirien.

"Hold," said Nerod. "You intend to involve Percivine in all this?"

"That is the plan, yes."

"You're not going to spring it on him in some rash manner, are you?" asked Marandir. "You're prone—"

Sirien cancelled out Marandir's voice briefly to think about his little brother. Though, it is not his intention to simply toss Percivine into the mix of the Solemn Hand's business, it is his intention to gradually bring him into the order. But he cannot address the future, or what might happen in the future, because he is not a Fenemerys, someone with the ability to receive visions of future events. So, what might come will have to be dealt with when it arrives.

"You're sure he won't just pop in on a moment's notice?" said Nerod.

"Sure of it," said Sirien. "He's recently gotten an apprenticeship scribbling for the *Frodrian Fox*. He'll be too immersed in his words to even bother coming home."

Everyone in the room appeared to be enjoying themselves. To many it was an eternity ago the last time they partook in a party like this. Several of them had felt the devastating impact of the murder of Sirien's mother, which left the Solemn Hand in pieces.

Astronitus constantly made his rounds to everyone in the room pouring more and more wine into their goblets.

"Drink up, all!" he said, a bit disoriented at this point. "It's a rather hot Aura's Bounty day, and luckily for *you*, the wine has been nicely chilled!"

While they all drank, they were subjected to a pompous speech by Thiurwold the Dwarf, droning on about his current campaign to be the next Minister of War for Uln Alzor, the Dwarvic lands.

Sirien looked around at everybody and felt a great deal of warmth, but admittedly was unsure if the drink had anything to do with this warm sensation. As he continued to wonder this, the Neledar holding a staff greeted Sirien again.

"Been a while, hasn't it?" he said.

"Quite a while, Pevarius," said Sirien, and enlarged his nostrils due to a strange smell. "Do you smell…smoke?"

"Oh right," said Nerod, "I smell it too."

Pevarius cleared his throat obnoxiously.

"Can't smell a thing," he said. "Must be my allergetic response to these summer days. Well, enjoy the rest of the gathering."

Sirien apologized to Nerod regarding the consistent interruptions from the other members. Nerod understood. Being Leader of the Solemn

Hand has its responsibilities, and this is one of them. Sirien hoped he could spend more time telling Nerod about the order and what their next steps would be. He also didn't want Nerod to be left alone. What he knows as commonplace, coming into a world like his can be overwhelming for another like Nerod.

"Really, there's no need," he told Sirien. "I do, after all, report to Astronitus, so I am used to this."

"Listen, Sirien," said Marandir, lowering his voice.

"Marandir!" said Siren, startled. "I nearly forgot you were still standing there."

"There's something I need to tell you. Things might turn in our favor sooner than we think."

"Care to elaborate?"

"Not more than an hour ago, I received word from a Captain Alemidili Thooch that she's taking Eoden Pinch on a secret voyage to the Naros Archipelago in search of some scepter called Vel—"

"Forgive my ignorance," said Nerod, "but who's Eoden Pinch?"

"General of the Army of Nell," said Marandir. "Apparently, they believe there is some sort of weapon hidden somewhere on the main isle that could change the tide of things."

"And they're certain?" asked Sirien hopefully.

"I'm assuming so. Then again leads like this appear all over. But make no mistake, if they don't find this so-called weapon, they will find Orcs ready to confront them. My contact confirmed zanilium plantations using the Wood-Dwelling Dwarves as their personal slaves."

"Absolutely disgusting," said Nerod, pinching the bridge of his nose with his eyes closed, "that something like slavery still exists this day in age!"

"The Orcs know no boundaries," said Marandir. "What's worse, I have a suspicion all that is connected to what's happening here."

"A good suspicion," said Sirien, "but we must be careful. We know Orcs are the natural allies of the Argoms, yet Nell houses far fewer Orcs than Argoms considering the latest events."

Sirien appreciated the information Marandir shared with him. However, he was not all too keen on coming to such a conclusion just yet. As Leader of the Solemn Hand, he needed to make sure all this stood in truth and not mere rumor. He hesitated to put the lives of those he cared for in jeopardy based on suspicion.

"It's no coincidence that these plantations sprouted around the same time Landseer Elwerth signed the Violet Veil Accord. I attended that ceremony and let me tell you that I did not see the Out and In Secretaries there, nor anyone from the Royal Family, but of course Elwerth's newest, and only of her Support Staff I might add, Talus the Dark, was. Why would he simply turn away from his ruling duties of Argoth?"

Talus the Dark, the infamous leader of the Argoms, now serves in a very high position in Nell, and anyone would wonder why an Argom, who holds the entire Argom race in the palm of his clawed hands, would ever dream of leaving that behind. But Talus is no fool.

With no signs of the In and Out Secretaries and the Royal Family falling silent, things have taken a dark turn. The In Secretary dealt with the home affairs of Nell while the Out Secretary dealt in all matters foreign. With Talus the Dark being the sole member of Elwerth's Support Staff, it should be no surprise Marandir has this distrust of the present state of things. If Talus the Dark is truly overseeing the roles of the In and Out Offices, all matters to do with Nell are only going to get worse.

CHAPTER TWO

THE MEETING OF THREE

Sun's Rain — Three Years Later

The splashing footfalls echoed through the misty forest. With every step the Neledar gasped for air and glanced back at something following him. A barrage icy bolts of magic shot passed the man's head; he ducked, missing them by centimeters at best. He kept running, not caring for the pains in his feet.

The Argom was approaching fast, hardly breaking a sweat, using his legs and clawed feet to give chase. But the Neledarian man did not give in to the Argom's petulant attacks. He leapt over fallen trees and over their enormous roots.

"I have nothing you want!" shouted the man, as he ran.

The Argom paid no attention to the Neledar's whimpering. The Argom kept shooting the white icy bolts from the tips of his fingers, each paired with sharp, crusty, black pointed nails, at the poor man, who dodged so quickly that he could almost twist his back in a full circle.

"Please! *Please!*" begged the Neledar, falling on his back and beginning to conjure small, yellow transparent magical shields, the Argom bashing through them with ease with his thick hands.

"Where are you to go now, Percivine Ogthorne?" said the Argom, glaring into Percivine's dark brown eyes. "If you choose to run again, this will only anger Lord Bartholev more. *Now—STOP!*"

Behind them, through the distant mists, an orange glow appeared. Percivine, on his back still, rolled the back of his skull on the muddy, wet floor so he could see, difficult through the pouring rain, where this glow came from. Something or someone had followed them both. The Argom ignored this to return to his task. At last, victory seemed only inches away for the Argom. Instead of casting another spell at Percivine, the Argom readied his sharp fingernails to stab the scared Neledar in the throat. Percivine clenched his left fist, swung at the Argom, and hit one of the fangs sticking out of the Argom's mouth. The Argom fell in the direction he had been hit, which gave Percivine just enough time to run again.

The Argom shook his head to get rid of the disorientation Percivine's fist gave him. He quickly cast one last bolt at the Neledar before he could no longer be visible in the rain. The bolt hit the Percivine's right foot. He toppled over, his cheek smacking the ground, while his right foot stayed frozen to the ground; his right leg bent down along with the rest of his body. He let out a screech of pain.

"W-what do you want?" asked Percivine, not trying to look into the Argom's burgundy, fanged face.

"Sirien Ogthorne, where did he go?"

"*I don't know!*"

The orange light grew closer…

"What are the whereabouts on your filthy brother?"

"I-I don't know!" exclaimed Percivine. "I haven't a clue!"

The Argom hit Percivine's right cheek bone, the same cheek he hit earlier on the ground, with his tail. "Lies!" spat the Argom. "Were you not with him just now?"

"I…I was not!"

"I've had enough of your—"

The Argom was beginning to cast his spell when another person's voice broke in.

"Enough, Tharacar," said the voice. "Enough. What are you doing to this poor Neledar?"

"He will not comply, Lord Bartholev," said the Argom anxiously. "He will not tell where his brother has gone to."

"Listen to me!" said Percivine. "Yes, I was with him, but I did not know we were to be separated. He told me to run this way. I don't know where he is, and if I did, I would never tell *you* where it is he's gone."

The ugliness of Bartholev greatly exposed itself more to Percivine as he bent down beside him. The man, who is not Neledar, had terrible cracks all over his pale grey face, dark circles around his orange eyes, and yellowed teeth covered by small lips. Percivine avoided looking into Bartholev's eyes, so he chose to investigate the epaulets resting on his shoulders over the charcoal-colored robes he wore.

"So, you say you don't know where *your* own brother is?" said the man. "How could that be?"

"I don't know!"

"I will ask you once more," said Bartholev, "tell me where your brother is?"

"I...don't...know!"

The Argom swiftly hit Percivine's face again. Blood now trickled down from a cut created by Tharacar's fist. Bartholev waved the Argom down.

"Answer the question," he said, "and your life will be spared, Percivine Ogthorne."

"*I don't know!*" said Percivine, more annoyed than scared.

"Very well," said the man softly, "I will not ask again. You've had your chance to answer, and now you will suffer for your insolence." He turned to Tharacar. "Do to him what you will."

Bartholev now began to turn away. Tharacar, thrilled at this glorious opportunity to kill, began to ready his magical attack. Just as he was going to unleash it square in Percivine's face, a conjured beam of sky blue struck Tharacar, sending him flying into a large tree, shattering his neck, and killing him instantly.

Percivine was frightened and bewildered. He wanted to know where the shot came from, but spent no time worrying about it. He found a sharp rock next to him and shattered the ice holding his foot. He got to his feet, turned, and began to run.

"Not so fast!" yelled Bartholev. He cast a spell at Percivine, and as quickly as it was cast, mysterious glowing red shapes appeared on the ground. The spell somehow dove into the shapes and both the shapes and magic vanished. "Runes? Clever! Show yourself!"

From nearby bushes, Bartholev could see them moving. He waited cautiously, and, at last, a figure walked out from behind them: an Elf with blackish hair and pale olive skin.

Bartholev laughed. "Looks like I'll be killing the both of you today."

"You can try," said the Elf. "But I won't allow it."

"Allow it?" said the man. "There is nothing to *allow*. You have interfered with the wrong person. This isn't your fight. Now run along like a good Elf before I kill you."

"Such big words for such a *small* man," said the Elf.

Bartholev grew angry. He gritted his teeth and began shooting spells from each of his hands at the Elf, the glowing runes eating up what came his way. Having had enough of Bartholev's foolery, the Elf conjured one final attack. One of the runes floated in front of the Elf and positioned itself to face Bartholev. The same sky-blue beam that killed Tharacar hit Bartholev, shooting him backwards.

Percivine headed towards the Elf who remained watching the spot where the man had been.

"W-who are you?" asked Percivine.

"There's no time for that now!" said the Elf. "We must escape while we still can!"

"*Who was that?*" he asked, panting deeply.

The Elf took off sprinting, with Percivine tailing behind.

"Are—you—going to—tell me—who—that is?" called Percivine, as they ran.

"Works for the Divination—Administration," replied the Elf. "*Their* side and is after your brother. Obviously, he'll stop at nothing!"

"So generally, he—decides to come—after me?" Percivine said, unable to catch his breath. "Makes—plenty of sense!"

"They know you're his brother. He is wanted by—the Administration. They'll get to you first before they get to him!"

"Why are they after my brother? What has he done? And who are *you* if I may ask?"

"I will explain this all to you later," said the Elf. "But first we must leave. Maradine Forest isn't safe at the moment. There's an ancient shrine of my people at the edge of the forest. We must get there, and quickly."

Choices were limited. Percivine could see no other feasible ways to escape the forest, so he didn't bother asking anymore questions. The Elf appeared to know what he was doing and where he was going.

The mist was not lessening, growing thicker as they headed towards the edge of the forest. Still dazed from the attack, Percivine wondered if it was just his imagination.

"Do you think we'd be able to find a unicorn in here?" Percivine asked the quiet Elf. "This is Ni'shorus after all, and my brother told me that unicorns are native to these Elvic parts."

"You won't find any in here," remarked the Elf, pushing ahead. "They're common mainly in the mountains."

The answer was subtle, without feel. Percivine tried to break the awkward silence between the two but thought it best not to say a word until they reached the shrine.

Why would anyone want to be after Sirien? he thought. He was just a regular person. He'd have never known his brother to put his nose somewhere it does not belong. Several uneasy questions nagged him, questions he didn't voice.

At last, he could see the mists beginning to rise. They were approaching the edge of the forest. In no time at all, Percivine could see a statue of an Elvic man in a small glade, with a marble archway over his head. The statue of the Elf had one hand clutched to his heart, the other holding a sword pointed at the ground.

"A lovely statue," said Percivine inspecting it closely. "Da'thanis, correct?"

The Elf raised his eyebrows, surprised that an outsider such as Percivine knew the identity of the sculpture.

"Sirien was often the traveler," said Percivine, "and would on occasion take me along. I was very young the last time I was here. Didn't realize this place was the same as the one my leg just got injured in."

The Elf bent on one knee and bowed his head in respect. He stood up.

"As you know, apparently," said the Elf, "this is Da'thanis, the Elf who slayed the Netherid demon we know as Karxas. This is where many believe he is buried…" The Elf pointed at the sword in Da'thanis's hand. "That's Elloc, the sword that slew Karxas during the War of the Netherid."

"And is it?"

"No one is really sure."

The Elf now pulled out a Wayorb, a spherical object used to communicate and meet with others. It began to glow as another voice spoke through it.

"You have him?" the voice asked.

"I do," said the Elf. "Ready the portal."

A door-like portal appeared, and at once they stepped through it. They landed in the middle of a forked dirt path.

"The left path takes us to Xerian where we can replenish ourselves, and the right path takes us to Borgsbury."

"We're in Nell?" asked Percivine. "Frodrir's not far from Borgsbury! I must get to my home at once! My dad will be worried!"

"No!" said the Elf. "It's too dangerous. We must go to Xerian. Now follow me."

Percivine felt like a child. This Elf was telling him what to do slightly more often than his brother ever had. Once again, he had no choice but to follow the Elf.

After about fifteen minutes down the path, they could see a village up ahead.

"We need to find a tavern," said Percivine. "I'm starved and rather parched."

"That is the plan," said the Elf.

The village of Xerian was still and peaceful. The hour was late, and the walkways were empty, and most shops closed. They walked a little further into the village. Percivine could see a tavern ahead, its windows aglow.

"There," he said. "That spot looks good enough."

"It'll have to do…for now," said the Elf darkly.

Once they entered the tavern, many eyes were cast upon them. To Percivine's left, a hooded figure sat quietly in a corner by the tavern window, slowly following them as they sat at a table close to the bar area of the tavern. An old, bearded barman approached them.

"Welcome to *Malebane's Tavern*," the old Neledar said. "The name's Zernobus Malebane, proud owner of this here watering hole. What will it be, lads?"

"Morgs Ale for me," said Percivine.

"Camel flask," said the Elf.

"Very good," said Zernobus. "Your drinks will arrive shortly."

Percivine nodded. He looked slowly back at the corner where the hooded figure sat, who turned away once Percivine met his eyes.

"I need to know: who are you?" Percivine asked.

Zernobus placed the drinks in front of them and went back to polishing old beer mugs behind the counter.

The Elf picked up his camel flask, took a large drink of it, and said, "Why do you need to know?"

"*Why do I need to know?*" Percivne huffed. "Sirien is my brother! If he's done something wrong, then I must know…Funny how you seem to know my brother, even though I haven't the slightest idea who the hell you are! And another thing, how did you know where to find me? Have you been following me?"

"I know you have…concerns," said the Elf, looking around at the eyes watching him. He paused to look at the figure in the corner, then returned his attention to Percivine.

"Quit toying with me, Elf," said Percivine. "Tell me what you know. At least tell me your name."

The Elf took another large gulp of his Camel Flask. "Faruin Abrandil is my name," he said.

"Now tell me, *Faruin*, what's all this about?"

Faruin moved his green eyes up and down while looking at the figure.

"Has Sirien told you anything…anything different lately?"

"No," said Percivine. "Not that I can remember, however. Why?"

"If there ever was a time when you were in danger your brother asked me to look over you and tell you what you need to know," said Faruin. "Have you ever heard of a secret society called the Solemn Hand?"

Percivine looked puzzled. "I think my brother's mentioned it once before. What's that got to do with anything?"

"It has everything to do with it," said Faruin. "You see—"

"Don't tell me all this time Sirien's been a part of that!" said Percivine.

"In a matter of speaking, yes." Faruin finished the last of his Camel Flask. "Shortly before your mishap in Maradine, Sirien contacted me by Wayorb to watch over you in case things got a little…messy, which they did."

"I don't need protection. I'm not a child."

"Yes, you certainly showed that in the forest," marked Faruin. "I am here on your brother's orders, so I kindly ask you to allow me to be with you, until the time is necessary for us to separate."

"On my brother's orders?" he said. "Who is my brother to be giving *you* orders?"

Faruin cleared his throat, glanced at the corner figure again, and looked back at Percivine.

"Why do you keep looking at that man in the corner?" Percivine asked. "He seems to be up to no good."

"Your brother is Leader of the Solemn Hand."

"I—" Percivine's jaw dropped. "W-what did you say?"

"You heard me," said Faruin, pushing aside his empty bottle of Camel Flask.

"How is this possible?"

"Five years ago, your brother and a certain few select individuals decided to secretly fight off the Argoms on their own," said Faruin. "The Violet Veil Accord has been disastrous to say the least. Unanimously, they chose Sirien to be the rightful Leader of the Hand. It began with the Original Seven, a titled coined by Sirien. They were: your brother, of course, Cosmera Rodriys—a healer from Edea; Elnius Bashh; Marandir Dibble, father of renowned author, Averwyn Dibble; there was Rufious Meed, a Dwarf no longer part of the Solemn Hand; Pevarius Garcinius, and another Dwarf by the name of Thiurwold Galon, now the Uln Alzor Minister of War. Over time, the Hand lost members and gained new ones. I've only become part of the Hand not more than a year and a half ago.

"That man in the forest you had the pleasure of meeting is known as Bartholev, whose name you know by now, and is on the hunt for your brother. The Argoms received word, none of us know how, that Sirien is the true founder and Leader of the Hand, and therefore they want him dead in order for the Hand to finally stop meddling with their plans. Sirien is now the most wanted man in all of Nell."

The brown skin of Percivine's face grew dangerously pale. He could no longer feel his fingers, and found moving his legs to be a very difficult process.

"Percivine?"

"That's why they were after us?"

"Yes," said Faruin. "They know you are his brother, so that makes you next in line to be just as deadly to their plans as Sirien. The Solemn Hand has been one of the few to have the courage to stand in the way of the Argoms' plans."

"But I have nothing to do with this!"

"You do now," Faruin said. "Your brother sends his *greatest* apology for this mess he's left you."

"I wish I could hear this from him…" The color started returning to his face. "Where is he now?"

"For the sake of his safety, and the safety of our own, he refused to tell anyone."

"But I'm his brother, I should know!" snapped Percivine.

"For that same reason, he did not say where he was to go," said Faruin kindly.

How could his own brother do this to him? Did his father know about all this? Percivine was all too confused and upset with his brother for holding this secret from him. He had never liked secrets. Like before, he had no choice but to trust this Elf before him. As far as he knew, Faruin had not steered him wrong.

"So…what do we do now?" Percivine asked. He just realized he'd not yet touched his Morgs Ale.

"Wait a second," said Faruin. "Do you mind if I drink this?"

"By all means," said Percivine, feeling ill to his stomach. "What are we waiting for?"

The solemn figure in the corner walked over to Percivine and Faruin in their robes of darkened yellow and green. He removed the hood, revealing a black-skinned face with rugged silver hair. The hair did not resemble the color of Astronitus's hair; it had a decent shine to it.

"Not very bright heading to someone in the way you just did," said Percivine.

"Is this him?" asked the Neledar.

"He is," said Faruin, finishing the last of Percivine's ale.

Percivine looked at them both, unsure as to what was about to occur before him. But much had happened already, such that normalities were not expected from where he stood.

"Oh no…Let me guess, somehow the two of you know each other, yes? Of course, I should have seen this from the start," he went on grumpily. "My brother has left me playing to solve the riddles of this maze. So now, I must guess who you are. Is that correct?"

"Almost," said the Neledarian man darkly. "You won't have to guess for I will tell you who I am. The name's Seleborn Alveroth, Warlock, member of the Solemn Hand, and trusted friend to your brother, and this here Elf."

"Of course, you are," muttered Percivine. "I suppose no introductions are necessary, for you must know who I am."

"I do."

"*Splendid!*" remarked Percivine, with a roll of his eyes.

"Come," said Seleborn. "We must leave this place. There are too many wandering eyes here. Thank you, Zernobus, for your hospitality."

"You're most certainly welcome, lad. Come back soon."

Seleborn gestured for Percivine and Faruin to head to the door. He left three silver coins on the table, looked around at the shady figures watching him, and made his way out.

"This way," said Seleborn, emerging outside.

"We're not going to Frodrir?" asked Percivine.

"Whatever for?"

"To go home, obviously!" said Percivine. "I need to know that my father is all right!"

Seleborn leaned in close to Percivine's face. "You are the second most wanted man by the Divination Administration. What makes you think they will not look for you there first?"

"How could that be?" said Percivine. "Do *you* honestly think an Argom will just prance right on into Frodrir?"

Seleborn sighed, and chuckled. "You are aware of the Violet Veil Accord, are you not?"

"Of...course," Percivine said.

"Then you should know that Argoms are quite common around here these days."

"These Argoms have allies who are shapeshifters," said Faruin. "It is very easy for them to get the shape of any Neledar, Elf, Dwarf, Troll—you name it! They can easily *prance* into any setting they want, undisturbed, and very dangerous."

"They wouldn't dare cause a disturbance though," said Seleborn. "Those of us who use magic can fend for ourselves if the Argoms did send any of their shapeshifters. I know your father, Percivine, and he is one of the greatest conjurers I've crossed paths with. He will be just fine."

"Yes, but he's aged!" said Percivine.

"We don't have time to discuss this now," added Seleborn, looking all around him as he had done in the tavern. "It's dark out, and we don't know who could be lurking about. This way."

Without saying a word, Percivine followed Seleborn and Faruin. This was all far more than he could have ever expected of his brother. In such a short time, he's discovered secrets about his brother that he'd never once come close to unfolding. All he could do now was stop wondering what his brother was doing and focus on where they were going now.

Not too far down the town's road, they came upon a villa smaller than the rest, with smoke issuing from the chimney.

"Whose home is this?" asked Percivine.

"A Dwarf's," replied Seleborn. "An old friend of your mother's…"

The villa differed from the rest: grass acted as the home's roof, and the walls were made of stone, with a thick pine door in the center. Many small plants and flowers decorated the home's surrounding area, and gave off faint light against the dark.

Seleborn knocked three times.

"*Go away!*" said a voice from behind the door.

"Open the door, Rufious," said Seleborn.

"I will not!" said the Dwarf called Rufious. "Who goes there?"

"Seleborn Alveroth and company."

"Prove it…"

"Watch this," Seleborn told the others. He kindly asked Percivine and Faruin to take a few steps back. He began to chant something which Percivine could not understand: it sounded like a portal opening. The ground rumbled slightly.

"*AGHHHH!*" the Dwarf yelled. "Enough! *Enough!* I've seen enough! Take this blasted Netherid away from me! Aghh!"

Slowly, creakily, the thick door opened.

"Get inside!" said Rufious. "I hope nobody saw that or felt the ground shake!"

"Thank you," said Seleborn.

"That's sure to have alarmed someone, Seleborn," said Faruin. "We best watch ourselves."

"I've always hated when ye've done that," panted Rufious. "Take a seat there, and don't move until I return!"

The Dwarf quickly exited the dining hall, into a room next to the fireplace.

"Seleborn," asked Percivine, "why are we here?"

The Dwarf returned, rather heated. "How dare ye come into my home the way ye did? Do you know someone could have seen ye, and then wha'? I've lived a quiet life, don't ruin that for me now! Why have ye come to do this to me?"

"We need someone to guide us to Relthren," said Seleborn.

"And of the millions of Dwarves in this world, ye decide to come to my home at all hours of the bloody night?"

"Well…yes," said Seleborn, glancing at Rufious up and down.

"What're ye looking at?"

"Your beard…A lot shorter than Sirien described. I could swear he mentioned it was brown…not orange. And your jewelry, you've removed it all."

"I need not be recognized here, and how many times must I tell ye, I want nothing else to do with the Solemn Hand!"

"I haven't come here on matters to do with the Solemn Hand," said Seleborn. "I've come seeking the help of a friend, or are you no longer part of that either?"

"I—" Rufious did not know now what to say. He tugged slightly at his orange beard and looked out the stone window to his right. Faruin caught this.

"Sirien wishes to know about Denefra. Is she all right? And your children?"

Rufious glanced furtively out the glassless window. "For her safety and the safety of my children, I refused for her to let me know where she has gone."

"Makes sense," said Seleborn. "Rufious, I don't think you've met Faruin before."

"I have not. I've met none of ye before."

"Faruin Abrandil—Rufious Meed, member of the Original Seven," said Seleborn.

"*Ex-member*, Seleborn," said Rufious.

"Pleasure," said Faruin.

"And I believe yer Sirien's brother," Rufious told Percivine.

"How did you know?" The question, he thought, felt foolish. Everyone he'd met thus far seemed to already know who he was.

"You look very much like your brother," Rufious said, again looking out the window. "And a lot like Merinni…"

"Excuse me, but are you expecting someone?" Faruin said.

"Hm? Oh—well, I am." Faruin's question startled the Dwarf. "A friend of mine is supposed to come by. It never takes him this long to arrive at my home. He lives on the other side of the town plaza."

"How's work been treating you, Rufious?" said Seleborn.

"Jus' fine," the Dwarf said. "However, Landseer Elwerth doesn't seem like herself. And that horrid Argom that follows her like a duckling to its mum. Disgusting."

"What do you mean?" asked Seleborn.

"She's dark," Rufious muttered. "The seriousness of her face is not a healthy one. She never smiles. The scleras of her eyes are always bloodshot, and she speaks with a heavy mumble. Most of us are afraid to have her repeat what she says."

"Why?" asked Faruin.

""In her seriousness is a harsh tone of attitude. Her temperament snaps even with the slightest fault. The other day, Fernius Phinean—I'm sure ye remember him, as he was part of the Hand once—had misprinted on his report to the Landseer, and she barked so loud that the guards were alarmed. She dismissed him from work rationally, and ordered he not be paid for the remainder of the day."

"That's awful," said Seleborn. "And can't His Majesty do something about all this?"

"He's too busy being the King. He's left Elwerth to enjoy running the government of Nell. Yes, she sends him daily reports, but must never ask King Erelon for permission. He's granted her that liberty."

Rufious gave a loud huff, and stared blankly through the window.

"I'm sure he'll come soon," said Percivine.

Rufious blinked at Percivine, confused, and nodded his head in appreciation.

"Rufious," Seleborn said casually, "earlier what did you mean by she's 'dark'?"

"Oh that," he said, taking periodic glimpses through his windows. "Well, it's not as it was before."

"Can you elaborate? We've no time for riddles."

"Do you remember the color of Estith Elwerth's skin?"

"I daresay, I rarely paid attention to her—those—details, but I would assume an off-brown."

"Very much so," said Rufious. "Not the same anymore, is it? There's a taint about her now. Refuses any medical attention. Listens to no one about it. But her appearance certainly has grown more on the purple side of things…"

"Interesting…" Seleborn pondered exactly what Rufious had just said, though dared not indulge any theories just yet. His thinking was interrupted when he saw something through the window. "I think I just saw straw-colored hair pass by out there."

"Before I forget, Seleborn," said Rufious, withdrawing a letter from his jerkin, "take this. As a final promise to Sirien. The last bit of help I'll be giving the Solemn Hand."

A faint knocking prompted Rufious to rush to the door. Opening it revealed another Dwarf with long hair and beard. They all immediately saw light blood coming from the places his facial jewelry entered flesh.

"Frerus!" said Rufious. "I was beginning to think ye weren't going to show! What was the hold up about?"

The Dwarf called Frerus did not utter a word. Seleborn and Faruin looked at each other. Rufious invited the Dwarf in.

"Everyone, I would like ye to meet my colleague and dear friend, Frerus Fondunus. Frerus—this is Seleborn Alveroth" —Rufious pointed to the right— "Faruin Abrandil" —he gestured his hand to the middle— "and Percivine Ogthorne, brother to Sirien Ogthorne."

Still Frerus said nothing, just kept staring blankly at them. They could not avoid his shriveled, sunken eyes. Rufious stepped cautiously towards Frerus, and asked, "Are you all right?"

Frerus looked dazed and unaware altogether of where he was. It appeared also that his facial expression made them believe that the Dwarf was currently elsewhere. Rufious now stepped in front of Frerus to examine this empty look he gave them. Frerus was completely blocked off from their view.

Something strange had happened. Rufious was silent now. He calmly stared at Frerus with the same dazed look Frerus had. Frerus stepped back.

"Rufious?" said Seleborn.

Rufious turned his head slightly to them, smiled meekly, and toppled over, slamming his head on the table. This brought them from their seats. Frerus stood looking down at his friend.

"*Blood!*" said Percivine.

A sharp dagger jutted from Rufious's stomach.

"You're not Frerus!" said Seleborn. "What have you done to him?"

"I've killed the other Dwarf like I did this one," said Frerus. In the blink of an eye, Frerus took the form of an Elf, one resembling Faruin.

Without thought, Percivine threw magical bonds around the shapeshifter. He could not move.

"It's a shapeshifter!" said Faruin.

Faruin summoned green-glowing runes on the floor that made a barrier while Seleborn began casting powerful jagged killing spells that looked like lightning at the Faruin impostor, missing with each. Percivine began to shoot spells at the shapeshifter, as vainly at Seleborn's. After nearly destroying Rufious's home, the shapeshifter taunted them.

"Is that all you've got?"

"Piece of shite," said Seleborn wiping sweat and dirt from his face. He pulled the dagger from the dying Rufious, who screeched a little when he did so. He looked closely into the shapeshifter's eyes, then struck the dagger straight into its throat, killing it instantly. Percivine released his bondage spell, and the shapeshifter hit the floor with a crash. Seleborn bent next to Faruin, who tended to Rufious's wounds.

"He's lost too much blood," said Faruin. He began chanting something under his breath. "I've managed to hold the bleeding, but there is nothing that can prevent from this Argom poison from spreading throughout his body."

They heard now mumbles coming from the Dwarf's mouth. "Come…closer," he said.

Seleborn leaned in.

"What is it, old friend?"

"I…sorry…" Rufious coughed. The blood was now choking him. "*Follow the letter to the last detail!*"

Rufious's eyes now gazed blankly into the ceiling of the cold house. They knew what had happened. Seleborn closed his eyes. A small hatred filled his heart. He looked at the dead shapeshifter and kicked it in the face.

"I will dispose of its body," said Faruin. "I think you and Percivine should properly give Rufious a burial."

Seleborn knew that was all he could do.

CHAPTER THREE

THE JOURNEY EAST

The death of a Dwarf really stirred Percivine. He had never witnessed a death before, and preferred not to experience another. Faruin had returned after disposing of the shapeshifter's body. They covered Rufious's body in a white cloth Percivine had found in what he thought was the Dwarf's room. Percivine and Faruin each carried the body from one end to the other, and carefully placed the body into a pit Seleborn had dug. However Percivine felt, Seleborn looked worse. He could see the distraught in Seleborn's eyes. He might have not known Rufious personally, but it appeared Seleborn had some sort of connection with the Dwarf. Each, with a little help of magic, lifted piles of earth and grass to cover the peaceful body. Blood seeped through the sheet from the area Rufious has been stabbed. Percivine quickly covered the spot of blood before Seleborn noticed it.

Many piles of dirt finally covered the small body, until a slight mound erupted from the ground. Seleborn knelt before the grave, where he muttered the following words: "You were a dear friend and father, you will not be forgotten."

"Seleborn," said Faruin, "we must get going. Here are the instructions he left."

"He's in mourning, can't you see?" said Percivine, surprised at Faruin's behavior. "Give him a few moments for gods' sake."

"No, Percivine, he's right…"

Percivine blinked rapidly at Seleborn.

"He's…*what?*"

"If we linger any longer, someone will notice that he's dead, and begin to wonder," said Seleborn. "We will have to find our own way to Relthren. The Argoms haven't pushed as far as Uln Alzor…yet. The

Dwarves will offer us sanctuary if we seek it. But first, we must get supplies for the journey east. There's a little shop that's convenient enough for us."

Seleborn took one last look at the grave and realized something: no grave marker on the mound. He looked over the ground—until he saw an object lodged in the dirt, under the flowers by Rufious's home. It was a rock. He picked it up and placed it over the spot where the body lay.

As they turned the corner from the Dwarvic-style home, Seleborn looked back, remembering a time when he and Rufious shared a moment of peace.

They walked down the pathway that led to the small shops of the little town that reminded Percivine a lot of Frodrir. As it was nightfall, most were closed. Fortunately for them, the shop that Seleborn sought still welcomed customers. They entered. A lone large, bald Neledar sat behind the counter, head down and snoring. Seleborn looked at Faruin and Percivine.

"Ahem…"

The man seemed to be sleeping. Seleborn tried the gesture once more. "*Ahem!*"

The man jumped, nearly falling from the stool.

"Gods," the man said, pulling himself together. "Can't you see I'm sleeping here?"

"Your shop door is still open," said Seleborn, "so I assume you must be open."

"Well—yes…yes I am, h-how can I help you three tonight?"

"We have a journey to Relthren, and would like three outdoor sleeping quarters, if you don't mind," said Seleborn kindly.

"Relthren?" said the man. "What takes you there?"

"I believe that business is our own," said Faruin.

"Oh right! Of course! Of course!" said the man. "Let me introduce myself. The name's Birus. All your outdoor needs are met here for a fair price, of course. Three sleeping quarters coming right up, any in particular?"

"Basic, if you please," said Seleborn.

Birus opened a door behind the counter, and closed it. They could hear the stumble of objects in the back. After a few short moments, Birus returned with three *basic* sleeping quarters or tents.

"Let me ask a quick question," said Seleborn. "Why are you open so late?"

"I never close," said Birus. "There are many adventurers like yourselves, coming through here for an odd reason or another. When they are short on supplies, where do they go? Here. I make a well profit at times. You've just proven that right now. Anything else?"

"Healing Powder and Healing Strips," said Seleborn.

Once again, Birus went through the door behind the counter, made stumbling noises, and returned with their requested items.

Birus quickly muttered something under his breath, then said, "That'll be ten zarks and five torks. Consider it a fair price. You all look beat, and it's too late to be gaining much from you anyway. Come again soon."

Seleborn dropped the silver coins like he had done at *Malebane's Tavern* and exited the shop spirited. Percivine looked back at Birus. He could see him prop his head on his fist, and return to his uncomfortable rest.

"Charming shop owner, wouldn't you say?" said Percivine.

"Your humorous sarcasm is a delight at times like these," said Seleborn. "Now, we must walk to the far end of the town, and from there we make our journey east into Relthren."

They walked through a quiet Xerian. Percivine envied the bodies fast asleep in their warm beds. He couldn't seem to remember the feeling of resting comfortably without having to worry about staying alive. Things had so quickly turned from light to dark for him. In just a matter of moments, he had discovered something extraordinary about his brother that, given an eternity, he never would have guessed on his own.

"Where shall we camp for the night?" he asked Faruin and Seleborn.

Seleborn opened the letter Rufious handed him moments before his death and read it aloud.

Solemn Hand,

> *You've no time to waste. From where you stand, travel east about two miles until you reach the border of Edea. Beware: The Midir Desert is rather hot this time around, and vigorously cold at night. Take plenty of water. I'd suggest*

making camp just on its outskirts. Make no worry; the people of Edea are quite welcoming to outsiders, lest you drink from the Pools. Best to start early before sunrise.

Continue heading east, until you reach an oasis more commonly known as the Pools of Nordorth. Once again— DO NOT DRINK THE WATER. Do not stop!

Through the biting sands you will go, and beyond the Pools lies the Halls of Adelvald in the Helin Mountains. These mysterious halls will guide you to Clepham, home of the Sand Dwarves.

Advice: Cut through the dense woods of Nerim Forest. No sense in going round. Once clear of green, you will cross the River Relthren into the Ebsurwald Hinterlands. Travel these hinterlands until you see a dirt trail travelling north and south.

Follow it south around the small mountains, until you reach a drawbridge with two titanic statues of Dwarves at the foot. You have made it to Relthren.

P.S.
I hope the journey comes easily.

"Should I hand over my legs now?" said Percivine.

"Well, you heard what Rufious wrote," replied Seleborn. "He's an expert. We'll have to trust his instruction. The Edeian border is two miles that way. Come on."

"Two miles?" Percivine was far too exhausted to think about the long walk.

"Yes," said Seleborn, "two miles."

"How do you know east is that way?" Percivine said suspiciously.

Seleborn placed a compass directly in front of Percivine, and showed him a folded map attached to Rufious's note.

"Oh…right," said Percivine foolishly. "I see."

"According to the map," said Seleborn, as they left the town's edge, "the Midir Desert will begin no less than half a mile to the border."

"No matter," said Faruin. "As long as we're undetected in heading to the border, we should be fine."

Percivine ached at Seleborn's and Faruin's words. He did not like the fact that they would have to be watchful of what lay behind them.

Percivine looked back. Xerian was nothing but a small glow in the distance. In such a short time, they had traversed fast and long. Surprisingly, he had little to no pain at all in his calves. He grew more excited about the prospect of further adventure, though hid it after having previously complained.

A little later Percivine looked back and could not see Xerian anymore. They were travelling at a good pace.

"How far have we gone, Seleborn?" Faruin asked.

"About a mile I would say. Would you like to stop?"

"No, just curious," said Faruin.

The vast open fields and meadows were a wondrous sight for Percivine. He found it difficult to absorb the idea that a desert lay beyond such greenery, though he could see it lingering ahead, barren and uninviting.

"Not too long now," said Seleborn.

Percivine had never travelled farther than the River of Zanbros, in the opposite direction. Trees were spread in great distances from one another. Small hills and pastures of farms covered the ground, making for the most tranquil nights Percivine had ever known. This had to be the peace his brother had once told him about.

"There's a sign up ahead," said Seleborn.

They quickly walked to the iron sign. It read:

To Edea

"Nearly there," said Seleborn. "Quickly now. We should not be bothered here. The night is calm."

"Thank goodness," said Percivine. He was happy to know gusts of wind would not be bringing sand their way.

After walking for a few minutes, Seleborn turned to them.

"Just over the hill now," he told them.

They reached the little hill, where they could shallowly walk into the dark desert.

"Down there," said Seleborn. "Looks like some sort of rock sticking out. It will give us more cover to let us make a fire."

Once at the base of the hill, they set up their camp beneath a large protruding rock. Faruin and Percivine made sure not to wander too far while they gathered small twigs to use as firewood for a small fire.

"Should we be worried about a flame at night?" asked Percivine.

"Why?" asked Seleborn. "We are well under this rock, and besides, the fire isn't that big."

Their tents were set, and the fire burned. Over the flames Faruin held a small iron pan full of sausage and ripe tomatoes. Percivine's mouth watered; he had missed his opportunity of eating at the tavern.

"Is it almost finished?" Percivine said.

"Almost," said Faruin. "Hold your patience."

A moment later, Faruin brought out two clay bowls from his pack. This appeared odd to Percivine. Why only two? Who exactly was not going to eat? This part he dreaded the most.

"Why are there only two bowls?" Percivine asked.

"I don't eat much these days…" Faruin had given a serving to Seleborn, and another serving to Percivine. He placed the remaining tomatoes and sausages next to his body just in case anybody else wanted seconds.

"So, I think I've figured it out," said Percivine, stuffing a mouthful of tomatoes in his mouth.

"Figured what out?" said Seleborn.

"You're the voice who Faruin made contact with at the forest, aren't you?"

"What gave it away?" said Seleborn cheekily. "Was it the similarity in tone?"

Both he and Faruin gave a chuckle.

"Very amusing," said Percivine. "As we walked this distance, it gave me time to think about it. I can manage to put things together. I very much do not like secrets, so therefore, if we're going to be stuck with each other for some time, let's not hold any from each other. Sound well?"

"Just eat," said Seleborn sternly.

Percivine's face grew red. He felt cross at Seleborn's response. He'd been pulled into this mess; he should be treated with more respect. After all, he was the brother to their Leader, was he not?

"You mentioned back at the tavern that you were a Warlock…" began Percivine. "I've always wanted to meet one. As much as a Mage."

"Well, here I am," said Seleborn.

"But you lied to me," Percivine went on to say.

"How is that?" asked Seleborn.

"Why did Rufious pretend to not know you? You were clearly very shaken by his tragic death. I could see it."

"If you must know," he said, "Rufious was once a great Warlock. Taught me a thing or two. After his departure from the Solemn Hand, Rufious advised Sirien that another Warlock would be in his best interest, so he recommended my talents to Sirien. Knew I would be as helpful as he had been."

Seleborn stopped there to clear his throat, and inhaled fresh, night air.

The stars above were bright, glistening by the light from Gylranor's two moons: Tarilon and Tarilmar. It gave them plenty of visibility, even without the help of fire. For a brief moment, a small, gentle smile broke across Sirien's face, but disappeared instantly when he remembered there were two others beside him. He whispered the word "Filiiri" beneath his breath.

"I'm sorry," said Percivine. "Did you say something?"

"Nothing," said Seleborn.

"Who's Filiiri?" Percivine asked.

"I would advise you not to ask questions," he snarled at Percivine.

"What's the matter with you?" said Percivine.

Faruin shrugged.

"Since we're to be with one another for some time," Percivine said, "I think it best if we got to know each other, wouldn't you agree?"

"I suppose that's all right," said Faruin. "What would you like to know?"

Percivine avoided watching Seleborn. Clearly, he was in no state of mind to be talked to at the moment.

"Everything," said Percivine. "How about who the hell you two are?"

"Isn't it obvious?" said Faruin.

"Hardly," replied Percivine sourly.

"Suppose I'll start since the beginning," said Faruin. "I started my youth in magic under my father. He had put me through the prestige Unin'shai School of Magic, where young Elves like myself were taught in the ways of battle magic, healing magic, environmental magic, or defense magic. Under these magicks, Elves choose their destinies. I, as you may have noticed, am a runecaster using battle magic. This in turn helped me valuably to enter the Solemn Hand."

"So you say," said Percivine, taking a scoop of eggs.

"During my studies, I realized I wasn't very good with my hands. That is where runecasting came in. What I used to dispel Bartholev's magic were simple absorption runes. They are for smaller casts and will relinquish themselves once magic has been detected. Expect them not to bard an assault of magic…I digress." He tucked away a spice pouch. "After my four years of intermediate magic were completed, I enrolled myself in the Unin'shai University of Elvic Magic in Edelas, located not far from the Annals of Elga'min. I took another four years, a fifth year if I was to specialize in environmental magic, but I did not.

"After completing my education at University, I went in search of formidable positions that specialized in my field. At the time, Elga'min was in search of freshly graduated students from the University to apply for positions as guards and watchmen. But I figured my prestige talents would be wasted just standing in a post, so I declined respectively. The Elvic military force looked for paladins to help fight the Argoms…Of course, I declined. Eventually, I found something that intrigued me. There was a minor obstacle: the position I desired required a specialty in environmental magic."

"What did you do then?" asked Percivine, clearing away the rest of his food.

"You know, you eat quite fast," noticed Faruin. "We've hardly touched ours."

"I haven't eaten anything in about two days. Don't pretend you wouldn't be hungry either."

Faruin ignored the comment and continued his story.

"I encountered an Elf by the name of Dedrinus Etwood," said Faruin, a slight tremor in his voice. "He was my mentor. Helped to shape the Elf I am today."

Percivine gave him an odd look, and asked, "You well?"

"I'm fine," said Faruin. "After a series of interviews, he decided to give me the position of Assistant Elf of Beautification. Dedrinus, Lord

Elf of Beautification, was responsible for the way many parts of Ni'shorus looked—landscapes, buildings, waterways, walkway. Ten years of work passed, and Dedrinus and I became close friends…"

Silence settled over them for a moment.

"What happened next?"

"We finished a project of restoring the University. It took us about one year. Then it all happened too quickly. The Triumvirate of Ni'shorus received a tip, and soon enough they sent us to oversee another project. Mind you, by this time Dedrinus had grown ill. Being a Fenemerys, he saw death coming to greet him. This news was hardly anything of sound to me. However—"

"Sorry," said Percivine, "but what is a Fenemerys?"

"Fenemeri have a small gift of foresight," said Seleborn. "Mainly common amongst Elves, but a select few others have been recorded in history as having this power."

"Interesting," said Percivine, staring at the embers. "You may go on."

"However imminent his death was," Faruin continued, "he was uncertain as to when it would occur. One of the workers accidentally made quite the discovery. But I digress. The tablet we had discovered was so well-preserved that its markings were easily visible. Granted, it was an old map, and incomplete. None of us knew any places like those which were shown on it, but there was something we all recognized: The Obelisk, drawn quite well. It was peculiar, yes, because the Green Grotto was destroyed over two thousand years ago, which only meant one thing: There's another way to reach that object of power.

"We theorized it was a piece of the Atlas," he went on, "a legendary tablet of four pieces that, when put together, shows a projection of Beled Ruun, home of the Mages, or at least we thought so. Dedrinus immediately took hold of the piece and kept it in his private quarters for safekeeping, until he could deliver it to the Annals at Elga'min.

"Each night we were at the University, I spent guarding Dedrinus's quarters with another Elf, who, for the time being, shall remain nameless. I remember the morning as if it were yesterday. I had told the other Elf with me to go on, that I could manage alone, and he did so…I closed my eyes for a few minutes, then awoke with a start. I, in haste, knocked on the door, but I could hear no response. I managed to break open the door…and the image I encountered could be no further horrific. There, in his bed, a trail of dark blood had formed a nasty puddle. Through the night, someone or *something* had slit his throat. By that time, he was pale and cold, and his eyes gazed blankly into nothingness. His last days were taken from him prematurely…I closed his eyes, and alerted the proper authorities.

"So, to summarize everything I have just explained to you, whoever killed my mentor was after that bit of map or so we believe."

"How awful," said Percivine.

"It gets worse, Percivine," said Faruin. "When the Elf returned, he helped to carry the body out. I had returned to Unin'shai with the body, to be buried next to the Temple of the Stars. Shortly after his burial, an investigation was held. They had me arrested under the suspicion that *I* killed him. I would not have done anything like that! They locked me away in the Citadel, and there I remained for months, until I made my escape.

"I won't go into those details, as they are not important," he continued. "Since then, I've been in exile—well, on the run, I should say. A year went by, and I stumbled across your brother's path. I had told him that I was in search of a new life, and he explained that a new and permanent life could be found there. I have served your brother faithfully now for two years."

Percivine's mouth hung open; the plate in his hands fell to the ground.

"L-let me see if I have this understood," said Percivine confusedly. "They have deemed you a murderer, and now are on the run?"

"I couldn't have said it better myself," said Faruin.

"And what of the piece?" asked Percivine, astonished.

"I destroyed it," said Faruin. "Dedrinus hid it so well that I almost couldn't find it. It's a good thing I did. I could not risk others coming in search of it. I might have destroyed some of the best history this world has given us, but no one else died because of it."

"Wow."

"It's not so bad," said Faruin. "I risked getting caught in the forest to help protect you, and I will do it again if I must. I Pledged myself to the Solemn Hand, and the Hand I shall remain with."

Percivine looked over at Seleborn, who seemed to be very deep in thought, gazing eternally into the campfire. He looked at Faruin, who merely shrugged.

"Quite the story, eh, Seleborn?" said Percivine.

"Yeah."

"Why don't you tell us about you? You're a Warlock, aren't you?"

Seleborn said nothing.

"Come on, Seleborn," said Faruin. "Tell him. Go on. There's no need to be secretive anymore. We're in this together, whether you like it or not."

"I never said…I disliked it," Seleborn said darkly.

"Then speak," demanded Faruin. "There you are, Percivine."

Seleborn exhaled. "Do you know the history of Mages and Warlocks, Percivine?"

"Not in the slightest," said Percivine, in the hopes Seleborn would reveal everything he wanted to know. "Well…maybe a bit. My dad's thrown me things here and there about them."

"In the year 1733 of the First Dawn, the first Mages appeared in this world. A Hrendai woman, or Elf of Iramar, named Erewyn De'ta'nith, the first Prime Magus, created what we know today as a great pylon called the Obelisk. But the Obelisk only serves a conductor of sorts from its true source of power: Ruric's Heart. It is said that Mages gain all their power from the Heart—allows them to channel the elements to use in their spells: fire, wind, earth, water, and time. The First Prime Magus infused a very small portion of the Heart's power into common crystals that she gave to grant them the power of elemental control, and they are known as the First Followers. After countless ages, those common crystals mysteriously vanished, and soon newborn Mages naturally entered the world with this type of power.

"Originally," he continued, "Erewyn was one of Ruric Vilinius's students. Ruric had become one of the first sorcerers on Gylranor to channel magic. Another of his students, Ulthdar Tilius, grew their counterparts: Warlocks. As Ulthdar and Erewyn grew in power, they began to hold different views on how to spread the teachings of their instructor. Ulthdar insisted the power of Ruric be used offensively to show its great prowess and influence others to follow in his ways, whereas Erewyn insisted a more passive manner to going about her master's teachings.

"Tilius went on to forge Ulthdar's Nether Scrolls, whose properties Raleroc, Orking of Darkwood, used to construct the great doorway, Undiniuf. Through it, Karxas and his horde of Netherids were able to enter this plane from the Nethermire, and by which they were sent back and sealed following Karxas's demise. Presently, the Kinship of Eradell—ancient alliance of Neledar, Elves, and Dwarves—guard Undiniuf, so that nothing of Karxas's magnitude ever escapes from there again.'"

Seleborn attempted to clear this throat, but only made matters awkward.

"Years after the founder of the Warlocks perished, one of his proteges established firm Warlock communities to serve as their centers for the Netheridic Arts. Three settlements on Gylranor contain Warlocks. There is a great priory in N'elen, where I had my training.

"Over the years, Warlocks' and Mages' dislike for each other grew into sheer cold hate, and eventually they fought each other in skirmishes and battles that would destroy the Warlock population by more than two-thirds. However, I am no such Warlock. I do not live my days to make the lives of others an unfathomable hell. I serve with your brother because he has found use in my talents, and, as Faruin said earlier, I have Pledged myself to the Solemn Hand. I certainly hope that answers your question about my being of a Warlock, Percivine."

"I believe it did, Seleborn," said Percivine. "Now tell me about *you*. You have such a mysterious veil over you? I've noticed something's been gnawing at you and I don't believe it pertains to Rufious. You might as well spill it. You have no other choice."

"But I do have a choice, and I refuse to tell you what it—"

"Seleborn," said Faruin gravely. "He's trying to make the best of this predicament we're in, why can't you?"

Seleborn grunted. "Very well," he said, clutching his teeth together. "Once upon a time I lived in the peaceful village of Borgsbury. I moved there from Mjorsten after my father died. What's left of my house, I have no clue, but I've managed to find shelter for myself since..." He gulped. "...Since my wife...died..."

"Your wife?" said Percivine. "I assume that's who Filiiri is..."

Faruin knew about this, but waited for Seleborn to carry on in his story.

"Yes, a darling wife she was. She had the most wondrous eyes, and the most beloved smile. She was beautiful…Ten years of marriage, and I remember each day like yesterday, until that fateful day …"

"What happened?" Percivine asked anxiously.

"My wife had gone out to harvest the Dern Tulips that grew by our gate when she called for me, and loudly. I had gone out, and saw an elder woman being attacked by an Elf on the other side of the road. It was no ordinary Elf, though: it was a shapeshifter by the name of Murgoy, whose identity I discovered at a much later time, one of the chief lieutenants of Talus the Dark."

"Talus the Dark? You don't mean—?"

"Exactly so," said Seleborn. "Anyway, the old woman was Clamantia—"

"Clamantia Clavenhorn?"

"Yes, her, Percivine. I remember seeing an old bloke with her at the time, too. His name was Hart, I think. How do you know her?"

"My parents were often indulged in their duties, so she cared for us constantly while they were away."

"I suspect they had knowledge that a member of the Solemn Hand was residing in the village," said Seleborn. "My wife and I intervened and chased the creature. We ended on the banks of Lake Irius. But we weren't alone. An assassin named Bartholev, who've you had the pleasure of meeting, waited for us. I don't know how he knew we were to be there. After attacking them both, both of us fell. Bartholev threatened to kill me if I did not tell him the whereabouts of your brother. I refused to tell him anything, and so therefore I would die…"

Percivine could see it was harder for Seleborn to speak. It was clearly a fragile matter, and he now regretted forcing Seleborn to speak about it.

"You are dismayed, and I must apologize for insisting you speak about this," said Percivine. "It is not necessary to go on."

"No sense in holding it in any longer," said Seleborn. "Now, where was I? Oh, right…Bartholev readied his attack on me. He cast the…the jagged spell…I knew my death was assured, but it never arrived. I wondered what had happened. Someone had guarded me against my…my attacker." His lips trembled. "Before my eyes lay m-my wife, dead by that bastard's attack! Motionless and pale. Blood seeping through her wounds. I couldn't bear it. I went mad. I began throwing spells wherever I could, until I was silenced by the grey-skinned person. When I awoke, they were gone, as was my wife's body.

"Since then, I vowed to hunt him down and slay him the way he did Filiiri!" Seleborn, angered at the thought, stared vigorously into the fire. After a few moments, hatred seething through his body, he began to bawl uncontrollably. "There is—is something…else I must say…Filiiri was not the only one Bartholev murdered that day…"

Percivine's heart hung beneath his chest, ready to fall.

"My…" The sobbing grew louder. "*She was with child!*"

Percivine and Faruin were in complete dismay. In all the time Faruin had known Seleborn, this detail, too, had never been spoken of. He grabbed a small piece of cloth from his pocket and handed it to Seleborn, who blew his nose loudly into it.

Seleborn shed his last tear and covered his face his hands.

"I am so s-sorry for your loss, Seleborn," said Percivine. "I did not mean for you to have to relive that dreadful day."

"I know you meant no harm," said Seleborn. "I've kept that in for so long, it feels good to finally have told someone about it. Thank you."

"Were you able to recover your wife's body?" said Percivine.

"I was not," said Seleborn. "I had to make my escape, however dreadful it was, in order for me to carry out her wishes. To this day I have no records or leads on her body's whereabouts. By now it would just be bone, even harder to identify."

Percivine quickly endeavored to change the topic.

"Filiiri is a beautiful name," said Percivine.

"Thank you."

Faruin felt it was time they tore away from such a dark subject.

"We've told you a bit about us, Percivine," said Faruin, "so I think it's your turn to tell us a little about yourself."

"That sounds like an idea," agreed Seleborn.

"I knew this would happen," muttered Percivine. "I should have kept my mouth shut."

"But you didn't," said Faruin. "Now out with it."

"I'm the younger brother of Sirien—"

"Tell us something we don't know," Seleborn interjected.

"Right—right…something you do not know…Hm…Where to begin? Where to begin?" He looked up at Tarilon and Tarilmar and said, "I know! Call it a bad coincidence, but I, too, have lost someone dear to me."

"Your mother…" said Faruin, much to Percivine's surprise. "Sirien's spoken of her before."

"Go on, Percivine," said Seleborn.

"I haven't said this, but you have my condolences," said Faruin.

"We have told your brother, and we'll tell you," added Seleborn. "Though we never met your mother, she would be proud of her sons."

"I've learned to cope with her loss," said Percivine. "But I am eternally grateful, as well, that my father still lives to this very day."

"What exactly happened?" said Faruin.

"My mother, Merinni Ogthorne, once served the nation of Nell proudly as Ambassador to the Orc and Goblin nations. Six years ago my mother was sent, which would be her last, to the Orc nation, to negotiate peace terms, but she was, again, unsuccessful. Upon her last days in Darkwood, she grew a bit ill, and was not fully immune to her surroundings. She had Orbed my dad that she would be at home within the hour, but she never made it back…Did Sirien say why?"

"There's been a veil of mystery upon it," said Seleborn.

"My father arguably agrees it was a shapeshifter. There was no trace of the murderer. A few days went by and my father created search parties to look for her, while Sirien and I stayed at the cottage in case my mother was to show up…but she did not…Finally on the fourth day, her body was discovered in a fountain in a courtyard of Elbynshire, mangled. My father refused to let me see her body at the burial. I now appreciate him for that."

Both Faruin and Seleborn looked dumbstruck.

"Certainly, your mother's death wasn't in vain," said Seleborn. "What we're doing here is because of her, and everyone else that has had to pay their life to this ongoing epidemic. You join us, and you will honor her."

"Here's a little something else about me," said Percivine. "I do not like secrets. I detest them with a passion. You ask me, and I will tell you. I have no choice now, do I?"

"I don't think you do," added Faruin.

They stayed silent for a few moments. A different thought ran through their heads: Seleborn remembered the day Filiiri had told him of her pregnancy. Faruin recalled the moment Dedrinus agreed to give him the post. Percivine recounted to himself the last words his mother spoke to him and his brother, before departing on her last journey, "*I will return, and when I do, we will go on holiday.*"

"Are we all right?" Faruin said.

"I'm better," said Seleborn, "better than most days."

"I miss my brother," said Percivine weakly. "I do hope he's off well in whatever it is he's doing."

"Your brother's plans are his own," said Seleborn. "If I had the knowledge of Sirien's whereabouts and his activities, I would have told you. I never knew what it was to have a brother or sister, but I'm sure what you must be feeling is something despicable."

"It is," agreed Percivine. "You're an only child?"

"Well, I wasn't."

"How so?"

"At a very young," said Seleborn, "possibly even younger than you were when your mother died, my father left my mother and my younger brother, and took me with him. He took me against will, wishing rather to remain with my poor mother."

"There is no love like the love of your family's," said Faruin.

"Can either of you tell me what exactly my brother does as Leader of the Solemn Hand?" Percivine asked quickly.

The question appeared out of thin air. It seemed to puzzle Faruin and Seleborn, as they looked at one another, sharing a silent conference.

"Well?" said Percivine. "Any of you going to speak?"

Seleborn swallowed.

"What's the purpose of you knowing? It's just going to anger you further."

"As I've already said, *Seleborn*, I dislike the very virtue of a secret, so I kindly ask you to tell me!"

"He's right, Seleborn," said Faruin. "It's not fair that we keep this information from him. So, go on, tell him what he wants to know."

Seleborn blinked rapidly at Faruin, with visible resentment.

"As I'm sure Faruin already told you about Sirien's formation of the Solemn Hand, I won't go into those details. He must have also told you of those that helped him make the Solemnd Hand a success—"

"He mentioned names," said Percivine. "Names of whom I've already forgot."

"Anyway," continued Seleborn, "the Solemn Hand is a secret organization—well, it was secret until recent events—that focuses of the well-being of those who suffer from the Argom Influence and Violet Veil Accord. The Hand attempts to foil the plans of the Argoms by whatever means necessary. Your brother, Sirien, handles the day-to-day activity of the Hand. He assigns a task to each of the members, individually or not, a task by which they are to complete without a specific given time.

"As you can see," he continued, "Faruin's task and my own task were to keep you safe from harm's direction while Sirien is away." Sirien halted the conversation shortly for a bit of water. All this talking was leaving his mouth parched. "Now I suspect you think by me telling you this I will 'accidentally' let slip the location of your brother and what he's doing, but think again. Like I've said before, we do not know what Sirien's up to."

"I knew that already," said Percivine. "Why had Rufious made such a fuss about never returning to the Solemn Hand? He made it appear to be a terrible society to belong to."

"You're just full of questions, aren't you?" said Seleborn.

"Yes," answered Percivine. "Are you going to tell me or not?"

"Long ago, years before our marriage, Rufious and Filiiri had been very good friends. I had met her through Rufious, even then Filiiri had the same charm up until her last days…Her death struck a blow at him just like your mother's did. Their loss he could not bare. He was filled with grief and remained distraught, unwilling to change. His depression took a toll on him. Rufious refused anything that had ties to Merinni and Filiiri, meaning the Solemn Hand. I took a visit to his old home in Bzor, and there he finally told me his reasons for leaving. I tried vigorously to get him to rejoin, but time after time it ended in failure. He moved to Nell, starting anew, found work within the Divination Administration and never looked back. This is theory, of course, but I don't think he truly could forget the Hand. I suspect he still wanted to watch over us."

Percivine frowned. He felt dazed. "I find it difficult to accept the fact that all this was occurring right under my nose. That I was this naïve, scribbling on parchment at the *Frodrian Fox*."

"Don't take it too personal," said Seleborn. "Your brother cares deeply for you, we know that, and you must realize his reasons for doing all this. It is to protect you."

"Your brother didn't want any of this," said Faruin. "He did not want you to get involved in the way you did."

Again, Percivine was getting the frustrating feeling that Sirien believed him to be utterly incapable of taking care of his own self. He wished his brother would have more faith in him, and not send his cronies to look after him like a poor, helpless infant.

"My brother needs to stop worrying," said Percivine reluctantly. "I capable of taking care of myself, and I have now come to the acceptance of what my brother has just offered me. He is my brother, and I will do everything in my power to make sure *he's* from harm's way."

Percivine thought he had rather impressed Faruin and Seleborn with his words, for they said nothing.

The sky lightened—dawn was upon them.

"Would you look at that?" said Percivine.

Over in the far distance, they could see the horizon. Never in his lifetime had Percivine viewed a full sunrise. It was a magnificent view. Being isolated for most of his life in Frodrir had prevented him from seeing such things.

"Hard to believe we've past the whole night talking," said Seleborn. "Look at that: The fire's almost out."

"I guess we'd better pack and get started," Percivine said. "We've got ways to go."

CHAPTER FOUR

RELTHREN

Sun's Blessing

They rapidly put their tents away and set out on foot. Seleborn threw dirt over the fire, burying all evidence of a camp.

Things became clearer as they stepped foot into the beginnings of the Midir Desert. What Percivine saw was more glorious than he imagined. He had pictured the Midir Desert to be a barren, arid, wasteland. In fact, this desert was the complete opposite. There were beautiful, jagged rock formations, and mesas and buttes filled with different types of cacti and other desert flora streaked with reddish-grey and green hues.

"This is my first time in a desert," said Percivine.

"Quite the scene, isn't it?" said Seleborn. "And we've only just entered the Midir. Throughout the desert one can find many small canyons and ravines, and oddly shaped rocks. Edea's main city—Beshera—is said to be nestled in a canyon surrounded completely by rocks like those, serving as a natural protection from the outside world."

"Wow," said Percivine in awe. "I would certainly like to visit that place one day."

"I've read that the Edeians gained their golden-yellow skin due to exposure in the hot, golden sun of the Midir Desert over time," said Seleborn.

Now things were getting interesting, making Percivine especially excited: a ruined watchtower loomed closer and closer. Seleborn explained it'd once been inhabited by the extinct Masixi, a race of cat people.

"My mentor has explained," Seleborn said, pointing up at the battered tower, "that the Masixi used these towers are primary lookouts for the great pyramids they sprouted."

Though tiresome, the journey to the ancient Dwarf city also bore many surprises. The temperature grew hotter, and they were dehydrated. As breathtaking the Midir Desert is, it did not give them mercy when it came to the heat.

"We must stop for a small break of water," Faruin told Seleborn.

They carefully drank out of their water pouches, as to not let any drop out of their sight. Once finished, they marched on. Percivine ripped apart cloth he had and wrapped it around his neck and over his head as to not burn himself. Faruin did so, as well, followed by Seleborn.

"By all that is good in the All-Essence," said Percivine, rubbing his eyes.

Unwittingly, they had approached the oasis Rufious had spoke of in his instructions. Hundreds of palm trees hovered over the Pools of Nordorth. Birds chirped, and flew away once they spotted them. An old wagon caravan lay ruined beside one of the Pools.

"What's this?" said Percivine. He picked up an old axe nestled within three leather rucksacks by the caravan's rotted, wooden wheel.

"Old mountain equipment it looks like," said Faruin. "We could use that, Seleborn."

"Right," said Seleborn. "The axe is a good start. Ah, look, rope! We'll take that. This caravan must have been here for years."

After they stuffed the rope and iron nails into their packs, they looked out over the glistening pools of fresh water.

"Spectacular, aren't they?" said Seleborn. "These pools contain some of the purest water you'll ever hope to drink. These pools are said to have been used by the Masixi to procure advanced medicines in case of disease and sickness. Some claim that one drop is all that is needed to create a potent medicinal remedy."

They decided to rest at the Pools of Nordorth and set up camp. Percivine looked at the shining waters of the Pools, tempted to taste it though he refrained.

"You must resist," said Faruin, who had silently come about. "The water is never to be touched. It's a crime punishable by heavy imprisonment.

I wouldn't underestimate the Edeians. We are most likely being watched now as we speak, and I can assure you these pools have been stamped with signal spells. Even the slightest touch of a finger will have a patrol howling over us."

Again, before the sun rose, they packed their things and continued east across the now abundant steppes. Now no tree could be seen, save for a cactus or two.

"We should arrive in Relthren in about three days' time," said Seleborn.

"Great," said Percivine.

Most of the mesas they had gotten used to were beginning to fade, indicating Relthren lay close. The Dwarvic part of the Helin Mountains came into view. The mountains were godly in their height; Percivine wondered the depth to which the Halls of Adelvald would take them. They travelled a little farther in, and soon saw old wooden boards with directions to the halls.

They followed a trail that gradually elevated itself upward to the Halls of Adelvald. Large doors of stone and wood barred them from entering so easily. The many markings on the doors were unfamiliar to them.

"That's not Dwarvic, is it?" asked Percivine.

"No," said Seleborn. "These halls weren't constructed by the Dwarves. No one has evidence to prove who built them, but more prominent theories suggest the Masixi constructed them."

"In we go," said Faruin promptly.

Carefully they entered the stone halls. Moisture dripped from the ceilings and wet grass covered the stone floor. They followed the combination of torches and sconces on the walls.

"Torches?" said Percivine. "Has someone been here?"

"Hard to say," said Seleborn. "With what little knowledge I have of this place, I can only imagine they've been lit for thousands of years. Rarely does one walk here."

"Comforting," said Percivine sarcastically.

Ahead, a blue light made its way into their view. What they saw next left them in wonderment: the first passage of Adelvald turned into a viaduct cutting across a cavern large enough to fit six Frodrirs. Beneath the viaduct, they could hear a running stream which settled their nerves as they walked along. High above, in the cavern, were more of the same designs they'd witnessed on the walls.

"And the Giants had nothing to do with this?" said Percivine skeptically.

"The Giants, or Titans, whatever you want to call them," said Seleborn, "once, long ago, settled these lands before being driven out by the Dwarves, retreating to the island of Ururazan. As I said, no one's found evidence linking the halls to the Giants or Dwarves. There has been great speculation that the Masixians carved these halls, and yet—"

"—there's no evedience to prove it," finished Percivine. "We know."

"But," Seleborn went on, "these carvings were made more recently."

"By whom?" asked Faruin.

"The Dwarves. After years and years of selfish expansions during the First Dawn, they were the ultimate cause of the Masixi's and Giants' extinction. They drove them from their homelands. Today's Dwarves regret what their ancestors did. Using what wisdom they had of Masixi and Giants, engraved these walls to depict the meeting of Masixi and Giants. Uln Alzor is littered with many Masixian and Giant ruins, so the Dwarves also made it illegal for anyone to touch or damage them further. The Dwarves think it a way to make amends for the suffering they put these races through. Nothing they do will ever bring them back, will it?"

The walk lasted nearly two hours but felt like only a few minutes, for they were deeply fascinated by Adelvald's ancient glory. The halls closed on them again, meaning they were nearing the end. They crept past a crumbling stone door that had been left half open centuries earlier and followed a set of steps tilting downwards. A small stone village lay yonder. To avoid any suspicion, they decided to travel around the Dwarvic village of Clepham, then back onto their original route.

"We have a midday's journey to Nerim," said Seleborn, "no time to stop now."

Percivine panted, and Faruin held him up in order for him to catch his breath.

The sand began to segue toward a greener terrain. The edge of Nerim Forest was upon them.

"This is a good spot," said Seleborn. He was unloading his travel possessions on the banks of a small rush of water separating the land and the forest, acting as a natural mote.

"Is it wise to camp so closely to the forest?" said Faruin. "Perhaps we'd be best inside of it. Wood-Dwelling Dwarves would never linger like this."

Seleborn pondered the matter. "Perhaps not. But we are not Wood-Dwelling Dwarves, and we're not in the Naros Archipelago."

They reached a lonely spot surrounded by a few trees and plants, still very close to the rushing water. Faruin had shuffled his way down to the stream and returned with spiked shrimp, slimefish, and some mollusks, which he quickly began to fry in a cast iron pan.

"Did you know the slime from a slimefish is so thick that water never actually touches its scales?" said Faruin. "The slime also serves a wonderful cooking oil, so in hindsight, it practically cooks itself."

"Got anything that isn't fish?" asked Percivine, gawking at the cooking slimefish.

"Well, I did go into the water to get these," said Faruin, attempting to keep himself composed, "so nothing that's not fish is in there. We have runnerclams and spiked shrimp."

"Shrimp, did you say? Can't stand the rest of that stuff. That'll do nicely!"

"Careful, though," said Faruin. "Before you eat the shrimp, ensure the spikes are limber enough. Heat usually does the trick. My cooking doesn't usually hurt, so you'll be fine."

After dinner they spent the next few moments preparing their camp, as they had done the previous two nights. Percivine usually had some difficulty propping up his tent, so Faruin had to help him. Once the tents were up, they sat around the small fire as they had done the first night; the previous night was unfriendly to them, so, quite exhausted, they had fallen asleep quickly.

"Something's been pestering at me for the past two days now, Perci," said Seleborn.

"What's on your mind?" asked Percivine.

"Faruin and I spoke about our past to you," he said, "but you have avoided telling anything about yourself. Thought you didn't like secrets?"

"After all that's happened," said Percivine, "there's been so much on my mind that it has been the least of my worries…I served as a writer for the *Frodrian Fox*—Frodrir's only news outlet. Thought I would enjoy it more, but it's not a very interesting profession; nothing exciting ever happens in Frodrir. Nonetheless it kept me occupied. Can't say reporting on who stole whose pottery is grand."

"It's decent work," said Faruin. "Besides, looks like you may have something more dire to write about now."

"Yes," agreed Seleborn. "However, I don't think I could spend my time writing so much…I'm more of a…physical person myself."

"Yes—" Before he could continue, Percivine remembered something odd. "Seleborn," he said, "since when have you called me 'Perci'?"

"What? Oh—that—well, I was thinking that your original name is too long to pronounce each time, so I figured why not shorten it by a few letters."

"A few letters?" remarked Percivine. "That's half my name!"

"I dunno," said Faruin. "I kind of like the way that sounds."

"You too, Faruin?" said Percivine. "I don't know if could get used to you calling me that."

"We can," chuckled Seleborn.

They enjoyed a few moments of conversation, until they were finally ready for bed. Faruin put out the fire while Seleborn packed up the remaining fried fish and loaves of Elvic bread that Faruin had brought with him. Percivine lay his head down and closed his eyes but awoke when he heard a faint whisper coming from deep in the forest.

"I heard something," Percivine told them the next morning.

"Probably the wind scratching against the trees," said Faruin.

"Whatever it was, it was unsettling. We should go around the forest."

"You know what Rufious instructed," said Seleborn. "It's best we follow his letter precisely."

The trio stepped gingerly over the rush of water and clambered over a large root far bigger than Percivine.

"Not too bad, is it?" said Seleborn. "There's light poking through the trees as I can see. Be on the lookout, though. Magic and runes at the ready."

They ventured through Nerim for what seemed like hours. The air grew cold, and the sounds of the forest dwellers echoed everywhere. Percivine looked anxiously all around and above; for a split second, he could swear he saw something move high up in the canopy. Then his own mind spoke to him.

It's nothing, thought Percivine.

That's what you perceive, said the other voice of his.

"The light's growing dim, Seleborn," warned Faruin.

Seleborn glanced upward. He knew they ought to wait until the new day began.

"You can't be serious…" Percivine said.

"What're you so worried about?" said Seleborn. "You escaped death in Maradine Forest. What makes this so different?"

"I hardly had the time to linger about. I had no choice, did I?"

"I've reached my limits with your wimpering, Perci," said Seleborn. "Shut your f—"

"Shh!" Faruin pointed up.

Percivine and Seleborn slowly looked up. An array of white, glowing objects hovered overhead, humming, drifting in one direction.

"Sylphs," said Faruin. "Spirits that inhabit the forests of Uln Alzor. Incredible. We've no such things back in Ni'shorus."

The sylphs' gentle humming attracted them. Made them forget what they had been arguing about. Percivine, with no control over it, felt himself following them.

Seleborn grabbed hold of Percivine's arm. "Where are you going?"

"I…don't know," said Percivine thoughtlessly. "Something tells me…we should follow them."

Faruin shrugged his shoulders and beckoned Seleborn to come along, who now felt as airily as Percivine.

The sylphs hovered graciously until they stopped. Percivine snapped out of the trance he indulged in, and said, "Look! We're at the edge of the forest!"

They could hardly believe their luck. Had the sylphs really helped them escape the thick forest? There was only one way to find out.

"No desert!" said Seleborn. "If I hadn't of seen it, I wouldn't have believed it. Good work, Perci!"

"Wasn't me! Thank those spirits."

"Their majesty is well-known," said Faruin.

Even more disquieting was the River Relthren, flowing brilliantly before them.

The three came to junction in the road, after having washed themselves and crossed the River Relthren. A wooden post with four boards stood at the center of the fork. The four boards leading southeast read "Loch Rell," "Bzor," "Great Dwarvic Dam of Melesnor," and "Relthren," the latter giving them great relief. The journey had long exhausted them. Being on foot differed greatly than riding on a mount.

They took the route leading to the Dwarvic capitol city. Many high trees blocked their view of the sun as they approached another sign: *Security Point Ahead.*

"What's that about?" asked Percivine.

"Can't expect the Dwarves to let just anyone prance into their beloved city, do you?" said Seleborn.

"I suppose not."

They continued down the path. Up ahead they saw two small toll stands made of blackened wood, with a Dwarf standing in front of each of the booths.

This must be it, thought Percivine.

"Halt," said the Dwarf with a red braided beard and heavy plated armor. "Who goes there?"

"Seleborn Alveroth of Mjorsten," said Seleborn. "That's" —he pointed at Faruin— "Faruin Abrandil of Unin'shai, and" —to Percivine— "this is Percivine Ogthorne of Frodrir."

"Two Neledar an' an Elf," said the Dwarf, as the second Dwarf, in the same plated armor and barely a beard to speak of, came in closer to them. "Wha' business have ye 'ere?"

"We are nothing but mere tourists," said Seleborn.

The short-bearded Dwarf whispered something to the red-bearded Dwarf. He tugged at his long red beard, then looked up curiously at Percivine.

"You're not by any chance related to Sirien Ogthorne? Sirien Ogthorne of the Solemn Hand?"

"I—" began Percivine.

"A mere coincidence," interjected Seleborn. "You can't possibly believe they're the only two Ogthornes of this world, do you?"

The red-bearded Dwarf raised one eyebrow and whispered something to the other Dwarf. The short-bearded Dwarf backed away to his stone construct.

"Ye are free to pass," said the Dwarf with braids in his beard.

"Thank you."

They calmly and quietly walked ahead, as the two Dwarves watched them leave with a careful eye, their battleaxes standing firm in their thick hands. After a great distance or so, Percivine turned back to catch a glimpse at the Dwarves, and saw them still eyeing them until they could no more.

"Why did you deny my relation to Sirien?" Percivine asked Seleborn. "And how do they know about the Solemn Hand?"

"That is very strange," said Faruin. "Do you think someone warned them of our coming?"

"I'm not for certain. Those Security Points are set up around Uln Alzor because, like I've said before, the influence of the Argoms hasn't tainted these lands. The Dwarves have yet to set every and any kind of precaution to maintain the peace. And as to your question about Sirien, I told them that, so they don't get the impression that we're bringing trouble with us."

"And we aren't?"

"I hope not," said Seleborn.

That did not make Percivine feel any better. How could he feel grand, if it was his fault that Uln Alzor no longer beckoned with the peace that Nell wished it had? The feeling was short-lived, however, for the trees were lessening and more sunlight was beaming on them, and in the short distance they could see a large mountain with a large iron gate built into its reaches. Two monstrous Dwarvic statues stood over the base of the drawbridge, welcoming outsiders. These mighty statues did not amaze them as much as what lay beyond: the Dwarvic city was an unprecedented marvel. Relthren, the City of Terraces it is also called, is great city of iron and stone, which stretches from one end of the mountain to the other. Many terraces and balconies stuck out from the side of the mountain allowing a fresher way to traverse the legendary city. To think the Dwarves had managed to build such a landscape was far more breathtaking than Percivine could dream of.

"Those are the Gates," said Seleborn.

Percivine and Faruin paid no attention to Seleborn, still dazed from the captivating scene before them. Only through tales had they heard of the wonders of Gylranor's best architectural experts and tinkerers. Percivine could now only wonder how the Dwarves built and secured a striking city such as this within and all along the edges of the mountain.

Two Dwarves, in the same plated, heavy armor, stood guard at the foot of the pathway leading to the Iron Portcullis. Behind them were two large, silver constructs. These machinations were called golems by the Dwarves. Each golem possessed limbs: two arms and legs, with their torsos and lower body connected by an energy, an energy unknown to Percivine. The golem constructs watched them as they passed onto the drawbridge. The iron drawbridge connected two platforms of the mountain. The entrance to Relthren lay a few feet away.

"Lower the bridge!" came a voice. A battalion of Dwarvic soldiers marched hurriedly down the path from the lowered bridge.

"Excuse me," said Percivine to one of the guards, "what goes on here?"

"Bit of trouble at the Aragorus Wall," said the Dwarf with a piercing on either side of her bottom lip. "Don' mind ye. Nothin' to worry aboot. Them Insectoids won' be causin' anythin' further. Can I help ye?"

"We're tourists," said Seleborn. "Longing to familiarize ourselves with such a grand city!"

"Then ye've come to the right place!" said the lip-pierced Dwarf. "Fer starters, I shall give ye lot a summary of how to maneuver through Relthren. Firs', ye are welcome to travel to any part of the city all along the various stairs and connecting roads. But I will sugges' seeking the Large Hall. There ye will find it connects internally from one end of the mountain to the other. All avenues and roads and smaller halls from every bit of the city connect to the Hall! Ye'll also find it to be quite the hub of commerce, from traders all aroun' the world. We've grea' taverns as well, if ye lot fancy a pint or five. Lastly, ye can take a lift to the summit that will give ye the best view of all of Uln Alzor, and will give ye a look into the numerous training grounds built by previous Dwarves for the development of the Thane's army. If ye would like a more scenic approach, I sugge' traveling along one of our countless terraces."

Percivine, Faruin, and Seleborn took kindly to the Dwarf's information, and entered through the visitor's entrance located on the right side of the gate.

Inside Percivine could hardly believe what he saw. Many walkways, halls, terraces, and homes built into the walls of the mountains overlapping them. The sights were evident in their beauty and culture. They clambered many steps and walked through flattened parts of the mountain and over many terraces until they reached another staircase, this one displaying more ornate carvings, busts of many important Dwarves of times past. This was likely the primary staircase to the Large Hall, as it was busier than the others.

The Large Hall was as grand as the Dwarf had made it out to be. The ceiling was higher than the tallest buildings of Frodrir, with statues and columns of immense height upholding the ceiling. Thousands of figures, of all races, paraded in haste through the hall. They spotted other Neledar and Elves, Ranoics and Goblins, and Neledar of the western kingdoms, and a Barb juggling maces. The many tunnels that connected the roads and avenues surrounded them, leading to all parts of Relthren. One, larger than the rest, had a symbol unfamiliar to Percivine and Faruin, but one that Seleborn recognized.

"I believe that road leads to where the throne of the Thane lies and the Uln Seat," said Seleborn.

"Uln Seat?" asked Percivine.

"The governing body of Uln Alzor."

"Can I ask again what our business here is?" said Percivine, overwhelmed by everything he is witnessing.

"There is someone I need to get in touch with…Someone who would make a great return to the Hand…He owns an antiquities shop."

"You brought us out here for *that?*" exclaimed Percivine. "My legs nearly broke off from the exhaustion I faced getting here!"

"Believe it," said Seleborn, focusing more on which way to turn rather than Percivine's whining. "Come. This way."

Seleborn led them to a smaller tunneled avenue, passing a silk merchant's booth, that ended on a terrace. At the end of the terrace was a large archway that led into a place called the Hall of Great Thanes, dramatically smaller than the Large Hall. It was here where many celebrations took place, where the Dwarves of Relthren feasted and drank into the hours of the day on several holidays.

"You, there!" called someone to Percivine. "Oi! You! Come hither this way, weary traveler!"

"Er," said Percivine. "What?"

"You're not from around here, are you?" said the Dwarf, wearing a brightly colored orange tunic and indigo breeches with a badge of some sort.

"What gave it away?" said Percivine.

"Humorous lad. Take this!"

A flyer was handed to Percivine. Across the top were the words, "PATHFINDERS GUILD."

"What is the Pathfinder's Guild?" asked Percivine.

"We've no time," said Seleborn. "We really must be—"

"You've dragged me along here," said Percivine tartly, "now you will bear me and my curiosity."

Seleborn grunted and said nothing else.

"Ah, a curious mind is a fruitful mind," said the indigo-breeched Dwarf excitedly, as if they were the first to actually stop and listen to what he had to say. "We are a league of explorers, adventurers, scholars, lore enthusiasts, and excavators who are tasked with upholding Uln Alzor's magnificent history, and we have recently stuck an alliance with the Society of Excavators from Nell. We make headquarters at the Thaneric Museum. The symbol of which is on this here badge; it hosts the Dwarvic Hammers of Döl Desdra and other magnificent artifacts! Should you be interested, the Thaneric is on the southern side of the mountain. One of our great archaeologists, Sorric Solthdar, is giving a *fascinating* lecture today on these remarkable etched tablets discovered not long ago in an old Giant ruin on the Isle of the Ancients, or for those of us who call it by its proper name, Ururuzan. Through the Large Hall, you'll see a tunnel marked with our personal emblem." He indicated his bronze badge again. "Follow it, and once out, make a right into Originator's Terrace."

"We need to get across the Hall," said Seleborn, oblivious to the Dwarf's words. "I believe he resides on the other side of the mountain."

Percivine frowned. "Why don't we investigate this Musuem? My father, as you may know, is head of the Society of Excavators, so why not pay a visit?"

"Ah, then you are familiar with such a craft?" said the Dwarf, greatly excited now.

"Another time," said Seleborn. "Come!"

"All right, all right," said Percivine, with audible disappointment that matched the little, indigo-breeched Dwarf's. A common misconception that other people have of Dwarves is that they are all the same size; it is false. They come in many sizes and heights, with tall ones reaching slightly over five feet!

As Seleborn walked ahead, he whispered to Faruin, "Who is he talking about?"

"Dunno," said Faruin. "Seleborn has always—how should I say—had a thin blanket of mystery over him. He never speaks of many things. That's why I was surprised when he told you about Filiiri, after mere moments of meeting you. Took me almost a year to get that out of him."

"If you two are done speaking amongst yourselves, I would like to continue," said Seleborn.

Many Dwarves were scattered across the Hall. Some played chess, others ate legs of ham and other juicy meats like swine, others poured thick ale down their throats, wetting their faces…Most of them took no notice of the three non-Dwarves parading through their great hall. They reached the other end and followed Seleborn as he made a left into a quieter market way.

"This is better," said Seleborn, looking carefully around him. "Now, I don't think he is too far from here."

A stout Dwarvic woman wearing a faded brown tunic-like dress had come out from her home to begin sweeping. Seleborn approached her.

"Excuse me," he said.

The woman looked up at him.

"Yes?"

"Can you point us to *Timeworn Antiquities*, please?"

"If ye're lookin' for the Minister of War, he isn't 'ome."

"And what of his cousin, Dunngarunax Galon?"

"Aye, I do believe he is there, up those stairs," she said, pointing to the shop, slightly larger than her accommodations. "I've got lots of work to do. Please make yer way. On ye go."

"Thank you," said Seleborn.

They followed the direction of the Dwarvic woman's finger to the stone steps that led to a shop, a sign with the name *"Timeworn Antiquities"* hanging over the door. They clambered up the steps and knocked on the thick stone door that resembled Rufious's door.

"Comin', comin'!" said a voice from behind the door.

The stone door swung open. A Dwarf, nearly five feet in height and clothed in sapphire chiton and black britches greeted them. What caught most of Percivine's attention was the arm that held the door open for them: it looked similar to that of a golem's with the same odd energy flowing through it. Percivine had never seen anything like it before. The Dwarf's right arm was connected in three parts: shoulder, elbow, and hands. Each prosthetic of an unknown grey material was held together by the blue energy that so mesmerized Percivine.

"Etharian be praised! Seleborn!"

"We've brought a visitor," said Seleborn. "Percivine Og—"

"OH! This lad needs no introduction—I know very well who this is! Percivine Ogthorne, Sirien's younger brother! It's a pleasure meetin' someone who's related to the same bloodline as Sirien. Come," said Dunngarunax Galon. He extended his artificial limb to shake Percivine's hand. "Come, and I'll fetch ye all some fine Dwarvic ale!"

"Much obliged, Dunn," said Seleborn.

The inside of the shop was littered with relics, trinkets, oddities, and other items filled with old history. They sat on shelves behind the main counter, on the counter itself, in display cases and cabinets along the walls, and even hung from the ceiling.

Dunn's shop, which also served as his home is structured very much like Rufious's. It's a cold place, though Dwarves were accustomed to the cold, bearing skin as thick as animal hyde. A large iron chandelier hung over them, as Dunn directed them to sit on the thick wooden table in the back of the shop.

"Sirien's plan didn't entail us stopping by like this, but we come with some distressing news, Dunn," said Seleborn. "You may want to sit down for it."

"Ye're scaring me lad, what's this all aboot?"

"Rufious…is dead…"

Dunn stared at them blankly. The three iron goblets he'd retrieved to serve the ale started to rattle on the serving plate he held.

"Dead, ye say? How could this be? Who told ye of such dark news?"

Over the next few moments, Seleborn explained to Dunn how the three of them had witnessed the shapeshifter put a dagger to the center of the Rufious's stomach. Worsening matters, he also explained to a now-nauseated Dunn how Frerus, too, had suffered from the fate of imminent death.

"I don' understand any of this," said Dunn, unable to comprehend what he'd heard. His face grew white. "Wha've they done? Who could do something so sinister? It could only mean…"

None of them really understood what it meant, but knew Dunn had a little more to say of the matter.

"…I had a feeling they would be after ye Percivine. None of us know where Sirien is or what he's up to, not even Nerod, who is ultimately Sirien's closest friend."

Percivine pondered these words for a moment. He always thought his father, or himself, would be the closest Sirien ever had. The words Dunn spoke did not seem to convince Seleborn very much. He could see a bit of fear in the Dunn's eyes. Seleborn also noticed Dunn tapping his first finger rapidly against the side of his goblet.

"There's something else you want to tell us."

"T-there is not," stammered Dunn, almost knocking over his goblet.

"Don't lie."

The tension was thick. Percivine and Faruin could only guess what Dunn needed to say.

"All righ'! All righ'!" snapped Dunn. "Ye should not be 'ere!"

"And why not?" asked Percivine.

"There obviously after ye!" said Dunn, pushing his goblet to the side. "This land is a peaceful land, and I want it to stay tha' way!"

"Are you joking, Dunn?" said Seleborn. "You're part of the Solemn Hand. You know wherever we go, there will be trouble."

"That may be, Seleborn, but nevertheless this is where I call home. Would ye want yer home to be troubled?"

"I suppose not…"

"We won't be—"

Dunn waved Seleborn down.

"I apologize fer my behavior," he said.

This came as a shock to the three of them. They did not expect such a change of heart from Dunn so fast. Dwarves had always been known for their haughtiness and lack of integrity.

However, no two stones are alike, Percivine's mind said.

"Rufious's death has left me feeling anger, a feeling I mustn't let get the better of me." He glimpsed at Percivine. Percivine quickly drew his attention away from Dunn's arm. "Yer mother was a good friend to Rufious."

"My mother had a lot of friends, or so my dad tells me," said Percivine. "How big is the throne room?"

"Er…Pardon me?" said Dunn.

"The throne of the Thane…how big is it?"

"Bigger than ye think, actually…It's been empty for almost three weeks. Thane Grin has been on holiday—"

The word "holiday" sent an electrifying feeling through Percivine's bones. It reminded him very much of the final words his mother had spoken to him, before her journey to Darkwood, the Orc kingdom.

"—in his mountain retreat city of Ilfesgard, near Mount Bedafn— the very same mountain where Olsius the Bearded, Thane of Uln Alzor, slew the Corrupted Dragon Hiimerion in 2D 1177; Hiimerion was one of the only few Corrupt Dragons ever to roam this world. The dragon's bones can still be found atop the cold mountain."

Dunn was very proud of it. He continued explaining that the events concerning the dragon would have been catastrophic if Olsius would have fallen under the dragon's frost flames.

Dunn's facial expression took on a solemn look. "That would have been the end of the Dwarvic race…It feels tha' such events are happenin' again…We Dwarves are proud creatures." After a pause, he added, "an' we will continue to assist the Neledar an' Elves in whichever way we can, me cousin 'as promised. Our advances in technology an' architecture will help us make so."

"How do you know that exactly?" asked Seleborn.

"Jus' look at me arm," said Dunn. "Percivine here can't keep 'is eye off 'em."

"Sorry for the stares," said Percivine. "I've just never encountered such—such—"

"Advancement?" said Dunn. "Yes, like I said earlier, we Dwarves are rather good at tinkering. It's taken us a century to perfect maggedium. Ah, but you don' know what maggedium is, do ye, lad?"

"Never heard of it," said Percivine.

"Maggedium is a fairly new energy force forged in the Fourth Dawn that networks the sensual energies tha' allows us to replace what has been lost. When our scaly neighbors of Agador began raiding our northern reaches, we knew it was time to think bigger! Morthdryn's Farmstead, anything past Mt. Bedafn really, is poorly secured. During the Era of Dwarves, the grea' Byeryn the Technologist fused the blue properties of stakratite with magic to produce such a revelation as maggedium. A realization struck him: he could siphon the energy released from this metal and use it as a power source but was unable to fully use maggedium without stakratite being maggedium's host to remain contained.

"It wasn't until almost twenty years later that he figured how to use maggedium without the use of the metal, and that's where Wayorbs came into play. Stakratite, if ye don't know, is a natural metal said to 'ave been Rosnios' actual tears long ago before the Great Cataclysm. We don' know how, we don' know why, but this precious metal's properties remain a mystery, and its energies now light our homes, our 'alls, our grea' roads throughout Uln Alzor, and powers our many apparatuses."

"So, this maggedium," said Percivine, "it is what powers the golems?"

"Very clever!" squeaked Dunn. "Precisely. Returning to my earlier explanation, the golems were created by Byeryn to defend our northern shores from Agador. Tha's the last time we've clashed with the Agadorians. After the success of maggedium, Byeryn discovered that stakratite could be used for many other things. Machines, lightin', artificial limb recovery. Feels like I never lost me arm."

"Me cousin, o' course," said Dunn proudly, "has been a large advocate for the empowerment of maggedium. He is, after all, a member to the Thane's royal court as actin' Minister of War. So…Rufious's death couldn't be the only reason you three showed up on my doorstep. What *really* has brought the three of ye 'ere to Relthren? I'm sure it wasn' to admire the splendor of me arm."

No one spoke a word. Faruin looked to the polished rock floor. Percivine looked at the gadgets and trinkets Dunn had laying around.

Seleborn merely looked at Dunn without blinking, which scared Dunn a little.

"Well? Seleborn, do ye 'ave anythin' to say?"

"Our main reason has been to discover if you knew anything about Sirien's location, but obviously you do not. We will leave you then. Upon Sirien's return, we shall see you at Headquarters, yes?"

Dunn was dumbstruck. His apparent behavior had caused the three of them to feel very unwelcome. He spent most of his time, and their time, worrying about the peace to be disturbed in the lands, rather than welcome them with food and drink after their long journey, especially Percivine's and Faruin's juncture in Maradine Forest. He was ashamed for his actions, and responded with, "Ye can't be leavin' so soon, can ye? I may not be the most hospitable host, but I do enjoy the presence of friends, an' new ones!"

"We don't want to impose," said Percivine. "Clearly, you're worried about other things."

"Please stay, at least for the night," said Dunn kindly, feeling guilty for his treatment of them. "I know ye three have travelled far to be here. I'll fetch us some fine mutton from the marketplace. Help yeselves to my ale. I've got a lifetime's worth down in the cellar."

"Dunn, it's all right," said Seleborn. "There's no need—"

"No need, ye say? There is every need. You came all this way to see me, an' I 'aven't been much help to ye lot. Let this old Dwarf make reconcile with his fellow friends. I won't be long. Make yerselves at home."

And with those last words, the Dunn hurried out the thick door and disappeared. Percivine was surprised by the Dwarf's sudden change, and now felt bad for having told him such a rude thing. This was a bit of a delight, however, for Percivine. He had never slept in the house of a Dwarf before, and found the experience to be enjoyable, now knowing food and beverages would be provided.

"It is very kind of Dunn to let us stay here," said Faruin. "Do you think old Thiurwold would mind? Seeing us here in his home?"

"I don't know," said Seleborn. "He's probably too busy dealing with matters of politics. I have a feeling he won't come home. Where the devil did Perci run off to?"

"I'm in the bedroom!" Percivine called from the other room. He returned quite shortly. "Sorry, I had to take a look for myself on how these Dwarves sleep. Their beds are made completely from mountain rock! Where the bloody hell is the comfort part?"

"He's invited us to stay the night," said Seleborn. "We will just have to make the best of the sleeping arrangements."

"I did notice a soft pillow and wool blanket. So, I suppose it won't be as bad as it looks." Percivine grabbed his goblet and poured more Dwarvic ale.

"I'll take some of that ale, too, Perci," said Faruin, extending his goblet to the iron growler in Percivine's grasp.

Seleborn removed his mantled cloak and placed it in one of the stone chairs. "That could have gone better."

"What are you talking about?" said Percivine, who took great pleasure in drinking the ale. "We've been offered food, drink, and somewhere to sleep. I say this has been the best we've seen in days! *Days!*"

"Percivine's right, Seleborn," added Faruin. 'It's just for the night, anyway. However…I feel something unbalanced."

"You sense unbalance?" asked Percivine.

"We Elves can sense a disturbance in nature. Something is not right. I can't explain it. The feeling's…just there."

"Are you a Fenemerys too?"

"No, Perci, we Elves…we Elves pride ourselves as being naturalists—having a special connection to this world."

"Should I start to my sleeping, then?" said Percivine.

"I'm sure you're more than hungry than the rest of us," said Faruin jokingly. "I recommend you stay awake."

After a few short moments of grave solitude, Dunn returned with a large husk of mutton and other assorted meats, hung over his back. He lay the husk of mutton on the table where they were seated and seasoned it with some of Faruin's spices. Dunn poured himself a goblet of ale before beginning to ignite the fire.

"It always helps to have a bit of lightheadedness before ye cook, isn' that righ', Faruin?"

"Er—yes…of course, Dunn."

With a quick snap of his fingers, Dunn ignited the fire. It grew and burned brightly, and the warmth made Percivine feel at ease. Since their arrival to Relthren, they had only experienced a cold mountain climate. A nice change to be sure. Seleborn helped Dunn set the large husk over the open fire, then Dunn placed two iron clamps at each end of the mutton, so it wouldn't fall into the pit.

"Ye'll love me Dwarvic food!"

The mutton cooked for about forty-five minutes before it was able to be served. Dunn asked them to talk about their journey. He was intrigued, and rather jealous, that he had not been a part of it.

"To think—travellin' through the Midir Desert! And see them sylphs! Jolly stuff!"

Faruin had chopped of vegetables that Dunn had brought back from the market—carrots, Dwarvic onions, and celery. While in Dunn's kitchen, Percivine had stumbled upon larger goblets to fill the ale in. He brought those out, took the measly goblets away, and poured the ale.

"I may have had too much to drink already," said Dunn, scratching his head. "I could 'ave" —he burped loudly— "sworn my goble' was much smaller."

Percivine chuckled alongside Faruin and Seleborn.

"No more for you then, Dunn?" asked Seleborn.

"No, no, keep it comin,' lads."

Dunn picked up a large iron knife from the table and began cutting off chunks of the mutton to place on their clay plates. Percivine couldn't be happier with this portion. He looked at Faruin's and Seleborn's plate and noticed they had relatively smaller chunks.

"Er...I don't think I could eat this much," said Percivine.

"Nonsense!" said Dunn, hiccupping and almost dropping his plate. "That's a fine piece. The ale will help ye swallow it down."

Percivine was worried it would not help him. Nonetheless, Dunn was being quite hospitable to make up for the earlier part of their visit, so Percivine began picking at it without saying another word. He was glad he finally had some "real" food to stuff down his gullet.

"So, Mr. Ogthorne, how is Relthren been treatin' ye?"

"I must admit," said Percivine, "Relthren was beyond any of my conceptions of it. A grand place for a grand people."

"It be grea' hearin' such things," said Dunn.

"The views are breathtaking. I am very curious to know more about those machinations you call golems."

"Ah, I'm will be glad to oblige ye on tha'!" said Dunn, through a burp. "I think I said this earlier, but we Dwarves 'ave advanced ourselves greatly in technology an' architecture. Mos' of the constructs ye see walkin' aroun' are over two thousand years old—never been touched or harmed. Thane Ebsurwald the Extravagant had commissioned Byeryn to initiate the project to 'ave these mechanical achievements built. Byeryn was able to funnel maggedium's great energy back into stakratite and use the metal to serve as the golems' power cores. Stakratite, alongside zanilium—a highly flammable metal, I migh' add—is considered some of the rarest metals in all Gylranor. Zanilium is also harvested deep beneath Relthren an' can also be dug on the island of Saluron, specifically in Darkwood. The mechanical guardians—don' let them scare ye. They won' harm ye unless ordered too.

"And ye know of the Wayorbs, don't ye?"

Percivine was surprised by the questions. "I have one myself," he said. "Why?"

"Guess who invented them contraptions?"

"The Dwarves," he said sarcastically.

"Aye!" Dunn hiccupped again. "A group of ancient Dwarvic inventors created them. We Dwarves have much to be proud of. We're revered among the many. If it weren' for us Dwarves, ye lads would not 'ave such means of communication."

"Noted, Dunn," said Seleborn.

Whether Dwarves or Elves were more pompous, Percivine found hard to decide.

"Fascinating." Percivine was surprised Dunn spoke with any clarity after so much drinking. "This has been the first time I've ever seen such a thing."

Soon, almost everyone had finished their plates. Percivine managed to only leave bits and pieces of fat from the mutton and some vegetables. He took one last swig of his ale, then placed it down before closing one eye. Faruin stumbled over to the bed Dunn had laid out for him. Seleborn grabbed their plates and Dunn's and took them to the wash area, where they began to clean them. Percivine could see Dunn asleep in his chair, hiccupping at different intervals. After Seleborn had finished cleaning the dishes, he and Percivine awoke the drunken Dwarf, and guided him to his bedroom. Once Dunn was fast asleep in his bed, they made their way to their own.

"Looks like Faruin already started in his slumber," said Seleborn. "Goodnight, Perci."

"Night," said Percivine.

The night was very still. Not a sound could be heard but the snores and heavy breathing of those sleeping in Dunn's home *and* someone murmuring in their sleep.

"Now take care of your younger brother, Sirien," said a woman, bending over to lightly kiss his forehead.

"I will."

"Promise me you'll not get yourself into too much trouble, Percivine."

"I…promise…"

"Astronitus, I must be off. The portal will appear soon. Take care of my two boys. She turned to a young Percivine and Sirien. Behave for your father, boys. I will return, and when I do—"

"Yes…mum—"

"Perci, *wake up!*" shouted Seleborn.

A large tremor rumbled through the ground. Percivine woke abruptly from the dream of his mother to see Dunn in panic, as Faruin and Seleborn quickly collected their things.

"What's going on?" he asked, stumbling out of his bed. The tremors kept on. "Seleborn, what is *happening?*"

"A warrior has been going from home to home saying we are under attack! They've advised us to gather in the Large Hall for further instructions."

Percivine felt dazed and confused.

"*What?*" he said. "Who's attacking? Is the Hall safe? Why put everyone in one place?"

"Dunn assures me the Hall was designed to house the entire population of Relthren, in case of an emergency. He says it hasn't been used in nearly a hundred years…I'm afraid that's about to change…Come, we must go. Dunn." He turned to the shocked Dwarf. "Grab your things; we are leaving."

Percivine grew cross. He did not appreciate Seleborn ignoring his question on who was attacking, but for now he had no time to ask him again—for Seleborn and Faruin already began making their way through Dunn's front door.

As they exited *Timeworn Antiquities*, they could see a mad house of adults and children raging along the mountain walkways towards the Large Hall. Percivine was almost hit across the face by the hammer of a guard as he stumbled in his efforts to not lose sight of Faruin, Seleborn, and Dunn. They swept past many people as they scurried to the Hall. They reached the entryway but were shoved and shunned by the scrambling crowd trying desperately to get in without any order.

"We're never going to get in like this, Seleborn!" said Faruin.

Seleborn looked all around him. He could see an opening between a tall, husky Barbish woman and a Ranoic man, who bickered amongst one another, trying to get ahead of the rest.

"…cannot get through this damned crowd!" said the husky Barb.

"Go that way, Olin!" said the yellow-feathered Ranoic man.

"No! That way won't work! This way!"

Percivine and company broke in between them and pushed their way deeper in the crowd. Percivine looked back at the woman Olin and the Ranoic stranger as they rushed by, glimpsing their expressionless faces. Instead of bickering, they could have made a run for the entrance the way they did.

On reaching the entrance, they were blockaded by two more guards, who crossed their axes in front of them.

"An' where do ye think ye four are goin'?" asked the guard with the artificial leg. "This is a time of turmoil, ye don' honestly think we're goin' to let ye come by, are ye?"

"We must get past!" demanded Seleborn. "We're simply tourists and want nothing to do what's happening now!"

"Hold back!" said the other guard, who sweat dangled over her fat, pierced nose. "It is highly suspicious that ye four wan' to leave at a time like this."

Percivine pulled Seleborn back and whispered something to him.

"I don't think it's best if we arouse any sort of suspicion."

Seleborn nodded.

"Very well," he said over the hollering crowd, "we will move back."

"Thas a good lad," said the nose-pierced guard. "Now back! *Back I say!*"

The bustling crowd tried pushing their way past the guards, but it was no use: they would not budge.

"What are we going to do?" bellowed Percivine.

"Dunn, do you have any suggestions?" said Faruin.

Shocked as he was, the Dwarf tried to relax, and to ponder the situation. He tuned out the maddening noise of the crowd and looked high to the cavernous ceiling of the Large Hall. His grey eyes spottted large hanging braziers. Their fire burned brightly. Dunn looked at the three, and back to the ceiling. He raised his stubby fingers, and before they could take another breath, a large explosion occurred on one of the braziers. The thick, heavy chains holding the brazier prevented it from falling onto the crowd.

"Go! GO!" said Dunn.

The two guards at the entrance loosened their stance, and were dragged into the crowd covering themselves from any falling debris. Percivine, Faruin, Seleborn, Dunn, and a few others rushed through the entrance. The two guards gave notice to this, and hurried back to block off any others from escaping.

"Fools!" said the guard with the maggedium leg.

"Where should we head?" asked Percivine, as three Dwarves ran past them toward the large gate.

"We should be fine…for now," said Dunn, panting. "How do ye think this city has lasted untouched for so long? Those blasted Argoms will have a hard time tryin' to get in! Now come! This way!"

They followed Dunn around a corner. A sudden *bang* ripped beneath their feet and through their bodies. A group of Dwarvic soldiers and one golem, stomping heavily, rushed by them towards the gate. Seleborn managed to halt one of the soldiers in plate armor, the mighty crest of a mountain of Uln Alzor glistening from the fire.

"What's happening?"

"They're tryin' to break in! Reinforcements have been called! The Thane has been notified!"

"We have no choice!" called Seleborn. "We must follow them! I don't know where the bloody exit to this city is, so we'll have to leave the way we came!"

Along the way, they felt more vibrations as the Argoms tried to make their way through. They ducked in order to avoid the falling mountain rock from plummeting into their skulls. Percivine felt guilty for snapping at Dunn earlier, for having accused them of bringing trouble with them. He'd been right after all…

Once they reached the Iron Portcullis, hundreds of soldiers stood at attention, awaiting further instruction. As ordered, four golems stood against the Portcullis.

"You four there, what are ye doing?"

A sharp, cold voice snarled at them. A hulky, older Dwarf in heavy steel armor and magenta hair and mustache marched towards them, the same crest of a mountain on the breastplate.

"Yes?" said Seleborn.

"Why are ye not in the 'All with the others?"

"We figured all the fun would be out of that place," said Seleborn.

"Is that so?"

Seleborn nodded.

"I don' know who ye think ye are disobeying orders, but now that we've got ye, ye will stay 'ere an' help us push those foul monstrosities back."

"But we are just tourists!" said Percivine.

"No' anymore," said the Dwarf. "I had gotten word of three unusual figures sighted 'ere in Relthren…I see that I just found them…"

"Please, you must let us go!" begged Percivine.

"It's no use, lad," said Dunn. "Ye're arguing with a Dwarf. Very stubborn of creatures. We'll just have to stay an' fight."

"I'm afraid we 'ave no extra armor to spare, so—"

"What seems to be going on here?" said a deep, raspy voice. The sound of the voice was not like any other Dwarf Percivine had heard; it had no accent, unusual for a Dwarf.

Standing next to the heavily armored Dwarf was yet another Dwarf, dressed in fine black linen vestments. To Percivine's surprise, the Dwarf looked remarkably like Dunn.

"Minister!" said the mustached Dwarf. "Ye must get to safety! It's dangerous out 'ere!"

It now rang in Percivine's mind: this was the cousin that Dunn had spoken of earlier, the evening before. With his lone working eye, Thiurwold Galon hardly observed them.

"I'm the Minister of War. I believe my being here is quite beneficial," said Thiurwold, a lonely ring hanging on the eyebrow above where an eye should be. He turned his head slightly in Dunn's direction. "What are you doing with them?"

"They call themselves *tourists*, but I don' believe a word of it. I insist that they stay an' fight!"

"This is not their battle, Tholfdir. Now let them depart as necessary."

Tholfdir felt extremely stupefied.

"Y-yes, Minister, but—but it is too dangerous for them to leave now!"

"The back entrance is far too distant to get to now. Cast a transparency spell on them, and let them leave as desired!"

"Right away, Minister," said Tholfdir.

"There's no need," said Faruin, cutting him off. "I'm an Elf, and we're exceptionally good at magic. I'll do it."

Tholfdir grunted and went back to ordering his Dwarves about. Thiurwold now walked up to his cousin.

"Thanks, cousin."

"Don't mention it," said Thiurwold. "I hope you didn't leave the shop in such a mess. I've just returned, and I would like to rest after this is over." He walked away from the scene, not acknowledging Percivine, Faruin, or Seleborn.

After a few short seconds, Faruin had managed to completely hide Percivine and Seleborn into nothingness. Faruin now cast the spell on himself with a wisp of his hand, and now, he, too, became invisible.

"Remember as soon as we pass through the side entrance," said Seleborn, "make a run for it. This transparency spell won't last forever. There will be hundreds of Argoms, I suspect, behind the Portcullis, make sure not to bump into one!"

Seleborn asked one of the soldiers to open the side entrance. As the door flung open, they noticed Dunn still standing there.

"Aren't you coming?" asked Percivine.

"This is my battle, my home," he told them. "Ye three best run along. I trust I will see ye soon! Now be off!"

The soldier shut the door behind them. Seleborn carefully opened the other side of the entrance, and could see, as he foretold, hundreds of Agorms blasting the Iron Portcullis with their dangerous attacks of dark magic.

"We must get across the bridge, once we do so," said Seleborn, "we will be in the clear. Remember don't bump into any of the Argoms!"

That was difficult too: the hundreds of Argoms stood cramped, each casting their icy bolts at the Portcullis. It was no use, though: there were too many of them. But then an extraordinary thought entered Percivine's mind. He remembered what Dunn had done in the Large Hall to distract the guards. He was going to cause an explosion. He slightly raised his hand, and began to conduct the distraction.

A few seconds later, a large wall of fire appeared, burning several Argoms into oblivion. The explosion was so close that its impact knocked over a good chunk of the Argoms down into the sharp, rocky underway of the drawbridge. Percivine was astonished—in one shot, he had nearly wiped out half the Argoms.

Their chance presented itself: they sprinted through an opening between the Argoms until they finally reached the other side of the bridge.

"We've done it!" said Seleborn. "Thank the Everlasting Realm for that explosion! Who on Gylranor could have done that?"

"It was me," said Percivine, with a smile.

Seleborn blinked at him, confused, but beamed nonetheless.

They ran further down the path back to a small forest patch. Their transparency spell was wearing off. Percivine took one look at Relthren, thinking, now, after the explosion, that it should not be too hard to push back the Argoms. He continued running after Faruin and Seleborn.

CHAPTER FIVE

THE SPRITE

At last, the transparency spell around the three of them wore off. They stopped running, in order to catch the remainder of their breath. As they bent over to inhale, there was a thunderous tremor beneath their feet. A terribly large explosion, larger than Dunn's or Percivine's, struck the side of the mountain, erupting fire and smoke.

"There's no chance in turning back now, you two," Seleborn told them. "We've got to continue forward. I'm sure the guards we met last time would want to know what the commotion's all about."

They retraced their steps back to the guards' booths, where they were blocked off. Apparently, the two Dwarves had already received word on what was occurring.

"We 'ave been ordered to not let anyone in or out," said the red-bearded guard.

"You must," said Faruin. "We're merely tourists, don't you remember?"

"What we remember," said the short-bearded guard, "were three *unusual* beings, with no business in Relthren whatsoever, and look at what's happened? Unlikely coincidence."

"We did no such thing!" said Faruin. "We did not plead with anyone!"

Percivine realized that the only way Tholfdir must have known about their presence in Relthren was because of these two idiotic guardsmen. They were the only ones to have ever spotted them this early in the path to the city.

"What *exactly* did ye three do over there?" asked the first guard.

"That's on a personal matter," said Faruin shortly.

"There's no sense in arguing with them, Faruin," said Seleborn. "The more we argue, the less chance we have of getting by."

"Ye should listen to yer friend, there, Elf," said the first guard.

Faruin's blood boiled. He disliked the way these Dwarves were speaking to him, and had a right mind to push them aside with the use of his runes, but he remembered his expulsion from Unin'shai, and decided to let Seleborn speak instead. He stood back behind Percivine, hoping to catch any more glimpses of Relthren.

"We made a visit to an old friend," said Seleborn. "Dunngarunax Galon, cousin to Minister of War, Thiurwold Galon."

The shot-bearded guard raised one of his thick eyebrows in suspicion. "The Minister of War? Really?"

"Yes."

"You can't tell me, with you being Dwarves, that you've never heard about the Minister of War's cousin?" said Percivine cheekily.

"W-we have!" said the short-bearded guard. "How dare ye suggest—? We know it!"

"Then I would advise you to let us pass, or else we will have to resolve letting Dunngarunax know of this. And you can be sure that he, in turn, will let his cousin know of your insolence."

Percivine thought he rather impressed the Dwarves. He also felt he'd frightened them, sort of.

"Are ye threatenin' us?" said the red-bearded guard.

"No," said Seleborn, "it's a fact."

The short-bearded guard shrugged. He was now not sure whether or not they were telling the truth. He whispered something into the red-bearded guard's ear. Percivine, Faruin, and Seleborn stood patiently waiting.

"All righ,' all righ,'" said short-bearded Dwarf, "We'll let ye through…"

"Very good—"

"…Under one condition," finished the guard.

"*Under what condition?*" said Seleborn, angered and ready to hit the guard in his face with his elbow.

"That ye tell us the *real* reason for yer…visit…"

"For the last time," said Faruin, "we have already told you our reason for coming! If you don't get out of the way, we will—"

Seleborn grabbed Faruin's arm, which had begun to form a fist.

"Ye will *what?*" seethed the short-bearded guard, squinting both of his eyes tightly.

Before anyone could make any other form of speech or action, another thundering explosion shook the ground. The two Dwarves were knocked off their feet. Seleborn now saw this as an opportunity to escape these incompetent guards, to pick themselves up. They began running away as the guards swore after them.

"Stop! *STOP!*"

"Faruin!" called Seleborn. "Use another transparency spell!"

Without any hesitation, Faruin waved his hands and cast another transparency spell. The two guards stopped for a second, bewildered, but continued to chase the invisible figures down the path. They threw themselves to the side of the road behind a large tree's bark. They overheard the guards as they ran past.

"We know yer 'ere somewhere! Ye can' hide from us forever! We know the way ye look!"

They continued to hide behind the tree bark as their spell began to fail. They watched as the guards disappeared behind a bend of trees and bushes.

"That got rid of them," said Percivine.

"For now," said Seleborn. "They can't leave their post for so long. They'll be back."

"So, what's next?" asked Percivine. "I feel like I still won't be seeing my father and home anytime soon."

"Do you know what a sprite is?"

"Aren't they those magical creatures that are supposed to help you out?" said Percivine, leaning against the bark.

"Correct," said Seleborn.

"Let me take a *wild* guess," muttered Percivine, "we're going to go see one, aren't we?"

"Precisely."

"What for?"

"If I knew that," said Seleborn, "I would not need or want to go and see one, would I?"

Percivine was in no mood to travel anywhere, anymore. He missed his father, his home, his brother especially. It has been a week since he'd last gotten any word from those he knew. He wondered where his brother could be. He wondered what his father must be going through, knowing his two sons were nowhere to be seen. The thought was dreadful to him.

"Where exactly are we to find one?" Percivine asked. "I was taught that they were only creatures in myth."

"I only know the location of one. And it won't be very hard to find. I'm sure Faruin knows what I speak of."

Faruin's eyes widened.

"You can't possibly—not there! You know I've been exiled from that place."

"We're not going directly into Unin'shai," said Seleborn. "The sprite resides in the Jeweled Lakes. He will appear, only, after we have given it an offering."

Although not fond of the idea of more traveling, Percivine was secretly excited to visit the land of the Elves. He'd seen extravagant pictures of the beautiful wonders of Ni'shorus, and always dreamt of traversing to it. His father had also taught him about the five Jeweled Lakes.

"Each of the Lakes is a different color for a different gem," added Seleborn. "The first is Lake Barenshai, the Sapphire Lake or the Lake of Knowledge; the second we have, Lake Orig'ai, also known as the Topaz Lake, the Lake of Nature; the third is Lake Al'hai, the Ruby Lake, the Lake of Relationships; the fourth lake is named Lake Henshai, the Emerald Lake or the Lake of Prosperity, and finally we have the last lake, Lake Isai, the Diamond Lake or known as the Lake of Harmony. Each of the five Lakes represent each of the aspects the Stars, created by the Elves, implemented in Elvic society as a way by which every Elf should live their life."

"It appears that you may know more about Elvic society more than I do," joked Faruin. "Perhaps you should also tell us about the Elvic Exodus from the Old Empire."

"Hardly," said Seleborn. "I only know this from reading Averwyn Dibble's *The Traditional Society and Customs of Elves*. Besides, you have nothing to worry about."

"What d'you mean?"

"Faruin here can as well cast transformation runes."

"Why runes?" asked Percivine, perplexed. "I just saw him use his hands back there!"

"I prefer runes," said Faruin. "They have a sort of…thrilling feel when used."

"Once it's conjured," said Seleborn, "you step onto it immediately. You are made to appear under a different guise. The effects will last a few hours."

"If I'm caught, you do realize I will be jailed for the remainder of my life, you do know that, right?"

"You have nothing to worry about."

"Here's a question," said Percivine. "Are we to travel by foot?"

"No, not this time," said Seleborn. "I have a contact in Unin'shai currently waiting on me to Orb them."

"Who?"

"In time you shall meet them, Perci," said Seleborn. "For now, he'll open the portal."

Seleborn withdrew his Wayorb, and whispered into the spherical object. It began to give off its usual golden glow. They waited a few seconds until they heard the voice of another, from the other side.

"Seleborn?" said the voice.

"Yes, we are ready," he told the Orb.

"Be warned," said the mellow voice.

"About?"

"It's not safe here. The Triumvirate received word from Nell about Percivine Ogthorne, and any who are involved in his escape. Throughout the city, there is a standing picture of both him and his brother."

"*What?*" exclaimed Percivine. "Never thought I'd be a fugitive-at-large."

"He is wanted. It is a decree from Omitay Handolan of the Triumvirate," said the unknown voice.

"Why would the Elves want our arrest, anyway?" said Seleborn, who just became a bit more concerned.

"All the Landseer's doing."

"You mean Talus the Dark's?" said Seleborn.

"Regardles," said the Orb, "she warned the Triumvirate that your trouble. The Triumvirate doesn't want any more disorder here, as we are dealing with the Argoms on our own front. The Landseer wants you found and brought back. She's even got your King to support her."

"This is absurd!" moaned Percivine. "I am not a criminal!"

"We know that," said Faruin. "What shall we do, Seleborn? I've already got a mark on my record. Now you've got one, as well. I don't know if we should risk anything else."

"We are to go…to the Jeweled Lakes," said Seleborn hastily into the Orb. "If there is anyone who I would want to receive advice from, at the present moment, it would be from a sprite. We are going, are there any problems? Open the portal."

"Have it your way," said the voice in the Orb.

"I think they are this way!" They could now hear one of the Dwarf's voices getting closer and closer. "I think I 'eard somethin' comin' from those trees!"

"Get in! *Now!*"

Seleborn pushed Faruin and Percivine into the portal. Just as the two guards approached, he threw himself forward, and found himself landing face-first into a muddy bank of a white-lit lake.

"I-I don't understand," said Percivine. "How could the Landseer do this? What's her motive for this? I am not the enemy!"

Faruin sympathized greatly for Percivine. He knew what it was like to be labeled a criminal for something you never committed. He urged Percivine to calm himself, but Percivine took no care of it. He wanted justice for the injustice the Landseer had set upon him and his brother.

"Sirien drags me into this mess, and now I'm stuck paying for it with my life!"

"Enough," said Seleborn. "Come on. The Lake of Knowledge is this way."

The glow of the white lake disappeared as they found themselves walking into another muddy bank, where this time the glow of the lake was an ornate blue.

This must be Lake Barenshai, the Lake of Knowledge, thought Percivine.

As they approached the calm waters of the Lake, the glow grew brighter, and, at the bottom, Percivine noticed, were actual sapphires, spread all throughout the bottom of the Lake.

This must be true of all the Lakes.

"Now what do we do?" asked Percivine, feeling at ease for the time being.

Seleborn brought both of his hands to his neck. To Percivine's eyes, he looked ready to choke himself. Instead, Seleborn removed a very peculiar necklace from around his neck, and held it up to show them. It dangled in the slight breeze.

"Do you know what this is?" he asked them.

"Er," said Percivine.

"That's some sort of pendant," said Faruin.

"This is an exact replica of Ruric Vilinius's necklace. Each Warlock or Mage was given it to wear, but each class had its own special significance from it. For Mages, the necklace meant that a little piece of their ancestor's soul remained in their own. For us, Warlocks the necklace was a symbol of power. As you can see" —Seleborn pointed out a small symbol resembling the face of a Netherid— "this signifies our power and control over the Netherids when we call upon them. Elvic customs state that in order to speak with the sprite, you must first give up an offering…Ruric's Necklace is what I've chosen to sacrifice."

"But won't you need it?" said Percivine.

"Like I said it's only a replica, a mere copy of his. This necklace holds no form of magic or power or anything like that. It's just a symbol."

"All right."

"Now, watch closely," Seleborn told them. "If I've done this correctly, the sprite should have no trouble in seeing us."

"Hold it!" said Percivine.

"What's wrong?"

"Won't the protectors from the city notice this suspicious activity?" he said. "It's nighttime, after all. Wouldn't you think they'd wonder what's happening?"

"Perci's right, Seleborn," said Faruin. "I think we should change our appearance, just to be on the safe side. Remember what the voice said: there's a warrant for anyone helping Percivine, and that's us. So, we must proceed with caution."

Seleborn sighed. "Very well. Let's do it quickly, then."

Faruin placed transformation runes on the ground that Percivine and Seleborn stepped on. Instantly, Percivine and Seleborn changed into two pale-skinned Elves, Percivine of green hair and Seleborn of orange.

Faruin stepped onto his own rune, which transformed him into a stubby, thick Dwarf with a long, black beard. Next, Faruin hastily gave them all new identities in case guards came and asked for their names.

"I think we're set," said Faruin. "We have our identities. Now proceed, Seleborn."

"Thank you, Faruin."

Percivine and Faruin took a step back and watched as Seleborn threw the necklace into the center of the lake, causing a light splash.

Nothing happened for a moment, until *the* Lake began glowing even brighter than before. They took several steps back. The glow of the Lake dimmed, before totally evaporating. They looked up and saw a small, scaly blue creature with webbed hands and feet, gazing down. The sprite, floating in midair, glided gently towards them. Its reptilian-like face seemed to smile at them.

"Which one of you has summoned me?" asked the sprite.

"That would be I," said Seleborn.

The sprite raised a cold eyebrow.

"Your offering was most…unusual," it said. "Never in the thousands of years I've spent at this Lake has a Warlock ever sought advice from this sprite."

"It's the necklace of—"

"I know what it is," said the sprite. "I'm merely…surprised."

"Where has the glow of the Lake gone?" asked Seleborn.

"I illuminate Barenshai, the Lake of Knowledge, as the Elves call it. With me out of it, it no longer can hold a glow."

"So you must mean the glow of the other Lakes come from your kind, as well?"

"My kind, you say?" said the sprite, recoiling a little at Seleborn's comment. "Very true, yes."

"I meant no disrespect," said Seleborn.

"It would appear," said the sprite, "that the arrogance of Neledar is truly as disgusting as I've been told."

Seleborn said nothing.

"How are you aware that I am a Neledar, and not an Elf?"

"We sprites are creatures of extraordinary wisdom and intelligence. You cannot fool us. Not even by the most potent of transformation magic."

"I see."

"I fear you do not," said the sprite. "None of you mortal races can *ever* know what we're capable of."

"I presume not," said Seleborn.

"Presume?" it said, almost interested in Seleborn's retort. The sprite glided closer to them. "You have not come to argue with me, have you? You are here on another important matter, I see…Yes…I see what troubles you. How can I be of assistance?"

"We come here in hopes that you can answer some questions we have."

"I will answer them in accordance with my ability, but we aware," the sprite said solemnly, "I give my responses with helpful hints, and not offer complete or blunt answers…I don't give heroes everything in one basket. A hero is someone who, with the help of others, strives through life's obstacles to achieve the goodness they seek."

"You think we're heroes?" said Percivine. "I don't even know where I'm going."

Oh yes," said the sprite.

"Why do you think so?" asked Seleborn, taking a step closer to the water.

"If I told you that," said the sprite, "then I wouldn't be keeping my promise of helpful hints, would I?"

"I…suppose not," said Seleborn meekly.

"Now, what is it you come seeking from me?"

"What can you tell us about the government of Nell?" said Seleborn. "As of late, a splendid source has told us that we are wanted for the aid of Percivine Ogthorne. We have done nothing wrong. Why is that?"

"Ah," said the sprite making a flip in the air, "I'm glad you asked. It seems that the innocent are now in guilty shoes. Indeed, there is something amok…All I can say is this: *From within the forms of government, there is the one who seeks power in bold, to rage, to havoc, to destroy…Not until a hero comes along to break the hold.* I greatly advise the three of you to not linger so much in your travels…Anything else?"

"Yes," said Percvine, who, until now, had rarely said anything to this encounter with the sprite. "I have something to ask of your wisdom."

"By all means," said the sprite, now focusing his attention on Percivine.

"I need to know the whereabouts of my brother," he said. "If you know anything about where he is or what he's up to, then, please, you must tell me!"

The sprite met Percivine's eyes, as he waited anxiously for a reply. Percivine waited for the sprite to stop giving him such an odd look. The look made Percivine think the sprite was not accustomed to such feelings from a mortal.

"Your brother is well and safe," it said, breaking its promise of hints.

Faruin and Seleborn straightened up a little at the sprite's response. Percivine's watery eyes opened fully. He fell to his knees, utterly relieved.

"Is your friend all right?" asked the sprite, with a hint of suspicion.

"I…think so," said Seleborn bringing up Percivine. "You all right, Perci?"

"It's a melody to my ears, knowing now that Sirien is safe."

"For now," added the sprite cautiously. "There may be a time again when your brother will find himself in danger. You might even find yourself in danger, as a matter of fact."

Percivine did not care. At least he could roam around a few moments without worry for his brother. He stared at the sprite.

"What seems to trouble you?" the sprite asked him.

"I find it hard to believe, still, that you are here in our presence. My father always taught me that sprites were nothing but mere watery spirits, and a myth."

"*Watery spirits?*" hissed the sprite. "We are no such thing! Bah! This once again proves the distaste I have for mortal arrogance. We are real; we have a physical presence, as you are aware. Anyway," continued the sprite, "we sprites were discovered not more than forty years ago, by one you know, Faruin Abrandil."

"Is that right?" asked Faruin.

"Yes. A Dedrinus Etwood."

Faruin blinked. He felt now slightly betrayed that his mentor—his teacher and great friend—had never spoke of this to him. Not even a shred of evidence throughout Ni'shorus ever proved this.

"He was very clear to keep our discovery anonymous. He feared that if the world knew of our existence that we would be taken advantage of. But what the Elf did not know was that we are creatures of extraordinary power, and no such thing would ever have occurred. However, he insisted the world was not to be trusted. Our Goddess made an extremely rare visit to the physical world to have conference with him. In this rare meeting, the Goddess agreed to let Dedrinus have his way."

"How exactly is it that he found you?" asked Faruin.

"Your friend was a Fenemerys, correct?"

"Yes."

"He had foreseen himself in his discovery of us. You may be wondering that his anonymousness failed—and it did. I am sure that you were his best pupil, but I am also sure that you were not his only. There would have been others he confided this information with, and before one could realize, the knowledge of our existence had spread secretly amongst the Elves. Soon the Neledar knew of this information, then the Dwarves, and soon the rest of the world was aware that such beings existed in their reality."

The sprite then added: "Your friend, as they say, would be devastated, and most angered about this if he were alive today."

"Don't let this deter you, Faruin," said Percivine, knowing his companion felt sickened and unappreciated that Dedrinus kept such a discovery locked away.

"Perci's right, surprisingly," said Seleborn, to which Percivine rolled his yes. Percivine, too tired, to retaliate, said nothing else. "We've got other present matters to attend to."

"It appears that I have done what's been asked of me," said the sprite, resuming his place over the center of the lake. "There is nothing else that you need of me. I am to return to home. I implement my luck into your…tireless efforts to help save the world. We will meet in the future. Until then…"

They watched as the sprite slowly sank itself into the depths of the Lake, not to be seen again. The water's original glow returned. They remained silent and still, a gentle night breeze sweeping over them.

Seleborn gestured his head towards Faruin at Percivine.

"Faruin?" he said.

"Just fine, just fine," he muttered.

"You don't look it," said Seleborn. "What's your problem?"

"I don't see why Dedrinus did not trust me with this information. He taught me, he took me under his wing for eleven years! *Eleven years!* I would think that was capable time for him to trust me, don't you think?"

"I never met him," said Seleborn, "but I'm sure he had his reasons for not confiding in you. You can't be so quick to elude him for his reasons."

Faruin turned to the other two. He looked at them quietly, then turned to look at the walled Elvic city just lying in front of them.

"I need to enter the city…"

Percivine was surprised, and Seleborn grinned.

"What for?" asked Percivine. "You nearly lost your mind when Seleborn mentioned going to the Jeweled Lakes."

"Hardly!" said Faruin.

"As you say," said Percivine, almost ready to laugh.

"I need to pay a visit to the Temple of the Stars."

"The Temple—what?"

"It's been far too long since I've paid my respects to Dedrinus's grave. He would have wanted me to do this, no matter the circumstance."

"But what's there to visit? I thought all Elves, when they die, vanish to the Stars?" said Percivine.

"They do," said Faruin. "We Elves, much like you, Neledar, have grave markers for those of us who have deceased and transcended to the Stars."

"I'll admit it's amiable, Faruin," interjected Seleborn, "but shortly before we arrived here, you worried that you would be caught and thrown back into the Citadel. What's brought about this sudden change? And, more recently, you were scolding your dead mentor…"

"I know," he said. "I might have overreacted a little."

"A little?" said Percivine cheekily. "I don't think that's the proper term for it."

"Hush!" snapped Faruin. "This is no laughing matter. I cannot pretend that I am not cross with Dedrinus, but maybe by my going to the Temple, a new feeling will wash over me, erasing that old one."

"And how do you expect to get in?" said Percivine. "Those gates appear to be heavily fortified."

"Once the gates open freely," said Faruin, "the paladins who guard Unin'shai welcome all outsiders freely."

"Yes, but you forget that I have a father who is extremely interested in anything having to relate to the Elves, *and*, you can't forget what that voice told us over the Orb: there is a warrant for my arrest, and anyone associated with me. I'm sure the security at the gates is going to be very precise and detailed in deciding who they let into their city."

"Perci has a point, Faruin," said Seleborn. "If we are planning to make a march into the city, we will need to properly prepare ourselves beforehand."

"Well, look, we've already got these hilarious identities over us," said Faruin, "so I really don't see what the problem is."

"You're not the only one around here who has worries about entering the city," said Percivine. "We can't rush into these things. We need to make sure the preparations are in order…Besides, what's the damn hurry?"

The next few moments were critical. Seleborn went over with them the plan for their entry, and the contingency plan in case of failure. Faruin also laid more transformation runes on the ground to further strengthen Percivine's incognito self. Percivine spent most of his time remembering his given identity, in case they asked for it.

"…I'll do most of the talking," Faruin said. "Once we approach, the paladins will alarm themselves to oncoming visitors. We'll do it like we did in Relthren…Tourists are what we call ourselves…nothing more, nothing less…"

"Which gate are we to pass through?" asked Seleborn. "The Northern or the Southern Gates?"

"Does it matter?" said Faruin. "Each of the Gates are at each end of the city…However, Lake Barenshai is closest to the Northern Gates. Might as well try to get past those."

"Then the Northern Gates it is," said Seleborn.

Seleborn led them around the muddy bank of the Lake. Percivine could see the white walls of Unin'shai extending upward as they neared them. An apparent topaz glow now illuminated their faces as they pased another familiar-looking muddy bank. Two guards dressed in fine, silver Elvic armor stood at each side of the ornate and lavish gate blockading the inside to rest of the outside world.

"Halt—"

The word sparked a familiar memory for Percivine all too vividly regarding Dwarvic watchmen.

"—it's a bit late for wanderers, isn't?" said the guard with the same olive-green tone just like Faruin, as the other paladin, of white skin, approached.

"We've just stumbled here after a stop in Norshuruk. We are extremely exhausted, and wish to indulge ourselves with food and beverage," said Seleborn.

The two paladins eyed them up and down for a few seconds.

"Is that so?" said the white-toned paladin.

"Yes," replied Seleborn.

"What were you three doing at the Sapphire Lake?" asked the olive-skinned paladin.

"Is that really any of your concern?" said Seleborn.

The olive-green guard raised his eyebrow. "It is my concern when you decide to speak with a sprite from near my city."

"It's a personal matter, and I think you should treat tourists with much more respect than that."

"Now let me—"

The white-skinned paladin quickly pulled back the other paladin and spoke to him in a low voice. The group, however, could still hear what he was saying:

"Do not lose your temper. Do you want these *tourists* to complain about us? The last time this happened we were—well, don't make me remind you! Now just do the routine security check and let them through."

When the guards returned to face them, the group acted like they'd not heard a word.

The olive-toned guard exhaled with frustration. Through gritted teeth, he asked, "What's…your…business…here?"

"Like I said earlier, we're just passing through for the night, hoping for some comfort in sleep, food, and drink. Nothing more."

The olive-toned paladin refrained from any further discussion. He then pulled out a picture of someone's face. He squinted at the picture, then at Percivine the "Elf" standing next to the disguised Seleborn.

"You look awfully like the man in this picture," he said to the incognito Percivine.

Percivine could feel an electrifying sensation up his spine.

"I don't know who that is."

"His name is Percivine Ogthorne. He is a highly dangerous Neledar. He is wanted back by Nell, and his presence anywhere will cause the infectious Argoms to come and harm the lives of others. We don't want that here."

Do I look like a Neledar to you?" demanded Percivine.

"Don't—!" began the white-toned paladin, grabbing the other's upper arm to help resist him from doing anything else.

"*Very well! VERY WELL!*"

The paladins returned to their posts and watched as the lavish gate swung open, presenting to them a quiet, lonely, cobblestone path surrounding many magnificent Elvic structures. The Northern Gates behind them shut.

"What was all that about?" Percivine said, surveying the scene.

"What do you mean?" said Seleborn.

"Why would that guard say that I look like myself in the picture?"

Percivine and Seleborn turned to Faruin.

"There's something I forgot to mention…" Faruin said.

"Of course you did," said Percivine as he exhaled.

"The point of the transformation is to make you appear like a different species of some kind, but it moderately changes your facial features. If someone were to look at the incognito specimen and the real specimen in a picture, they would be able to see the similar features in both. But there have been very few cases in which runes of transformation failed—unless you give your identity away, of course."

As they continued to listen to Faruin's knowledge on the matter, a shadowy figure walked towards them…

CHAPTER SIX

TEMPLE OF THE STARS

Slowly, the shadowy figure approached them. The figure could see them still conversing about the effects of transformation sorcery. As they drew nearer, Seleborn said something in a dark tone: "You will not come any further. You will stop and turn around."

The covered figure was alarmed that they had noticed them. The figure was also rather impressed the way they had lured them. The figure removed their mantle and two long pointed ears sprouted into the air. A yellow-skinned Elf, with bright green eyes, and long brown hair, stood before them.

"Twy'leden!" said Seleborn. "What's the idea approaching us like that? We could have hurt you!"

"I did not mean to alarm," said Twy'leden. "I see you made it here without any trouble, I presume."

"Well…I wouldn't say quite that," said Faruin. "I think we may be most wanted by the Dwarves, but nothing too extreme, or illegal."

"I don't suspect you'll be wanted there like in Nell and Ni'shorus. Uln Alzor is not yet so tainted."

The Elf greeted Seleborn with much enthusiasm, and soon noticed another Elf standing between Faruin and Seleborn.

"I believe introductions are in order," said Seleborn. "Twy'leden, let me introduce to you Percivine Ogthorne—well, Percivine Ogthorne in disguise."

Twy'leden bowed slightly before Percivine in a pompous manner.

"Perci," said Seleborn happily, "this is Twy'leden Paros, one of the newest members to the Solemn Hand. He currently works as Assistant Elf for Beautification, under the new Lord Elf…Dedrinus's…replacement…"

"And my successor," said Faruin.

Seleborn knew he spoke on a fragile matter of Faruin's, so refrained from saying anything else.

"Come, come," said Twy'leden. "I'm sure you three are exhausted. We'll go to my house, so you can properly rest."

Twy'leden led them up the cobblestone street and up a small incline. Percivine simply enjoyed himself. He'd always heard of the illustrious architecture of the Elves, and now, through the shadows, he noticed many arches, unusual greenery, domes, and Elvic statues as they walked the street to Twy'leden's home.

Twy'leden's home was everything Percivine thought it would be. Vines stretched along the marble face, over the door, of his home. The interior was far cozier than Dunn's had been. Percivine could see many more fixtures covered in elegant fabrics, and actual warm beds that had no base of rock. It was a delight to be in a comfortable, familiar sleeping environment. Now he was ready to set his stuff down and eat. Twy'leden showed them the room they would be sleeping in, then directed them to a table.

Twy'leden had served them a very odd but delicious Elvic meal of herb-baked woodcock and Elvic wine. They enjoyed these pleasurable comforts in front of a fire, which helped ward off the night's chill.

"So…" Twy'leden said. "So, I am eternally surprised to see *you* here, Faruin." He eyed their disguises. "I see Faruin's work always gives the best results."

"Mind if we get rid of these transformations?" asked Seleborn.

"By all means, please," said Twy'leden. "I'd like a closer look at Sirien's brother."

Percivine expected this.

Nothing more inviting than an Elf wishing to inspect you, he thought.

Faruin quickly got rid of the transformation effect this time, using rune-less magic, and was elated to be himself again.

"My, my," said Twy'leden, between sips from a gold-encrusted goblet, "you certainly do look like your brother."

"Thanks," muttered Percivine.

"Dunn was here earlier," said Twy'leden.

"*He was?*"

Their eventful stay at Relthren had all but remained in their thoughts. Too soon. It was a surprise to hear that Dunn had just paid Twy'leden a visit.

"Yes."

"How could that be?" said Seleborn. "Relthren must have been on lockdown after what occurred there."

"He explained it all too clear to me," said Twy'leden. "It appears that those Dwarvic golems of theirs did the trick. Dunn said Thiurwold, as Minister of War, ordered that hundreds fall to the Iron Portcullis and push them back…but he had also mentioned something out of the ordinary…"

"Like what?" asked Percivine timidly.

"That a *mysterious* entity had caused some sort of an explosion on the viaduct. Dealing the Argoms with fiery damage, and knocking half their force over it. You three wouldn't know anything about that, would you?"

Percivine swallowed and nearly choked. It was him, after all, who had caused the explosion.

"We know nothing of the sort," said Seleborn. He had caught eye of Percivine's nervous features. "Whoever it was had helped us to make a great escape."

Twy'leden made a disapproving face. It almost seemed that he did not believe them but said nothing more on the matter.

"He suspected that you three would arrive promptly since I was your contact here," said Twy'leden.

"Why didn't he just Orb us to tell us this?" asked Seleborn.

"He thought it too dangerous," said Twy'leden "With all the mess that's going around, I hardly think it would be wise to contact you…anyway…Nell's in dire need."

It now struck Percivine who this Elf was. For the time being he had tried, with great difficulty, to understand where he's heard this voice before, and now he realized: Twy'leden had been the voice Seleborn contacted through the Orb, when they'd arrived at the Lakes. It was him who had told them about the warrants.

"I didn't mean to alarm anyone," said Twy'leden, noticing the suspicious eyes of Percivine meeting his own. "I only wanted to warn you of the troubles brewing around here."

"You must know where my brother is then!" said Percivine.

The shout almost startled Twy'leden.

"I-I'm sorry, Percivine, but Sirien's whereabouts are his own, I'm afraid. He's given us no lead as to where he's been. His strict orders to protect you, however, have pursued I should say, quite nicely. His instruction has been very precise to the last detail."

"If you think being on the run like a criminal is *nice*, then so be it," retorted Percivine.

"Did I offend you?"

"*No*," hissed Percivine. He was very distraught that, yet again, another member of Sirien's so called Solemn Hand is utterly clueless as to where he might be. "I've lost my appetite."

"Very well," said Twy'leden. "You can empty your plate in the bin over there" —he pointed to a chrome bin lying next to a kitchen counter— "and you can set your plate in the sink, there."

Percivine got up abruptly, and set to wash his dish to release his frustration. He cleaned noisily in the background as Twy'leden began to speak once more.

"I was sorry to hear about your friend Rufious, Seleborn. You have my deepest condolences."

"Thank you, Twy'leden."

"Did he have any family?"

"Y-yes," said Seleborn, "a wife and two small children."

"I was led to believe that they weren't living together?"

"That is correct. He believed his involvement with the Solemn Hand was too great a risk to have those he loved close by. So—he sent them to Edelas, to work among the Elder Elves within the Annals of Elga'min."

"Ah, I could think of no safer place, and a bit surprising. The Elves of Edelas aren't usually so inviting to outsiders to live amongst them. The archivists there dabble in potent spells of arcane, and would act as great defenders of that place, if the moment presented itself."

"Agreed," said Seleborn.

"Are they aware of his death?" asked Twy'leden curiously.

"Not that I know of," said Seleborn. "I've not yet had the chance to write them explaining what has happened. I know she will be devastated, but I'd like to think his death was not in vain."

"That sounds plausible," said Twy'leden genially. "Perhaps, upon your return to Headquarters, you shall write to her?"

"I think so."

"I see Assistant Elf of Beautification is treating you well," said Faruin apprehensively, looking at the luxuries Twy'leden's home presented.

"I manage," said Twy'leden. "I don't understand how you ever liked doing that sort of stuff, Faruin."

"Unlike Mormac, Dedrinus was wise and held compassion for what he did."

"You'll have no argument from me. How he ever got a recommendation from the Triumvirate is beyond me."

"They had no choice, did they?" said Faruin gravely. "After all that, they needed another Elf, and promptly, to continue the work."

"The meal was delicious," Percivine cut in nimbly, thanking Twy'leden only for the portions he had eaten before losing his want to eat.

"Happy you enjoyed whatever parts you did ingest."

Twy'leden slightly lifted a finger, and all their plates lifted accordingly before making their way silently toward the sink. Percivine grumbled even more and began to wash the rest of the filthy dishes.

"You don't have to wash them, you know."

Percivine muttered something and kept washing the rest of the plates.

"What's the matter with him?" Twy'leden asked.

"Sirien's secrets have left Percivine feeling a bit sour and resentful," said Seleborn. "Perci *hates* secrets."

"You would too if you were in my place!" snarled Percivine from the kitchen sink.

"That makes sense," said Twy'leden. "Now that we're settled in comfortably, would any of you mind telling me why you're really here?"

"If you spot me some Elvic mead, I would certainly be glad to tell you our reason for being here," Seleborn said.

A freshly clean chrome goblet and carafe hovered straight towards them. With a flick of his wrist, the carafe poured its contents into the goblet, and landed itself gently in front of Seleborn.

"There you are," said Twy'leden. "Mind you, though, these have been aged for one hundred years. It helps to pass the time, sometimes."

"Understood," said Seleborn. "But I think Faruin should speak. After all we are here for him."

Twy'leden raised an eyebrow.

"The exile returns…"

Faruin breathed heavily, but very quietly. He rather wished Seleborn would not have said that in short.

"Well, Faruin?"

"I need to visit the Temple of the Stars."

"What for?" Twy'leden now poured himself mead. A slight trickle of sweat ran down his nose. "What's your reason?"

"You know, Twy'leden," said Faruin. "Do not sit there and pretend that you are without a clue!"

"I've already paid my—"

"I don't give a damn! Go again! Doesn't he deserve more than just one visit from you? *You were there the night he died!*"

"Control your tone," said Twy'leden. "I had left. Don't you remember? Or has your exile so clouded your memory?"

Percivine, who just about finished washing the plates, overheard Faruin. He was almost too sure he knew what Faruin was talking about. He recounted in his mind the story Faruin had told them about the night Dedrinus died. He also remembered Faruin speaking of another Elf with him that night, one who "*shall remain nameless,*" as Faruin had put it. Twy'leden was the other he'd spoken of.

Faruin got up from his seat and stormed into the room Twy'leden had prepared for them earlier.

"It's a pressing matter for him," said Seleborn, as he finished the rest of his mead. He got up and went after Faruin.

"What was the purpose of omitting that last bit?" asked Percivine.

The following morning, Percivine awoke to the sounds of two bickering voices.

"…would have wanted the both of us to pay our respects together!"

"*Very well!*" agreed Twy'leden. "I will take you to the Temple. I have some business to attend to. I will return in about an hour. Be ready." He wavered before the door. "There was no sense in lying to them about that night. You know quite well his chambers were watched, not by us, but by the Elvic guards."

"Yes, but during my rounds!"

"What had happened to you that night could not be put as your fault! You could not know the shapeshifter intended to put a po—" He took notice of Percivine's presence, said nothing else, and left.

Percivine pretended to ruffle through some parchments Twy'leden had lying around on an end table.

"So, what part of that did you hear?" seethed Faruin.

"Very little," said Percivine. "What did the Argom try to do to you?"

"Well, you heard Twy'leden. Be ready by the hour."

"Where's Seleborn?" asked Percivine.

"He's gone off to the market to buy food for our journey ahead. He won't take long; I am sure of it."

Faruin thundered back to the room, pressing heavily with each step he took, and shut the door, not wanting to be disturbed until the hour came.

Percivine found the present situation a bit awkward, so he painstakingly continued to rummage through the messy parchments. Many were rather old, with parts of them faded. There was one headline, dated ten years ago, that did attract his gaze.

LORD ELF OF BEAUTIFICATION FOUND DEAD!

The picture beneath the headline was horrific. The Elves had not restrained themselves from publishing a gruesome picture of the lifeless body. Dedrinus, staring blankly into space, lay in his bed, blood dripping from the deep gash on his neck. Percivine found it difficult to tear his eyes away from the illustration. Before he read any further, he ensured Faruin was still locked in his room.

> Dedrinus Etwood, renown brother
> of the Omitay of the Elvic Triumvirate,
> found dead in his bed. Who could have
> done such a dastardly thing? Who would
> want this prestige Elf dead? Who? It's a
> mystery that no one comprehends
> besides Faruin Abrandil.
>
> When questioned, the two there that
> night, Abrandil and Twy'leden Paros,

watching over his quarters that night knew not how it had happened. The proper authorities state that one of the them had slipped away for a night walk, while the other, Abrandil, stood behind …asleep.

New suspicions have arisen. How is it that Abrandil did not hear anything or anyone come pass him? It's nearly impossible. However, there are those who believe otherwise.

"I know Faruin," said Twy'leden Paros. "He wouldn't hurt the tiniest of insects, let alone kill an Elf. Whoever did this must be brought to pure justice! You cannot assume that Dedrinus was killed by one of our own."

A most touching statement. Abrandil has been brought in by authorities for further questioning, a recent source tells us. Will he be convicted of the charges set against him, or will the proper justice be thrown upon Abrandil like any normal murderer? A standing trial will be conducted on the Fourth Day, at the Eighth Hour of the morning.

Many who knew Abrandil now fear for their own safety.

"I always knew something was funny with him," said Mormac Ik'sadd. "I attended the University of Elvic Magic with him. We were quite close, I should say, and there were, at times, when Faruin seemed fishy to me. I don't know anymore. To think he could be the killer of one of the greatest Elves known to

Elfkind—it's a horrid thought. My husband and I now must keep our eyes wider than ever. Who knows if he comes after one of us next, or worse, one of our children? It's dreadful, utterly dreadful!"

A tragedy indeed.

"He was a very gifted Elf, I'll admit. Top of our class," said Il-dendryn Os'sid. "After graduation, I went along to work with Faruin for the special project at the University under the supervision of Dedrinus. I never—I never expected Faruin to have committed a crime such as this. I hope he gets what he deserves. I am outraged to think it was him— SIMPLY OUTRAGED!"

There you have it, one and all. This tragic case for this poor Elf is simply not in good terms. How could someone ever feel the need to take the life of another? It's a disgusting habit that one should not pick up on.

Abrandil is currently being kept in the Unin'shai Citadel—the heavily fortified fortress for the most dangerous of criminals. If the world does not get him, then surely some of the other captives will. His justice will arrive in a timely manner, and those who write to inform the public of current events, we simply ask that you sleep with an eye open. For none of you will know if there are any more Abrandil's running amok.

Percivine was filled with resentment and disgust by the way the papers had spoken about Faruin; to think that they were accusing him without any proper evidence. He understood now why Faruin feared returning to this place. To his horror, he found another parchment dated only several days after the one he'd just read.

> …been found guilty for the murder of Dedrinus Etwood. Once the Triumvirate rules for his punishment, they will release the information to the general public. Please stay intact with your local news parchment offices.

Percivine did not need to rummage through the rest of the parchments to know Faruin's punishment. But it all sounded too odd to him. Why, if they thought Faruin a murderer, would the Triumvirate exile him and put him upon the rest of the world? It made no sense to him.

He quickly placed the parchments the way he found them. He could hear Faruin's steps in the next room, walking with a heavy foot to the door. The door flew open.

"What are you doing?" Faruin said with a cold voice.

"Just sitting here," said Percivine. "Not a crime, is it?"

Faruin glared at Percivine. His nostrils flared, before he returned to his room.

I suspect things aren't as well as we thought, said the voice in Percivine's head.

Really? I hadn't noticed, said Percivine to the voice.

I suppose seeing Twy'leden imposed upon his old post, recounting Dedrinus's death, and his exile, must bet the root of it.

I should say so, the voice said.

He could see a point in that, but still, after how hospitable Twy'leden had been to them, surely Faruin could learn to look past it.

"The things being written about you, Faruin," said Percivine sharply. "I know the maggot who wrote this piece." He slid the news parchment he read earlier about Dedrinus Etwood in front of Faruin. "He's a Dwarf I used to work with at the *Frodrian Fox* until—you know? He was always snooping about, trying to find the best leads, and it looks he got what he wanted."

Seleborn eventually returned minutes before Twy'leden's arrival. Once they were ready with their transformations, Twy'leden sealed his door with a locking enchantment before setting out. The part of the city he lived in was not as dense as the next part of the city they entered, which was cut off by a river.

They crossed over a small stone bridge to reach the bustling Trade Province of Unin'shai. Hundreds of Elves, big and small, rushed through the dazzling shops and boutiques, all aligned perfectly. Percivine saw one small kiosk that sold precious gems which hovered over the owner's head. To his left, he could see a shop that sold very rare plant life—at once, he figured the shop must sell them for very expensive prices.

They reached the end of the busy Province, and entered the Natural Province. Many fabulous trees, plants, benches, magically lit lamps, and exquisite walkways marked the area. Most of the greenery here was present in several parks that made the area what it was, with a home or a shop here and there. Faruin explained that this was the area most students from the University of Elvic Magic, studying environmental magic, came to do much of their research for theses and valuable experiments.

At the very back of the Natural Province stood a unique building with two star-shaped objects floating on the domes of the primary structures, which lay against the great wall of Unin'shai. At the very center was a large building with a blue colored dome, where a vague blue beam of light that shot up into the sky. Percivine was sure that was the Temple of the Stars.

"We're nearly there," said Twy'leden. "That blue beam you see there is what we Elves believe to be the Gateway to the Stars. Please remember to be very quiet, for there are others there who are paying their respects, as well. The Elvic priests won't take lightly to us if we do."

"You needn't worry," whispered Faruin to Percivine. "Dedrinus's grave marker lies outside the walls of the Temple."

"There!" pointed Twy'leden.

Percivine and Seleborn, having never been here before, followed Twy'leden's yellow finger to an empty, moderate-sized, marble epitaph jutting from the lush ground. The design of the marker was one that someone would have expected: a column at each end of the marker, with what appeared to be vines sticking out from each end. In the very center it read:

Dedrinus Etwood
Great Elf, friend, and mentor to the many

Faruin knelt slowly before Dedrinus's memorial monument. He held both hands to his heart, and began to shed tears.

"I—*I'm sorry!*" he croaked. "I wish—I wish I could have done more for you…You deserved not to die this way."

Twy'leden knelt beside Faruin and placed a hand over Faruin's back. Twy'leden gave him a reassuring look.

"*Quiet,*" said an Elf covered in white and gold robes, as he walked by. "This is a place of sanctuary and mourning. You will refrain from any further noises."

Percivine and Seleborn watched as the Elvic priest shuffled along and stepped away for a bit, to let Faruin have his peace with the last remnants of Dedrinus. Faruin's cries were largely muted, as the voices of two Elvic women, one of them clearly sobbing, drew closer.

"…body won't be harmed anymore," said the woman holding the handkerchief in her hand.

Faruin and Twy'leden retreated mournfully from Dedrinus's shrine and returned to them.

"The soil is now the only protective barrier he needs to be at peace, Ora."

The two Elvic woman could no longer be heard as they drifted far away from them.

Percivine gave Faruin a suspicious look. "I thought you said once an Elf dies they head to the stars?"

"They do…well, in a manner of speaking, anyway."

"I just overheard those two Elvic women speaking about how the soil will protect him. How is it, you say, that Dedrinus has no physical form left?"

Twy'leden cut in: "As Elves we have been privileged with Fenemeri, I don't suppose you've—?"

"Heard of them?" said Percivine. "Yes, I've heard of them."

"It has been carefully researched, the afterlife for an Elf as a Fenemerys," said Twy'leden. "Since their minds are so attune with magic and the Stars, we believe the Stars use their powers to rid Fenemeri mortals of their impurities—meaning their bodies—and cast them into an immortal journey through space and time, where they remain for the rest of eternity. Faruin should have been a bit *clearer* when he explained this to you."

"So, not *all* Elves simply become nonbeing after death?" Percivine asked for clarification.

"Precisely."

Faruin said nothing. He was too busy remembering the last time he and Dedrinus had had a conversation. He gazed into nothingness and began to march solemnly towards the Temple.

Once inside, Twy'leden instructed them that they must remain silent, for there were others in deep prayer and meditation. The Hall of the Temple was lined with polished rows of marble on each side of the doorway. A long blue carpet was laid at the center of the opposing rows, which in turn led to an altar upholding the beam of light. In here, the light was much brighter and more visible than from the outside.

Percivine, Seleborn, and Twy'leden sat on the very last row as Faruin slowly walked up to the altar. Many of the Elves in the Temple watched with curiosity, for none of them had ever witnessed a Dwarf giving an offering to the Stars.

From within one of his trouser pockets, Faruin withdrew a white flower he'd picked right by the marker. He took one step further towards the altar and placed the flower in the very center. After a few moments of waiting in solitude, the flower rose up, followed by Faruin's eyes, along with Percivine's, Seleborn's, and Twy'leden's, watching from their row. The flower dissolved, and at the moment, Faruin knew that Dedrinus would receive it momentarily.

"I will bring you the justice you deserve. I swear it," he whispered.

Faruin bowed his head in respect and proceeded out the doorway, trailed closely by Percivine, Seleborn, and Twy'leden.

"Thank you," Faruin said to Twy'leden. "None of this would have been possible without your guidance."

Twy'leden nodded with a stiff smile.

"Come," he said, "let us make our way back."

As they clambered down the marble steps of the Temple, they were halted by a grey-skinned man.

"Not so fast," said Bartholev.

Seleborn's blood boiled. The man standing before them was the very same who'd killed his wife, Filiiri. He ached to lash at him but was far more concerned at revealing his identity than killing Bartholev.

"What do *you* want, Bartholev?" asked Twy'leden. "It would be wise if you returned from the scum hole you came from."

Bartholev laughed darkly.

"Do you honestly think I'm going to take orders from a filthy Elf?"

Percivine, too, began seething from his bones. This was the very same man who had chased him menacingly through the forest. He wished for a split second that he could attack this man, severely torture him until he revealed anything of his brother—if he could.

Bartholev looked at the two Elves and Dwarf.

"Funny to see a Dwarf here, don't you think?" said Bartholev, showing a nasty smile full of crooked teeth. "I couldn't help but notice you four stumped over that idiot's grave." He snorted loudly. "He was only getting in the way of things, anyway."

Faruin's face reddened. He wanted the simple satisfaction of making Bartholev bleed.

"*Don't you* ever *call him that again!*" spat Twy-leden. "*Do you hear me?*"

Bartholev had no intent to listen to Twy'leden's threat. He merely saw it as useless words. He got in closer to Percivine and inspected his face.

"What importance was Etwood to any of you?"

Percivine swallowed nervously, Maradine Forest flashing before his eyes.

"I don't think that's any of your concern, is it, Bartholev?" said Twy'leden. "Our business is our own, and we will not discuss it with the likes of you."

Batholev now glared at Twy'leden, offering a threatening gesture, which Twy'leden returned.

"You look awfully like Percivine Ogthorne," said Batholev, slightly turning his neck towards the disguised Percivine. "Ever heard of him? It would be…absolutely…*hilarious* if he was under—let's say—spells of metamorphosis, wouldn't it?"

"Do I carry Neledarian looks?" said Percivine.

"You should mind your attitude, Elf. I wouldn't want to *accidentally* hurt you."

Deeply, Percivine knew Bartholev would want no greater satisfaction than hurting him. He was a smart man, however, he suspected that this disguised Elf was indeed Percivine Ogthorn.

He could tell…It must be the only reason why he's saying such things…

Percivine continued to glare back at Bartholev.

"What's given you the right to be here?" demanded Twy'leden. "I don't see fit to let murderers wander loose, especially here. If the Triumvirate discover Nell's presence like this—"

"Murderer, you call me?" chuckled Bartholev. "No, no, I'm not a murderer. I'm here on strict business. I'm here on Landseer Elwerth's orders, you see."

He pulled out a parchment showing the authentic signature of Estith Elwerth. Percivine's jaw nearly separated from his face and fell to the ground. He could hardly believe it—the Landseer, the *Landseer*, giving free reign to such a person. It could not be. Seleborn's face turned bright red, and Faruin glared at Bartholev. And what of King Erelon? Is it not his word over hers? Where was the King in all this? *Where?*

"I forgot to mention," said Bartholev in an oily voice, "King Erelon has been on holiday for the past fortnight. He trusts her judgment and Lord Talus's. And he's not due back at all …anytime…soon."

"FILTHY LIAR!" snapped Seleborn, as he pushed Bartholev back with a dark jolt of magic.

"Feast on my power!" shouted Bartholev, hurling jets of white-hot magic their way and and dodging every single one which made Bartholev even angrier. "You'll regret this!"

Each time Bartholev shot an attack, Twy'leden cunningly deflected it with protective shield magic. Now Bartholev shot savage attacks from both hands, a maniacal expression on his face. All who'd been surrounding them had vacated the Temple, until it was just the five of them. Bartholev panted, still shooting inconvenient spells back and forth. At last, he ceased any further attack. It might have been that Twy'leden was just far more powerful than Bartholev wanted to admit.

"I'm surprised you don't have those disgusting Argoms by your side!" Twy'leden called to Bartholev, who drew in closer.

Bartholev was now inches away from Twy'leden's face. Twy'leden neither feared nor dared move back.

"I'm going to kill you," he whispered softly. "I'm going to kill you and everyone in that ruddy *order* you belong to. Wait and see. Your precious day will come."

Bartholev spat on the ground and looked up at the Elf named Percivine. He winced slightly at Percivine's face, and disappeared in front of them using the little device around his wrist.

"Where'd he teleport to?" said Seleborn.

"I don't know," said Twy'leden, "but I don't think any good can come from this. He's tainted this place of sanctity. How in this world did he find you here?"

"Has the Landseer lost her mind?" said Faruin. "To think she would allow that piece of dried shite to roam free, unharmed by authorities."

"And where exactly is King Erelon?" said Percivine. "It's hard to believe that the King would leave her with such power for so long, and what exactly did he mean by that last bit? What's he playing at?"

"I'll admit that was bewildering," said Seleborn. "I don't like this. Not a bit."

To avoid being targeted by paladins or the Temple clergy, Twy'leden rushed them out. That evening, they sat around quietly Twy'leden's table, with occasional bursts of discussion about their encounter with Bartholev and the King's whereabouts. Something was dreadfully wrong with Landseer Elwerth, but what could it be? They were beginning to conclude that she was corrupt and abusing her power, or, even worse, being more of an ally to the Argoms.

"We can't conclude that bit yet," said Seleborn. "What it comes down to is how much the King trusts her judgment. He's obviously given her reign to do absolutely almost—"

"—yeah, she probably disposed of him—" Percivine muttered under his breath.

"—anything. All we know for fact is that we have to assume the King remains on his holiday, and will return soon."

"Not how Bartholev made it seem," said Faruin.

"You don't think he—?" started Percivine.

"Hard to say," said Seleborn.

"If what he did to me in the forest is any indication as to what he can do," said Percivine, "then it might be safe to assume it."

"Like I said," said Seleborn, "we cannot assume anything yet."

The next morning, while everyone slept, Percivine attempted to cast himself in transformation. He did an acceptable job; this time he came out looking like a Dwarf, with a pierced septum and a frizzy black beard. He did not mind the appearance. He did not want to be cooped up in Twy'leden's home any longer. He decided to take a stroll to the Trade Province, to take a look at the treasures the Elves had in store for him.

Once he arrived at the Province, a little stall caught his eye. The vendor explained what his goods for sale were: "Magic Conductors".

"Might I interest you in one, good sir?" said the vendor, dressed in a red jerkin and one of these conductors hanging around his neck by a piece of lace.

"Er," said Percivine. "I'm just looking. What exactly do they do?"

"Ah," said the nameless vendor excitedly. "I'm glad you asked." He picked up the magical conductor: a rod-shaped instrument with a wider end for better grip. "This particular tool hones one's magical abilities when, for instance, in combat. You use it like this" —he flicked the conductor at a stone he had next to him. It floated a bit, and settled back down on the surface— "and like this" —he kept flicking his wrist, pointing the conductor in many directions— "and finally, once you grasp the concept, you'll be able to use your magic in a more controlled manner."

Percivine knew that many can control their magic, but he decided to flatter the vendor.

"Have you sold many?"

"Er—one, just one."

"One?"

"Yes," said the vendor "to an elder couple of Elves. I don't think they were using it the way it was intended to. My return policy is quite lenient. I'm sure they'll be back. Interested in purchasing one?"

Percivine wanted to help the Elf, but unfortunately had no money to speak of.

"I—I've got no money. I'm merely browsing today."

The Elf sighed with disappointment. "You wait and see. These conductors will help to modernize the world. I will become famous when it does. But first…I must think of a better name to call them. Let's see…"

It appeared that the merchant had almost forgotten that Percivine was still in front of him.

"Have a good day," the Elf said, and returned muttering things under his breath, probably thinking of a name for his goods.

He roamed around the marketplace for a couple hours more, seeing unique objects, plants, herbs, and wildlife only common in Ni'shorus. His next visit brought him to a plant and herb shop, owned by an Elvic woman, who looked as young as he did, but realistically, she may be hundreds of years old. He was quite allured by her scent, and her wondrous red eyes.

"Hullo, how many I help you today?" she said kindly.

For the smallest amount of time, he wished he was not a Dwarf, so that Percivine could look her straight instead of looking up.

"I'm just browsing…This is very nice, what is it?"

In a pot next to one of the shop windows rose a beautiful orange flower, with a bright green stem. He attempted to touch the bright orange flower.

"Careful not to touch the center!" said the shopkeeper. "Do you know what that is?"

"A very beautiful flower?"

She covered her mouth, and chuckled. "They are called Fire Traps. Native to Uln Alzor…One touch of its inner mouth, and consider your finger severely burnt. Don't you know?"

Then, it dawned on him: he's disguised as a Dwarf from Uln Alzor. Uln Alzor where this flower normally blooms. She must either think Percivine's a simpleton or isn't going to assume all Dwarves are familiar with flora of the region.

He quickly pulled it back in horror. The shopkeeper laughed.

"They are highly dangerous, but they are just so beautiful," she said."

"I've always wanted a plant that could kill me."

She laughed again.

"See anything you like?"

"Afraid not," said Percivine, feeling guilty. "I'm window shopping today. Just for looks. Forgive me."

"Not at all, not at all," she said. "I fancy doing that myself from time to time."

He took another look around the flower shop, then turned to the woman. "Have a good day."

In such a short time the Province grew busier. More and more civilians and outside traders flocked and migrated like birds. He had a hard time trying to get by, as people continually pushed him about.

I've got to get out of here, he thought.

Several minutes turned into an hour, which became two hours. Finally, he saw the wall separating the Province from the other. There were shops here, but not very busy as the center of the Province. He noticed a small eatery, separated by a small alley against the Province wall—very lonely, very quiet, somewhere he could be at peace, and eat. He froze in his tracks. There, coming from the entrance of the eatery, was Bartholev, followed by a skinny, pale Elf in tattered clothing, who shook nervously as he trailed him. Percivine saw them enter the alley. As he approached, he could hear the Elf speaking shakily.

"…s-swear I-I know nothing else!"

Sound familiar? asked the voice in Percivine's head.

"Lies," said Bartholev, readying an attack the same way he had on Twy'leden. "For me to even consider sparing your life, you need to tell me what you know."

"I—I'm just a lowly shop owner!" cried the Elf. "W-why would I know anything about Percivine O-ogthorne?"

Percivine's thick ears quivered.

"My source tells me that he was spotted eating here."

"*Your source lies!*"

"I doubt that," said Bartholev.

Suddenly, without a breath, Bartholev grabbed the Elf by the throat and slammed him against the solid wall, nearly giving the poor Elf a concussion. Percivine could see the Elf's face turning blue. The Elf pointed a finger at Percivine and gasped, "*H-help…me…Please…*"

Bartholev quickly turned, and was thrown back. Percivine's bolt spell hit Bartholev center in the back. He hit the wall and collapsed on the floor.

"Go! GO!" said Percivine to the Elf. "Close your shop, and go!"

Regaining his breath, the Elf nodded and sped off. Percivine walked darkly up to the still body of Bartholev. He kicked him square in the face and said, "I hope that'll teach you not to harm others." He swung his leg again, hearing a crack coming from Bartholev's nose. "Consider that a gift for the hospitality you showed me in Maradine."

He peered out from the alley, ensuring no attention was drawn. After it was clear to move, he hurried back to Twy'leden's home. Once there, he was scorned by Faruin and Seleborn for not telling them his destination.

"I needed to stretch my legs," he told them. "Anyway, you didn't tell me where you were off to, Seleborn!"

"Faruin said he told you!"

"But you didn't specifically tell *me!*" said Percivine. "Did you now?"

"That's not the point," said Seleborn. "It's far too dangerous for you to be roaming the streets of Unin'shai alone. And by the way, who transformed you? Faruin was this you?"

"Not my doing," said Faruin.

"I did it myself," said Percivine. "Not a bad job, right?"

"Well—no," agreed Seleborn.

Just before Percivine told them about his third encounter with Bartholev, Twy'leden's Orb began glowing bright purple. Twy'leden rose from his place at the table and grabbed the Orb that rested on an end table.

"Twy'leden! Twy'leden!" said the voice excitedly. "Are they there? Is Percvine there with you?"

"He is," said Twy'leden. "Well, don't leave us in suspense, Nerod. What's all this about?"

"Sirien sent Astronitus word! He'll be back tomorrow!"

Percivine's heart almost popped out of his chest. Could it be? Could Nerod really be telling the truth? If this is someone's idea of a twisted joke, he would lose hid mind. One thing Percivine learned in the course of his journey, was to expect the unexpected, but this was, as Nerod put it, wondrous news!

"When did he contact you, Nerod?" asked Twy'leden. "Where has he been?"

"Not more than thirty minutes past. He was very vague with the details on his whereabouts. I'm sure he'll tell us all soon."

"How's my father?"

"Percivine!" said Nerod. "Not sure if you remember—"

"I do," said Percivine.

"Astronitus is well," Nerod said through the purple Orb. "Sirien asked me to stay at Headquarters and look after him. He'll be very glad to see you Percivine. All of you! Now we must get underway. Sirien's requested a meeting of the Solemn Hand upon his return. Everyone should be here soon. I'm going to open the portal. I hope everybody's ready."

Nerod's voice could no longer be heard. A few seconds later, a purple, Neledar-sized gateway opened before them. First Twy'leden entered the portal, followed by Faruin. Percivine hesitated a moment before entering the portal. He was finally going to be in the same presence as his brother and father.

He entered, wearing a hopeful grin. At long last, the Oghthorne family was to be reunited once more.

CHAPTER SEVEN

HEADQUARTERS

Aura's Gaze

There it sat: Ogthorne cottage. It seemed to have been an eternity since he'd last set foot into it. The humble double-story home stood quiet, ready to welcome them warmly. Observing and smelling the many plants all along the little pathway felt like a new sensation to him. He even wanted to climb the vines sticking to the side wall of the cottage to alleviate some of his excitement. Faruin, Seleborn, and Twy'leden headed for the door, while Percivine stood behind, admiring what he'd missed for so long.

"Aren't you coming?" said Seleborn.

"I'm breathing it in deeply," responded Percivine.

"I'm sure your father would want to see you, so come on."

They stood on the steps leading to the front door. It was about to happen. Twy'leden knocked on the door. They waited.

He knocked again, but no one answered.

"That's odd," said Twy'leden.

He knocked again. Still no reply.

"I'll check around back—" said Seleborn, but was cut off when the front door slightly creaked.

"W-who's there?" said a most familiar voice.

"Old friends," said Seleborn.

The door opened wider to an older man of snow-grey hair and stress wrinkles probably caused by wondering if his sons were all right.

"Dad!" said Percivine.

"Percivine! My boy! *My boy!*"

Percivine Ogthorne and Astronitus Ogthorne embraced one another.

"It's so good to see you, son, so good!"

Astronitus looked up.

"Seleborn—Faruin—Twy'leden—so good to see you as well! Please, do come in!"

The lanky man gestured them inside but put his hand out in front of Faruin's chest once, stopping him.

"He's here again," whispered Astronitus into Faruin's ear, loud enough that Percivine heard the message.

Astronitus guided them inside to where a small spiral staircase spun upwards, and where many Mage-related artifacts dusted the shelves and tops. Astronitus took them through a small dining hall that connected the little kitchen and where they met two surprises.

Admiring a relic on a console table by a window was a scarlet-haired Elf dressed in unmistakable ornate cloth vestments and a green shawl. Opposite him, at the other end of the table, sat a shaved-headed Neledar with a scar and Dwarvic band on his upper left eyebrow.

"Happy to see you upon your return," the Elf said, offering a smile of good measure. "Twy'leden, truly a shock to see you among them."

Twy'leden rushed to where this very important Elf stood, placed his right hand over his left shoulder, and lowered his head.

"Omitay," said Twy'leden. "It is indeed—"

"Handolan, I have asked you endlessly to stop this," said Faruin curtly.

"Might you walk me outside?"

Faruin hissed but knew refusal would not be in his best interest.

"Astronitus," said Handolan "again you have my thanks for your hospitality."

"As always, Handolan," said Astronitus kindly.

After another awkward silence, Percivine decided to ask Twy'leden about the Elf.

"You referred to him as 'Omitay,'" he said, recalling an order of his arrest, "one of the Triumvirate, if I'm not mistaken."

"That's enough of that," said Astronitus, watching Twy'leden's worried face that he might have said too much. "Let's all sit in the dining area."

Percivine and Seleborn began to cramp around a polished, wooden table and accordingly started to take their seats. Nerod enthusiastically shook hands with each of them and shook Percivine's slightly longer than the rest. Percivine's only met Nerod a handful of times since Sirien spent most of his time adventuring. He can't remember Nerod having a scar the last time they saw each other.

"It's a pleasure to see you again, Percivine," said Nerod.

"Percivine," said his father, "Nerod and I have worked at the Society of Excavators but in different departments. He's not my personal assistant."

Pericivne wondered, however, how close he really was to Sirien, because not even he knew of Sirien's whereabouts.

"But you must be starving!" said Astronitus in delight. "We've prepared food for this very occasion."

Percivine was undoubtedly hungry. He never got the chance to eat back in Unin'shai, for Bartholev had taken that pleasure from him. Without any words to say, he awaited the meal that his father intended to bring out.. They continued situating themselves comfortably into the chairs and waited.

"So, Nerod," said Seleborn, avoiding Faruin's disgruntled gaze. He had returned from walking out Handolan looking even more flushed. "Tell us. What's the latest since our departure?"

"We've Pledged two new members to the Hand—twin Elves—a brother and sister. The brother's a bit arrogant but I've seen his skill in magic. His sister is a Fenemerys, and saw fit to recruit her as well. It will be very beneficial to us."

"Great," said Seleborn. "This will be Percivine's first encounter with a Fenemerys."

"It would be to many Neledar," said Nerod. "By the time Sirien returns, we should all be here, ready to conduct the meeting. And it appears," he looked at Percivine, "that you are now part of the Solemn Hand Seleborn tells me."

Percivine lifted an eyebrow.

"Have I?" he said. "I haven't even been—what did you call it?"

"Pledged," said Nerod. "A custom of this order's to initiate new members."

"Well—that. I think Faruin and Seleborn mention it previously."

"Nonetheless," said Astronitus, "you are part of this now, son."

There was yet another awkward instance. Percivine thought of the grand secret Sirien had hid from him for five years. Nerod could see the disturbance upon his face, and said, "Don't be upset at your brother, Percivine. I know it must be a lot to take in after recent events, but he means well. He values you and your protection. That is why he saw fit to not tell you about any of this until you were ready. It was his dream to have you alongside him in all this. Albeit, a bit sloppy in some aspects."

"This was not the way I wanted to find out," said Percivine. "My leg nearly got punctured by an Argom, for reasons unknown to me. How long more must I wait before Sirien the 'Savior' returns?"

"He'll explain everything," said Nerod gently. "I've been told to refrain from telling you too much. Ah—looks like supper is ready!"

Astronitus, followed by many floating plates and bowls full of food, entered the small-scaled room. With a large bird at the center, the feast looked lovely. They were to indulge in baked turkey, a salad of potatoes and corn, spiced wild greens, a thick stew of hog's bacon, and fluffy biscuits infused with Ranoic lunasong pepper flakes.

"Eat up! Eat up!" called Astronitus over the ruffling of filled plates. "There's plenty for everyone. Percivine, do share, the bird's not only for you, and do mind the biscuits, I may have added a bit too many lunasong pepper flakes."

Percivine turned pink and withdrew his grasp of the same turkey leg Seleborn had gone for.

They quickly emptied their plates and dove in for seconds. Percivine enjoyed most of all the missed comforts that his home always offered. After supper everyone washed up, as the sun was setting over the distant line.

"So, when's everyone expected to arrive?" Seleborn asked Nerod.

"Soon, I hope," said Nerod.

Though new to Percivine, he wondered as to the sorts Sirien had become entangled with. Having a full gut pleased him, helped undermine some of the anger he'd felt for his brother previously. However, he kept a watchful eye on them. They laughed and cheered at this reunion, acting as if nothing ever so serious came to be. It felt strange watching these people find joy where there was none. Now, he would have to endure more of it, something even his father did not seem concerned about.

"Sirien's departure has presented great difficulty in hosting meetings," said Nerod. "The Administration is on full alert what transpired in the forest between he and you, Percivine. The Administration also plopped one of their investigators, Darus Dillory, in Frodrir's local policing office. Came snooping about very recently."

"I was lucky Nerod was here when it happened," said Astrontius.

"For what purpose?" asked Faruin.

"He came to question us about Sirien's whereabouts, but obviously we refused to tell him anything. He threatened to arrest us, and if we refused further, to cast the Argoms on us; I welcomed his threat with much enthusiasm. That really set him off."

Seleborn took the liberty of explaining to Nerod and Astronitus their encounter with Bartholev at the Temple.

"What in Blinn's fortune?" said Nerod. "Twy'leden, you especially must be careful. They might believe you three lingered behind. Do you know how they managed to find you of all places?"

"Didn't seem too much of a problem," yawned Twy'leden. "He's just full of words, no action. And I daresay Bartholev's magical ability is that of mediocre. But, alas, we aren't sure how he was tipped off about our location."

"Did anyone recognize him?" asked Nerod.

"No," said Twy'leden. "I'm sure the passersby just thought we were mad."

"Things brings me to another grave point," said Seleborn. He felt this was the best time to tell them about Rufious's death. "We have also suffered a regrettable death."

"Who?"

"Three months ago," Seleborn began, "not long after I encountered Perci and Faruin in Xerian, we journeyed to Rufious's home, as per Sirien's plan. We were attacked. It was a great surprise to us. A shapeshifter took the form of an old friend to Rufious, cornered us, and eventually succeeded in stabbing Rufious."

"*How many more must die?*" said Astronitus, covering his face with his hands. "When will it end? Yliki was found dead holding a worn copy of Edemard the Believer's *A Short History of Gylranor*, then Joric—his arms and legs bound, a rope around his neck, hanging from the branch of an aphorus tree. Now Rufious? Percivine, your mother meant a great deal to him, just like he was to Seleborn. There must be an end to this. Is one of us betraying the rest?"

"Someone or something is after us," said Faruin, "wanting to keep us shut. Now this mysterious force is unleashing a fiercer storm."

Astronitus turned to his son.

"My boy, word travels fast."

Percivine was confused.

"What have you heard?"

"I've heard of your exploits in Relthren," Astronitus said with pride. "Dunn Orbed me the night after the attack on the city, and told me what you three did in order to escape."

"I feel we were the causers of such a mess," said Percivine. "To make matters even *better*, we fled like cowards."

"You weren't meant to stay there and thank the gods for Thiurwold's intervention, or else it would have been a bloody mess. You may have figured over the past few months the reason as to why I made no form of contact. Yes, I could have Orbed either Faruin or Seleborn, but it was your better protection that I did not, I was—"

"More worried about Sirien, yeah," finished Percivine.

His father stared blanky at him. He did not expect for his son to say something so absurd. Everyone in the hall remained silent, and a bit worried.

"*I beg your pardon?*" said Astronitus.

"Yes, dad, I do know the real reason why you made no such effort to contact me," said Percivine hastily. "You worried over precious Sirien, that is why you paid no attention to your other son."

"Perci—"

"There's no need," said Percivine. "I get it. You worried that if something did happen to Sirien you would have to settle for less than what you wanted—"

"Percivine!" Nerod cut in. "I assure you that your father made no such attempt to—"

But Astronitus waved him down.

"It's all right, Nerod," said Astronitus calmly. "If I were in his situation, I would lash out at my father, too."

"You're telling me that you made no effort to contact Sirien?" asked Percivine suspiciously.

"Exactly," said Astronitus. "Sirien begged me to not lift a finger to try to discover where either of you could be. You two are the only family I've got left. Not trying to do anything to help you was a complete tear within me. And just look at what you have recently endured. Rufious's murder…The murderer knew you would be there…

"The Wayorbs are wondrous inventions that the Dwarves have shared with us, but they are not perfected. You see, Percivine, there have been a few instances where when you contact someone, someone else, at random, could be overhearing your conversation…The communication is projected through another frequency, and ends up being heard by those we do not know.

"This is the sole purpose why Sirien wanted not for me to contact the both of you. He feared that, if communication was reached, one of those rare instances might occur, and the whereabouts of the Ogthorne brothers would be discovered. At first, I questioned his motive, but soon I realized how ingenious this plan was. Much suffering I felt, as I was not to lift a finger to touch my Orb. I would have to wait it out. I waited on your mother for years on her constant trips to faraway lands. That is why, this whole time, I knew you would return. My worries were less, and not so much stress involved."

What a fool he had been. Percivine did not seem to know how to speak. He tried to utter words, but only weird noises escaped his dry mouth. He wanted to apologize to his father but was afraid his father would reject such an offer after how cold he had been to him.

"Dad, I—"

"You needn't say a word, Percivine. You have every right to feel this way. Over the past, I may have acted like Sirien matters more, but you are mistaken. I value you both equally, and no matter the circumstance, you will always be my sons. I do not play favorites, and I never will."

Summer was nearly over and still no sign or word of Sirien. Though extremely composed, Astronitus grew worried about his son's whereabouts. Nerod had assured Sirien would be back in a day's time. From Nerod's consistent urging, Astronitus agreed to hold a meeting with the rest of the Solem Hand.

There was a tap at the front door.

"I'll get that," said Nerod, and sped off to the door.

"I'm really thankful you all are all right," said Astronitus, as they could hear Nerod opening the door to unknown guests, and saying, "Off to the dining area!"

From the archway, they saw two orange-skinned Elves walk in. Beaming brightly, Nerod followed. The Elvic woman's eyes seemed most drawn to Percivine. The Elvic man next to her held his chin high, his grey eyes scanning the room.

These Elves were not dressed in anything as grand as Twy'leden and almost looked alike facial-wise. Each wore a brown, sleeveless garments, a white shirt guard beneath the brown jerkin, and charcoal-colored britches.

"Everyone," Nerod called to attention, "I would like you to meet the newest members to the Solemn Hand: Vaureth and Viri'el. Do take a seat wherever you'd like."

Vaureth and Viri'el bowed before them. Once they greeted them, they took their seat. Faruin found difficulty not taking watchful glances at Viri'el, who hardly has paid any attention to him.

"Thank you, Nerod," said Viri'el, her opal hair sitting neatly in a bun."

"How's the farm?" Nerod asked brightly. "What was it you grow there, again?

"Quite well," said Vaureth proudly. "A field of parsley and green onions. We prefer not to slaughter living animals."

"Most noble, yes," said Astronitus.

"With the growth of our farm," said Viri'el, "we've had to hire help. A young girl named U'rindrel."

"Excellent!" said Nerod.

"She usually arrives after her classes," continued Viri'el. "We know her family well; they board the house next to our city flat."

Percivine watched everyone with much detail: these new faces aroused his interest in who might be part of all this. Just then, an eerie voice floated over his shoulder.

"I'd like a word with you in private."

He turned and saw his father looking right at him. He somehow should have known that the familiar voice was his father's. He followed his father quietly into the hallway, near the front door.

"You well, son?"

"Spectacular. Didn't even see you leave your seat."

"I hope this is not all too overwhelming for you," said Astronitus Ogthorne. "You know it was in our best intention to reveal this all to you at a proper age."

"Proper age?" Percivine said indignantly. "*Proper age?* I've spent much of Sun's Blessing jeopardizing my life for things that made absolutely no sense to me at all! I don't understand how I couldn't get a rat's arse load of news from either you or Sirien."

"I've already explained to you the situation, Percivine, why must you dwell on it so? Besides, you're here, safe and sound, aren't you?"

"I—" His father was right. After all the anguish he'd put up with, he was, after all, safe and in good terms in seeing his father. For a second, this wise observation stymied his tongue. "You know I detest the very nature of a secret, dad. I don't like being shunned when it is not necessary. I'm only four years younger than Sirien. I think I've been the proper age for a while now."

Astronitus looked at his son and smiled, the length of which was awkward.

"Dad?"

"Oh—I'm sorry, Percivine," he said removing the smile. "I just— well, I just can't believe how grown up you and Sirien have become. If only your mother were here to see all this."

Percivine knew that, to his father, the subject of his deceased mother was a delicate one, so he refrained from speaking.

"Not a day goes by when I don't miss your mum, Percivine," said Astronitus weakly. "You must understand that by not contacting you or Sirien I managed to prevent your downfalls. I couldn't do anything to help your mother. If only...I—"

Percivine was eager to hear what his father had to say, what sounded so mysterious, but they were interrupted by a loud *knock* at the front.

"No, no, don't worry, Nerod," Astronitus told Nerod Nilius, peering in through the archway. "I'll get it. Go back and enjoy the company."

Astronitus slowly and cautiously walked to the front the door. With a hand readied to attack, and on slightly opening the door, he said, "Password."

"*Fat hog*," came the womanly voice.

"Enter," said Astronitus.

Percivine was amused: this must be the way Nerod had let Vaureth and Viri'el in earlier.

A Barbish woman of golden skin and advanced age, a Neledarian man, wearing a vine and straw hat covering his bald head and about the same age as Nerod, and Dunngarunax Galon entered Ogthorne cottage.

"Astronitus, you old cod!" said Cosmera Rodriys. "It's good to see your ancient face, again! Where's that arsehole, Marandir?"

"Last I heard he was still in mission with the Goblins," said Astronitus.

"So, old Marandir ain't goin' to show 'is face then?" said Dunngarunax Galon.

"Not likely," said Astronitus. "Where's your cousin, Dunn?"

"Bah! We 'ad a row two nights ago abou' whether he'd be comin.' Tha' power-hungry tosspot will no' be comin.' Personally, I think all this government business 'as gone to 'is 'ead. Percivine Ogthorne!" He shrieked in delight. "Elated tha' you three made it ou' of Relthren in one piece!"

He marched over and nearly crushed Percivine's hand with his thick hands.

"You too, Dunn!"

Cosmera and the Neledar standing behind Astronitus looked carefully at Percivine. The old woman walked forward, her golden skin glowing in the candlelight.

"Cosmera Rodriys, Mr. Ogthorne," she said, and gently put out two fingers. "We've heard so much about you from your father. This here" — the quiet Neledar walked up next to Cosmera— "is Linaus Olvea, an outstanding alchemist."

"Botany more than alchemy, but a pleasure to meet you, Mr. Ogthorne," said Linaus, as he fixed his hat. "I own *The Herb and Vial* shop here in Frodrir."

"Son," said Astronitus brightly, "Linaus, here, is the one who constructed the alchemy station in our small library—"

"Astronitus," began Linaus.

"—and with his knowledge of the plant, helped to mold the very gardens in the back!" Astronitus finished loudly. Linaus offered a wooden smile and turned to Percivine. "Sirien has been rather gracious to us all. It's a sound feeling to know he's all right, don't you think?"

"Yeah, sure," said Percivine, needing no reminders that he still walked in his brother's shadow, even if Sirien was not around. "I have been told you are a healer, Miss Rodriys—"

"Call me Cosmera, and yes I am. Work at a small ward that primarily treats younglings. Heard you boys went to the Pools at Nordorth. You know, they are very sacred to my people. Nordorth the Augur used those waters to give the Midir life. Did you bask in their magnificence?"

"They were exquisite," said Percivine. "The water almost—"

"Where's the food, Astronitus?" asked Dunn loudly, overbearing Percivine's conversation with Cosmera. "I'm starved."

"Always pondering with your gut, eh, Dunn?" said Linaus cheekily. "I see some of us have already eaten."

Astronitus laughed. "There's more than enough for everyone, Dunn. Go on in and help yourself."

Dunn nodded and vanished beneath the archway, followed by Linaus.

"Everyone here?" asked Cosmera.

"We're still waiting on two and Sirien," said Astronitus. "I'm sure they'll be along momentarily. Why don't you go on in?"

"I would like to, but first, I would like to use the lavatory, if you don't mind."

"Not at all," said Astronitus.

"You battered old piece of bark," she said with a smile.

"Wrinkled raven," he said, returning the same kind of smile.

Astronitus watched as Cosmera went up the spiral staircase.

"You two seem…very friendly," Percivine pointed out.

"Yes," said Astronitus. "She's been a good friend to both your mother and I. If there ever comes a time, gods forbid, I would recommend you come to her. She's a very good healer."

"Dad," said Percivine, "what's the knowledge on him?"

Astronitus's eyes landed on Linaus.

"Linaus?" he asked.

"Yes, him."

"He's always been a quiet one," said Astronitus, sitting on a wooden chair next to a shelf. "Pledged shortly after Joric's gruesome death and Thiurwold's appointment as Minister. Never once stepped into his shop before that." He observed Linaus a little closer now with this brown eyes. "Seems a bit upset this time."

"Upset?" said Percivine. "At what?"

"It's not wise to mention Thiurwold in front of him. For as long as I can remember, Linaus has a misguided perception of Dunn's cousin."

"Why?" asked Percivine.

"Let me see if I can remember…" Astronitus leaned back in his chair, pensive, until finally it came back to him. "Oh yes, I remember. Ever since Thiurwold's election as Minister of War, he's had little to no time to partake in Solemn Hand matters, and this infuriates Linaus greatly. He says Thiurwold should not be so, as he puts it, 'in love' with the government; that there are more important issues ensuing among us. And, of course, Thiurwold sees different: He believes that he owes his loyalties to Uln Alzor as well, and not just solely to the Solemn Hand…There is something strange about the way Thiurwold works…"

"Strange?" said Percivine.

"Yes, Percivine, strange," said Astronitus, looking afraid to elaborate. "I don't know if I should be speaking about this, but you're my son, and I've kept so much away from you already."

Percivine was rather thankful for this.

"On Thiurwold's last visit here, months ago, I overheard him in conversation with someone through his Wayorb. Thiurwold thought he had closed the door to the room properly, but mustn't have been aware of it. Of course, I didn't go eavesdropping."

"What did you hear, Dad?"

"I dunno, really," said Astroniuts, pondering. "Might've just heard things. Heard something about a plan or something like such."

"A plan?" said Percivine. "Probably on matters do with Uln Alzor. Highly classified stuff, I suspect."

"Perhaps" said Astronitus. "You must not think I dug my ears into his matters. I've been taught better. Please," he begged to his son, "you must not tell a soul what I just told you. It sounds dark, I know, but we don't know exactly what he meant by that. It could have something to do with government, like you said! Just keep your lips sealed!"

"Dad, you seem affright. Are you well?"

"S'nothing."

"It's all right to feel angry, dad, but now's not the time. I didn't mean for you to have to relay that bit of information to me. If it set you off, I apolo—"

"Don't you dare apologize, Percivine," said Astronitus, getting up from his chair. "I should not have let it excite me so much. Forgive me!"

"I heard about the consortium between the Society and the Pathfinders Guild," said Percivine, hastily changing topics. "Congratulations are in order."

"Did I tell you that?"

"Had to hear it from a Dwarf in Relthren," said Percivine.

"Exciting, isn't it? After Faruin and the other Elves discovered the missing piece to the Atlas, a resurgence of interest in all things Mage sprouted again in both our leagues, so our very own Felefor Depository here in Frodrir—with permission from the Society of Excavators—has seen fit to resume our searches. You know how much I go on about Mages. Now's our chance to continue the path that will lead us to Mage civilization."

"I'm happy for you, dad," said Percivine.

"Thank you, son," said Astronitus, misty-eyed. "Since the Museum of Nell in Elbynshire manages all institutions like ours across the land, the curators their make broader decisions. They agreed to a commission from the Divination Administration to further exploit our efforts. As head of the Frodrir Society of Excavators Chapter, naturally I was opposed to any such intrusion from the government, but their finances will certainly help us very much. I hope I shan't come to regret it. Now where the Netherid is your brother? We can't be kept waiting all day long, can we?"

"Does it really matter how late Sirien is?" said Percivine, looking at the door in hopes that someone would knock. "You even said earlier that the whole of the Solemn Hand isn't even here yet."

"You're quite right, son," said Astronitus.

Clunk.

Somebody was at the door. Could it be Sirien this time? Percivine waited as his father cautiously made his way to the door.

Clunk.

Astronitus opened the door Percivine shuffled around to try and see who could be at the door, but his father's head blocked any means of doing that.

"Password."

"*Fat hog,*" said a man's voice.

Unfortunately, it was not Sirien. It was another elderly Neledar, but not nearly as old as Astronitus, carrying a staff with intriguing circular and pointed markings on it, as well as a younger Neledarian man sporting white-streaked brown hair. The two Neledar panted as they entered.

"Pevarius, Trobius!" said Astronitus. "Why are you breathing that way?"

"We were followed!" said Pevarius.

"Trailed, more likely!" said Trobius, sweat sliding down his temples. "An investigator followed us here. He thinks we know where Sirien is. Expect him here in no time! And Borak barely made his escape!"

"Where is Borak now?" asked Astronitus.

"We don't know," said Pevarius.

"All right, all right," said Astronitus. "Come in. Quickly." He peered out to see if anyone approached, then closed the door with a loud slam. "We're clear."

"Is this your son?" asked Pevarius.

Before Astronitus could answer, a harsh *thumping* noise beckoned at the door.

"Shh!"

"Quiet!"

"Tell the others, and Percivine—hide!" his father hissed.

Percivine scurried off to a room next to the spiral staircase, where he left the door slightly ajar to listen. He saw Pevarius and Trobius run into the dining room.

Astronitus, ready for an attack, opened the door. "Password."

Percivine could not hear, this time what the figure outside said. It must have been "fat hog" for Astronitus let the figure in. Percivine was surprised: the figure was no ordinary person. An Orc, grabbing a piece of cloth from a red pocket on his frock, wiped sweat from his faded beige forehead and nose. As the Orc went to put the cloth away, it got stuck in his nose ring.

"I think a need a smaller band for my nose," he said.

Percivine walked out of the storage room toward his father and the unknown Orc as they conversed.

"…nearly got hold of me," the Orc was saying. "Did Pevarius and Trobius fare all right?"

"Yeah, they're in the hall, Borak," he said. "I'm glad to see you. Haven't seen or heard from any investigator. Where are they now?"

"Last I saw of him was in the brink of Frodrir." Borak spoke no more, because a Neledar approached him in complete confusion. "And you must be Sirien's brother Percivine."

With a mouth opened, he nodded stupidly. He could not believe he was in the presence of an Orc, those whom, along with the Argoms, were previously at war with. The Violet Veil Accord must have included other stipulations besides the Argom Influence.

"Son?"

Percivine quickly snapped out of his daze and shook Borak's pointy-nailed hand.

"P-pleasure to meet you…er?"

"Borak is the name," he said. He clamped his hazelnut hair into a tail and dusted off his rough beige skin. "Excuse me."

Borak departed himself from their vicinity and through the archway, where Percivine heard everyone cheer "Borak" as he entered the room.

"Hard to believe?" said Cosmera's voice.

They could hear footsteps stomping heavily. Cosmera Rodriys made her way down the spiral staircase.

"Quite," replied Percivine. "But I am not here to pass judgment."

"One of several Orcs that do not agree with the way the Argoms run things," she said, approaching them. "He's very valuable to us. We were, at first, suspicious of him, but he's proven to be a very trustworthy, helpful, and friendly Orc. Sirien was wise to Pledge him into the Hand."

"If Sirien trusts him, so do I," said Percivine.

"As you should," she said, and made her way to the hall.

As Cosmera left, Nerod leaned out of the archway.

"Looks like everyone's here, Astronitus," he said. "But where in Inilizul's name is Sirien?"

"That's what I'd like to know," said Astronitus.

Percivine grew impatient. Most of the food was gone, there was hardly any beverages left, and the atmosphere grew bothersome. He wished Sirien would hurry so he wouldn't have to worry whether his brother had been killed or not. He watched everyone as they conversed amongst each other. It seemed to be a meeting that had grown into a kind of welcoming party. He was also anxious because earlier they'd said an investigator would arrive on their doorstep, and investigators *investigated* thoroughly.

"I know who's to come, too!" said the Neledar Trobius. "Dillory. The very same who bothered Astronitus. Seems pleased to be assisting the Argoms."

"Let him come," said Nerod. "We've nothing to hide. No one knows we were meeting tonight."

Percivine moved from his lonely spot and placed himself next to Faruin and Seleborn, who were listening to Linaus.

"I have my suspicions, but you mustn't tell anyone, especially Dunn!" Linaus said. "He won't like to hear it. I can't be for certain, but that cowardly Dwarf will have to answer to me if I do discover he has a part in this!"

"That is a very serious accusation, Linaus," said Faruin. "But you have my word I won't tell a soul."

"Do I have yours, Seleborn?"

"You do," he said.

"And yours?"

Percivine was surprised he spoke to him.

Linaus drained his goblet. "After all, you did just hear me say these things. I would grandly appreciate it if you kept it shut."

"My word," said Percivine.

"Thank you."

The old figure of Astronitus Ogthorne appeared before them. He leaned over to Linaus, and said, "I need a word. It's urgent."

"Pardon me."

Linaus placed his goblet in front of Faruin and followed Astronitus on a brief jaunt outside the hall, still visible to the rest of the Solemn

Hand. As Faruin and Seleborn were about to tell something to Percivine, the middle-aged Neledar with blue hair, who also seemed a bit under the wine, called out to him.

"Trobius Stout, Mr. Ogthorne," said the lopsided man. "Earlier we" —he hiccupped— "didn't have the chance to properly introduce ourselves. Your brother's said so m-many wonderful things about you. Come to think of it, where is Sirien?"

"I haven't a clue," said Percivine.

"Ah well, knowing Sirien he will be late. It's already nightfall."

"I think you've had enough to drink, Trobius," said Seleborn. "You're becoming a bigger drinker than Dunn."

"Nonsense," said Trobius Stout in his wheezy voice. "I'm just right. Just wait until that insect Dillory comes—I'll show him a thing or two."

"Now, now, Trobius, you mustn't lose your temper," said Seleborn.

"I'm not scared of that tosspot."

"So, what do you do, Mr. Stout?" asked Percivine, pretending to be interested in the question.

"I'm an archivist," said Trobius, hiccupping again, "for the Divination Administration."

"Good work, then?" asked Percivine.

"Why yes, yes, it is!" Trobius said excitedly. "I frequent the Museum of Nell on my recesses and have occasionally bumped into your father or Nerod on important business."

"Interesting," yawned Percivine. "Who held the marked staff?"

"Pevarius?" said Trobius. "That's" —he pointed at the Neledar covered in teal robes, and conversing with the Elvic twins— "Pevarius Garcinius. He works as an undersecretary to Ambassador Dibble. Perhaps you've heard of him?"

Percivine tried to think of a Dibble, but nothing popped into his head.

"Marandir Dibble?" said Trobius.

"I've heard that name before!" said Percivine. "Faruin's mentioned it to me in Xerian, and Cosmera mentioned him upon her arrival here."

"Well, I'm not sure if your father has ever mentioned it to you, but that Marandir Dibble succeeded your mother as Ambassador after— well, you know the rest. He's also a part of the Solemn Hand."

"I see," said Percivine. "Well, I would like to meet him someday."

"He's away, far away, deep within the Goblin lands discussing—I can't say much—so I won't," said Trobius. "Ah, Dunn, there you are!" Dunngarunax Galon wobbled past them, holding a goblet of Morgs Ale in each hand. Trobius grabbed him by the shoulder and wondered off at to the end of the table.

"Charming fellow," said Percivine. "Wouldn't you agree, Faruin?"

But Faruin had not heard a word Percivine said. He was far too busy gazing upon a majestic beauty deep in conversation with Pevarius.

"Faruin?"

Both Percivine and Seleborn followed Faruin's eyes to Viri'el. Percivine and Seleborn looked at each other. Percivine winked at Seleborn joking, gesturing him to watch what came next.

"She's quite beautiful, eh, Faruin?"

"Yes…she—*what do you think you are doing?*" Faruin caught himself before he said anything embarrassing. "I don't know what you're talking about! I'm exhausted! I faded away for a bit!"

"With eyes open?" laughed Seleborn. "Come on. We don't care if you think she's beautiful."

"She is, after all," added Percivine.

"Shut it!" said Faruin and took a large gulp from his goblet.

Percivine glanced over to the archway and saw Linaus and his father break apart. He sensed what his father wanted to speak with Linaus about but held off on any assumptions. He got up from his seat and approached Astronitus.

"Where are you going?" asked Seleborn.

"To speak with my father. I'll be back."

As he walked towards Astronitus, he noticed Linaus looking darkly at him. He paid no more notice to it and halted his father before he could get comfortable.

"You all right, dad?" said Percivine.

"Splendid," said Astronitus. "Why do you ask?"

"What were you and Linaus talking about?"

"That's private, son."

"After keeping all this from me for so long, do you really think it's wise to hold off on another secret from your son?"

Astronitus glared at him. He was not fond of the way Percivine approached him.

"Here is not the place to talk," he said. "Let's go back out to the hallway."

Percivine could see from the corner of his left eye that Linaus was still looking at him. He probably knew what they were going to discuss once they left the hall.

Astronitus let out a great sigh. "Linaus has just informed me of something," he said softly. "I don't want to put these bits together, but it somehow seems to fit into what I told you earlier about Thiurwold."

"What's he done now?" asked Percivine. "You've not been doing an estute job at keeping this secreted."

"No, no!" said Astronitus. "You've got it all wrong, son. For many months now Linaus has been coming to me with weak pieces of evidence about whether Thiurwold could partake in dark works. I felt it was the right time to let him know about what I heard that one day. He tried to configure it with the rest of the maniacal stuff he's come up with about Thiurwold. I thought he was getting ahead of himself."

"You don't believe him?" said Percivine.

"Honestly, I think it's a load of muck," said Astronitus. "But I don't want him knowing that now, do I? Ever since I met him, he's been a lonely, quiet boy, with little friends or people he can trust. Yes, he's a bit loopy, but aren't we all? Now—we shall not speak about this anymore! Yes?"

Percivine nodded stiffly.

"Excellent," said Astronitus. "Where is your brother? Everyone's getting worried and the hour is—"

Clunk.

That same noise again. Astronitus walked cautiously forward and looked out through a window. As he had earlier, he quickly told Percivine to hide himself in the room, and for everyone in the dining area to be silent.

"Quiet!"

"*SHH!*"

"No one say a word!"

"Nerod, Cosmera, it's him!" said Astronitus. "Come here! And he's with two of his cronies! Dim those lights!"

Percivine heard his father open the door, and say, "Who is it?"

"Investigator Dillory," said a nasally voice. "Good evening, Astronitus. We were out for a stroll and thought we'd stop by to pay you a much-needed visit."

"A stroll?" said Cosmera. "Odd time for a stroll."

"A source has told us that Sirien might be making an appearance tonight," said Dillory. "Care to elaborate on that?"

"The source must be drunk," said Nerod, looking up and down at Dillory's leather armor and black cowl. "Goodness—is that what investigators are wearing these days? Not the usual cape and breeches?"

"Charming," said Dillory. "You know, it is unwise to lie to those who serve Landseer Elwerth with the utmost loyalty. Something you clearly lack."

"Right." Nerod smirked. "As those who do not work for the government, but for the Society of Excavators, we wouldn't know what that would be like, would we?"

"Watch your cheek," said Dillory. "We *are* commissioned by the Sanction Service to find Sirien on behalf on the Administration. Take not of my words. Have you heard of what's happened to Shelina Sendrik and Avalon Imbartus?"

"No," said Astronitus, "because we don't even know who they are."

"Well, apparently, about a day ago, they were found dead in their Administration offices—"

"*No!*" came Pevarius's faint voice.

Dillory raised his eyebrows and curled his lips in a devilish way.

"Two poor, mistaken, outspoken fools, I might add," said Dillory. "Investigator Hendlen and I were there to remove the bodies. Such...a...pity. They will be missed."

"Unsurely by you, however," said Cosmera.

"Quite unusual to have all your sconces and candles out, wouldn't you think?" said Dillory. "Especially when things are so dark out."

"I would say so, sir," said the investigator with a purple streak across her face.

"As a matter of fact," said Astronitus, "they're dimmed. Not a crime, is it?"

"But surely you would need to see properly at night," said Dillory. "I know, in darkness, a light is most valuable to me."

"Is there anything else we can help you with?" asked Astronitus impatiently.

"Not hiding Sirien in there, are you?"

"Like we told you earlier," said Nerod tartly, "he's not here."

"You should mind yourself, wretch, or you might find yourself in similar fashions like Avalon or Shelina."

"*Is that a threat?*" barked Astronitus.

Percivine wished he could rush out of hiding and lash out with full might at this Dillory character.

"It's a promise," said Dillory, swiping his finger beneath his chunky nose. "You would be wise to not say such treasonous things to an official of Nell, Astronitus."

"You just mind *yourself*, Darus," said Astronitus, returning the same threatening tone. "You watch *yourself* that I don't lose my temper at you, and that's *my* promise."

Percivine could hear Dillory let out an oily laugh.

A silence fell between them, until Dillory spoke again.

"I'm going to take a look around your home."

"Not a good idea," said Astronitus. "You haven't got the right to search my home unless you have the proper documentation and warrant. As you have neither, you will refrain from stepping one foot in this house."

"Very well," said Dillory, who sounded like he was speaking through gritted teeth. "You have had your day, reptile, but you just wait. We will come for you, and whoever else dares step in our way!"

"We look forward to it," said Nerod.

The front door slammed shut.

"Put a seal on it, Nerod," Percivine heard his father say. "Everyone—do not brighten the lights until we are secure that Dillory has past."

Percivine made his way back into the hall, where many whispers could be heard among the members.

"I think 'e might have been responsible for their deaths!" said Dunn.

"If he was, then he did it in great secrecy," added Vaureth.

"I think he's gone," said the wheezy voice of Trobius Stout, as he looked out one of the large windows. "I'm surprised he didn't take a peep through any of the—"

"He...comes..." said a most stirring, feminine voice. "Blood and sweat...The moments of...combat...Aid is what he will—"

Vaureth quickly grabbed hold of his twin sister before she hit the ground with a loud *thump*.

"It's her foresight," he said, gently laying her on the floor. "She hasn't learned to control it very well yet. Viri'el." To his fallen sister: "What did you see? Who was it? *Viri'el?*"

Cosmera Rodriys approached the feeble Viri'el and pushed Vaureth out of the way.

"She needs a healer's touch, but," she looked at Vaureth, "yours was...just as suitable."

Cosmera hoisted Viri'el's back upright and spoke softly to her: "It's all right, dear. Don't exasperate yourself. Tell us when you are ready."

Viri'el stood still, and, at a final second, slowly opened her weak eyes.

"There we are," said Cosmera, beaming. "Well don't just stand there, Dunngarunax, you befuddled Dwarf! Bring the woman a seat!"

Until now, Dunn had been too busy drinking from his goblet. He clumsily brought over a chair and helped Cosmera situate the young Elf in it. Her brother huddled close by.

"Give her some room!" said Cosmera. "It's in her best interest if you don't hover around her like a pest!"

Vaureth backed away without a word. He muttered something under his breath and watched his sister. At that very moment, Faruin caught wind that Vaureth was looking right at him. He quickly moved his eyes from Viri'el and pretended to be admiring the ceiling of the hall, much to Vaureth's disbelief.

While everyone remained in the hall, waiting for Viri'el to recover, Percivine left the room to compose himself. His father followed him.

"You all right, son?"

"Who was that man, dad?"

"An idiot, more or less," said Astronitus. "It's nothing to concern yourself about, Percivine. You know investigators are the police force of Nell and are overseen by the Divination Administration. With Elwerth's Violet Veil Accord in full swing, many have turned sinister."

"That gargoyle of a Landseer needs a lesson taught to her!" hissed Percivine.

"I couldn't agree more, but we should try to at least mind our language," said his father. To shut Percivine down quickly, he added, "Yes, she is an abusive woman, but none of us fully understand the stresses of her position. We know for a fact that something about her is not right. Calling her names isn't going to reward us victory."

For the sake of not arguin, again, Percivine remained closed on the topic. He told his father that he would prefer to adjourn upstairs to his room and recall memories of Merinni.

"I'll make sure no one goes up and disturbs you," called Astronitus, as Percivine made his way up the spiral staircase.

"Thank you," Percivine called back. He clambered up the stairwell to the top floor of Ogthorne cottage. There were two slim hallways on either side of him. He remembered it all too well: once you climbed the stairs, there was a smaller hallway leading to his room as well as Sirien's. Located at the other end of the small hallway was his parents' room, and a meager study. The top floor was dark, and every step he took creaked on the wooden, polished floor.

And there it was—his room. He shuffled over to the door when a banging noise struck his door!

"*W-who's there?*"

No reply. He opened his door, and slammed it shut behind him. His heart raced. Sweat trickled down his nose.

The door shook. Percivine readied himself.

"WHO GOES THERE?"

Still no reply. The door opened slowly, and without Percivine's help…A figure stood at the very center of the room, panting heavily. The shadows made it hard for Percivine to decipher the anonymous face.

Percivine lit the room. "*Show yourself!*"

"H-help…me…" the raspy voice said. The figure had no strength remaining to speak, and began to topple over.

Percivine ran and grabbed hold of the figure before he hit the floor. He looked into the Neledar's pale face.

"*Sirien!*"

CHAPTER EIGHT

THE OTHER OGTHORNE

Cosmera Rodriys remained slumped over Sirien Ogthorne's bed, carefully placing and replacing old wrappings with new ones. She sprinkled Healing Powder over the deepest wounds across his body, especially the gash over his chest. He had been severely beaten and cut. His father sat opposite Cosmera, watching carefully. His other son, however, remained outside the door to Sirien's room, pacing nervously back and forth, much to Faruin's and Seleborn's anxiety.

This must have been what Viri'el had foreseen the night upon Sirien's return. There *was* blood and sweat from the pain Sirien felt, all over his bound body of wrappings and dressings. He wished he could have done more to prepare for his brother's untimely arrival.

"He's going to be all right, Perci," said Seleborn.

"It's been a week, Seleborn, *a week!*" said Percivine. "And still he remains in this state. Whoever did this certainly knew what they were doing."

Every time he got close to the door handle of the room, he gazed at it for a few seconds, then returned to pacing. Why should he be worried about entering? After all, it was he who'd first caught sight of his brother in bad shape. It was *he* who had alerted everyone about the situation. He should have no right feeling this way. What kind of brother was he? He contemplated these matters backwards and forwards, all throughout his mind.

What kind? What kind? thought Percivine.

Control yourself, said the voice in his head.

Sirien will want to see me when he wakes.

Then you must stay.

But I won't be there, because I'm too cowardly to face what's in store.

Was this it? Was this the *true* reason why he dared not enter the room? To see his brother, all bloodied like this? He'd never seen Sirien injured before, and the very sight made him queasy.

If it was me in there, not him, surely, he would be right next to me, hoping for my recovery.

"I'll go in and take a look," said Faruin.

The door shut.

"Are you ever going to go in?" said Seleborn. "I'm sure one of the first things your brother would want to see when he wakes would be you. If you hadn't of been there, who knows how he would have been able to survive?"

The night Sirien stumbled into Ogthorne cottage and tried desperately to open the door to Percivine's room, Percivine ran to grab his brother as he fell forward before Sirien's face smacked the floor. He dragged him to his bed and rushed downstairs to retrieve Cosmera.

The door opened. Faruin popped out with a grim expression on his face.

"Well? How is he?" Percivine asked anxiously.

"There's still a lot of blood," he said. "Cosmera has been doing all she can to prevent the bleeding from—"

"*Well, she's not doing enough!*" snapped Percivine.

"Perci!" said Seleborn. "Don't speak like that! She's doing her best, and you must remember that magical wounds take longer to heal than normal ones!"

"Who do you think could've done this to him, Seleborn?" said Faruin.

"I don't know," replied Seleborn, "but whoever it was intended to kill him."

They could hear someone approaching the door from the other side. Percivine froze in place. The door opened. Cosmera poked her head in, her eyes landing directly on Percivine.

"Are you going to come in?" she asked.

Percivine hesitated for a moment. He looked at Faruin and Seleborn, and back to Cosmera. Reluctantly he nodded his head, and walked slowly to the door.

"Not a fast boy, are you?" said Cosmera. "By the time you reach the door, we'll all be in our graves."

Percivine hurried at the insult. Cosmera removed herself from the face of the door. He took a first step into the room, and was suddenly blasted by a heavy odor of iron. To his horror, he saw a tray full of blood next to Sirien's bed.

"I should have tidied that away!" said Cosmera. With a graceful flick of her wrist, the tray of blood vanished.

Percivine could not see his brother's face. His father was blocking it.

"No, no, it's all right, son," Percivine heard his father say. "Try not to excite yourself. You need rest, deep rest." He turned to his other son, who nervously walked closer, and said, "He's in a very fragile state, my boy. He is not to get up for anything! You must make sure he stays in bed, got that?"

Mouth hung open, Percivine nodded. All he could do is nod it seems. The state of shock left by Sirien's appearance made him feel skittish.

"Excellent," said Astronitus. "We'll be downstairs if you need anything. Come on, Cosmera."

"Hold," said Cosmera. "I need to address—this last—dressing—there we are!"

Astronitus and Cosmera walked out of the room. All he could hear was Sirien Oghtorne's faint breathing. Percivine came up close to his brother, and sat in his father's chair. He found a cloth lying on a nightstand and gently dabbed it along Sirien's bruised, sweaty face. Sirien's black hair was messier than Percivine could ever remember. He felt like crying. Sirien had always been the stronger of the two.

He heard a whimper.

"Shh, shh," said Percivine. "It's all right, I'm here, Sirien."

Percivine carefully examined his brother's body more in depth for the first time since Sirien's arrival. He swallowed against sudden lightheadedness. He tried to steady his breathing and dried his sweaty palms on his lap.

Sirien whimpered again. The agony of Sirien's mortified Percivine and wished he could do something to ease his brother's pain. But what could he do? He knew nothing of the medicinal world.

Cosmera had worked endlessly to ensure all of Sirien's wounds were cleaned and dressed nicely.

Perhaps she didn't add enough, thought Percivine. What if he grabbed the Healing Powder, and simply doused the wound again? He grew frantic, wanting to speed up Sirien's recovery process and be useful like Cosmera.

"Yeah, that might work," he said.

He quickly grabbed the Healing Powder, and poured it heavily on Sirien's wound. Sirien let out a loud moan. The Powder, however useful it may be, still stung immensely. He grabbed Cosmera's bandage to replace the ones he removed. All he could do now was hope that the bleeding would stop. He waited.

After a half-hour of patient waiting, Percivine noticed something: blood no longer ran from Sirien's wounds into the bowl. The foul stench of blood was beginning to ebb. The bleeding had stopped! He quickly opened the window. He also realized Sirien's heavy breathing had begun to ease. He had done it! He'd helped his brother! He took away the blood-filled bowl. So pleased with himself, Percivine he did not realize that the bowl quivered in his excitement, and that he was spilling blood across the floor.

He grabbed some of the bandages to soak the spilled blood and laid the bowl to rest on the nightstand next to Sirien's bed.

"*Why do you have blood on your clothes?*" rasped a voice.

He turned, stomach sinking. Cosmera stood there frowning at him.

"Who did this?" she said, examining Sirien.

"I did," said Percivine. "Is there a problem?"

"You're not supposed to add this much Powder, it will cause irritation to the wound, and—" She cut herself off, as she noticed Sirien's condition. Her eyes widened. "You did this?" she asked. "Well, you're lucky, boy, that it worked. Next time, however, make sure you consult with me before applying any of *your* own remedies."

She took a look over at Sirien one more time, and left the room.

From behind him came another voice: "Kind of a whiny one, isn't she?"

Percivine froze. He knew that voice. He grew nervous—he'd not heard that voice in so long, he was afraid that, in turning around, it would be nothing more than imaginary.

"*SIRIEN!*"

Percivine could hardly believe it. His brother was well.

"I felt you addressing my wounds," said Sirien Ogthorne. "I would've thanked you, Percivine, but I could hardly speak. You did wonders on me. However, did you know that would work?"

"I didn't," said Percivine. "I know I shouldn't have done it. I'm no healer, but it was a lucky guess. I wanted to help you. To see you—like that—it was dreadful."

Sirien nodded. "Where's dad?"

"Downstairs with the others."

Filled with brand new energy, Sirien picked himself up.

"Sirien—don't!" shrieked Percivine. "You're still too weak!"

"Nonsense," said Sirien. Prepared to throw himself out of bed, he saw the worried look on Percivine's face, and so merely placed his back against the front of the bed. He remained there, legs hidden under the sheets.

A silence burst into the room. Percivine wondered whether this was a good time for him to ask Sirien where he'd been all this time. He did not have to worry. Sirien already knew the anxious look on his brother's face.

"So," he said.

"So…" said Percivine.

"I suppose you're wondering where I've been."

"Just a bit."

"I know I have a lot to account for," said Sirien.

"You don't say?" said Percivine tartly.

"I deserve that," said Sirien.

"You deserve a beating from me," said Percivine. "But I'll wait until you're fully recovered, and then I'll knock you off your *arse*."

Sirien chuckled nervously, knowing there is no humor in the situation.

"You've had dad and I worried about you!" said Percivine. "Poor dad knowing that both his boys were out and about, swimming in a pool riddled with danger, and did you bother contacting either one of us? *NO!* I would think, at least, you would tell dad what you've been up to…Oh, but he covered for you well—very well! Saying that you did not want anyone accidentally hear you when you Orb him? Ha! A load of dung if you ask me!" He began to seethe. "And another thing, I—"

"Look, I know you're—"

"Shut up!" snarled Percivine. "I spent weeks in hell, if you hadn't noticed! You wouldn't believe the mess I've been through, all because someone didn't want to us to know where he was or what he was doing! You know I detest the very nature of secrets...I never understood why you brought me to Maradine that one night. But now I get it—it was your way of introducing me to all this. Thanks for that, by the way. Believe me, my life couldn't have been any better!"

"Percivine, I—"

"I was chased and nearly killed, and did you care to come and intervene to help? No, you didn't! You ran off like a scared girl!"

"That's why Faruin and Seleborn were there!"

"But it gets better," said Percivine. "I witness Rufious get stabbed in the gut by a shapeshifter—worse, Relthren is nearly capsized because of my presence! Ruddy explosions! And then we encounter Bartholev, *again*, in Unin'shai, and Twy'leden had to fend him off before he realized that it was me in disguise. Funny thing, I was informed that I am now one of the biggest criminals to walk all of Eradell! Fancy the joy I must have felt when Twy'leden told me!"

"I know you're upset with me," said Sirien, "but you must understand that—"

"Upset? *Upset?*" snapped Percivine. "That feeling doesn't—"

"*Will—you—for—the—love—of—Gylranor—shut—your—MOUTH?*" said Sirien. "Let me speak!"

Percivine fell stiff and silent.

"Yes, the way I planned to make you aware of all this, wasn't the brightest, I'll admit. But you must understand that it had to be done. A few days before our mishap in the forest, I received a threatening letter from someone within the Divination Administration, saying that, if I don't cease with my meetings of the Solemn Hand, someone will be set out to deal with me personally. I took no notice. I thought someone just wanted to let off steam, but never thought it would come this far. Someone had come to our door, attacked dad and injured him on his shoulder. Imagine my surprise when I heard Elwerth had lost it and put out warrants for our arrest. To think the Administration could sink no lower.

"Anyway," he continued, "after I warded off the intruder, that's when I realized they knew where everything was happening—our home! Upon your return from the market, I knew it was time to show you what I've been building the last five years. I had to take you with me. It was dad's wish for you to come with me. He didn't want them to find you at home and hurt you. I wish there would have been an easier approach to show you, but I had no time. Dad knew all about it. In two days' time, I concocted what I thought was one of the most complicated plans I'd ever made. And it worked, didn't it? We're all alive, aren't we?"

"Worked out *perfectly*," said Percivine lividly.

"After we got separated in the forest, I knew there was no going back, and that I would have to trust Faruin to protect you until you reached Xerian, where you would next meet Seleborn. I had told them they needed to seek out Rufious. I went ahead and Orbed Rufious to expect you. Though reluctant, he agreed."

"He almost didn't let us in!" snarled Percivine.

"I said he would be reluctant," said Sirien. He continued: "From the forest, I went to the Elvic town of Jidi'us. There I transformed myself into an Elf. I don't know how they did it, but a few days later, that filth Bartholev made his way to the town, and casually asked around for me. He did not want to cause an uprising among the Elvic folk, so once he heard that no one knew of me, he left. I left Jidi'us, and traveled south on the River of Jerdane.

"I followed it until I came to the River Junction and followed the River of Zanbros until I reached Borgsbury. I have a friend there by the name of Terrien Waterborn, but his cowardice of 'harboring a criminal,' as he put it, did not help me whatsoever. I came upon Mrs. Clavenhorn's home. You remember her, don't you? Seleborn offered me his home, but I thought it would be best that I don't draw any more attention to his home after Filiiri died."

So Seleborn's home must be intact, Percivine pondered. *Sirien will be pleased knowing this since his uncertainty about the state of his home lingered over him.*

Just another secret, replied the voice in his mind.

"Without any hesitation, she allowed me shelter for a fortnight. Her life hung in jeopardy, but she didn't care. My safety was more important, she told me. I had to give myself enough time to not be caught."

"And you weren't disturbed?" The question had come out of Percivine's mouth, without him realizing he still had anger towards Sirien.

"Not one bit," said Sirien, placing a hand over his dried chest wound. "Anyway, if trouble arose, I wouldn't worry too much about Mrs. Clavenhorn. She's a rather competent spellcaster."

"After I left Mrs. Clavenhorn's, I spent a week travelling back here to Frodrir, but was delayed when I stumbled upon Bolhana. It's in complete despair. It's no longer a Neledar settlement. It's been overrun by Argoms, and who knows what else? After the slaughter there… *especially* the innocent children…I knew it was time for the Solemn Hand to act. No more death, no more destruction! If the Administration had no desire to silence them, I would take matters into my own hands!" Sirien's tone of voice changed and caused him to pant. "I managed to remain unseen, but what I did see were the last remnants of Neledarian opposition trying to kill what Argoms they could—bless their souls…

"I made my return to Frodrir," he said. "As soon as I set my first step back home, I Orbed dad to let him know the news of my return and to call together the Solemn Hand once more. I'm pretty sure you're wondering how I got into this state. Well, I'll tell you. I walked straight home from Frodrir's outskirts, when I saw three people approach me, from the direction of Elnius's home. Just by their conniving, twisted faces, I knew they meant trouble."

"It might have been the investigators!" said Percivine. "Before you arrived, Dad, Cosmera, and Nilius were confronted by an Investigator Dillory. I heard everything. He threatened Dad, and asked whether he was harboring you here at home!"

"Did you get a look at him?" asked Sirien eagerly.

"Unfortunately, no," said Percivine. "Dad had ordered me to hide. He must've known about my warrant. I found it surprising that Dillory did not ask for me."

"It could have been him," said Sirien. "They ambushed me, and one of them, a tall woman with a sort of purple mark on her face, slashed my chest with a very sharp sword. They got what they wanted and scurried off. They must've known it was me. No one does anything like that for no reason, do they?"

"Could've been a bunch of morons looking for a rush," suggested Percivine.

"Yeah, maybe," said Sirien. He looked at his brother, who appeared less cross than earlier. "There you have it. The Argoms finally got smart and grew tired of the Solemn Hand always thwarting their plans. And who do you think they went after? The middle finger of the Hand—me! Thoughts?"

Percivine opened his mouth, but nothing came out. He may have overreacted prematurely without actually knowing the reasons Sirien had for doing what he did. A soothing feeling settled over him, though. Now that he knew the truth, he could no longer stay upset at his brother, who might have died if not for him.

"I am glad you're here now, brother," said Percivine.

"As am I, Percivine, as am I. Faruin and Seleborn did a grand job in keeping you safe."

"Never thought I'd say this," said Percivine, "but they truly have been the best in playing their parts."

Sirien beamed. There was a knock at the door.

"Can we come in, son?" said the voice of Astronitus Ogthorne.

"Do as you please. It's your home."

The door swung open. In walked Faruin, Seleborn, Cosmera, and Astronitus.

"Looks like Percivine has the makings of a fine healer," said Cosmera. "Were you locked in argument just now?"

"We're fine, Cosmera," said Sirien.

Cosmera reached over to check Sirien's wound, which had nearly healed itself.

"Very good" she said. "I can hardly see any blood. It was very lucky that the Powder didn't irritate his wound and skin, Percivine. Be a bit more mindful next time. Such luck isn't so common in the healing ways."

"There's a first time for everything, Cosmera," said Astronitus. He turned to his son, and said, "You gave us quite a tear, son. I'm glad to see that you're up and doing well."

"Thanks, dad."

"It's a sight to see my two boys with each other again. It would make your mother extremely proud."

"Are you well enough to walk?" asked Faruin.

"Let's find out, shall—?"

"Don't even think it!" said Cosmera. "You may have recovered from the great gash on your chest, but you've still got others that need attending to! No time to get ahead ourselves."

"All right, all right," said Sirien. "I can't express how sorry I am about

Rufious's death, Seleborn. I know he taught you a few things as a Warlock."

"Thank you, Sirien," said Seleborn. "But how did you—?"

"Percivine told me. I think we're all caught up npw…Any leads as to who the shapeshifter could be?"

"I haven't told anyone," said Seleborn, catching the attention of Percivine and Faruin, "but I've been thinking for a while that it might have been the very same one that had led me and Filiiri to the lake, Murgoy."

"Evidence?" said Sirien.

"Solely by thought," said Seleborn. "I know there're hundreds of shapeshifters out there. I have this wrenching feeling in my gut that it's him."

"Percivine has also informed me of what occurred in Unin'shai," said Sirien. "Glad to hear Twy'leden showed that piece of scum that we can meet trouble with trouble."

"I think he suspected that Percivine there with us," added Faruin. "I had noticed him eyeing Percivine's disguise more than the rest of ours."

"Yes." Sirien nodded. "If only transformation magic had a better effect than it does now. Where's Nerod?"

"Hard at work," said Astronitus. "We're still examining these old Mage tomes we came across. Lots to do. I wrote asking the Pathfinders Guild to lend aid if they could spare it. Sorric, a kindly Dwarf, has been cataloging for us."

"He should be here," said Sirien, holding his wounds.

"Sirien, you're not well enough. You're too weak. The meeting can hold off for a—"

"It cannot wait!" snarled Sirien. "I've waited too long as it is!"

"Don't excite yourself!" said Cosmera, in a thunderous voice. "You're going to upset your wounds, and you're going to damage the intricate work done for your injuries. Now, *rest!*"

Sirien did as he was told, but being instructed had become tiresome and demeaning.

"Has he done what I asked?" Sirien said coldly.

"It's been a bit hard for him," said Astronitus. "The investigators raise suspicion every time they see someone from the Society of Excavators wandering into the Administration District. On his last attempt, Fernius stopped him in his tracks."

"Fernius?" said Sirien. "I knew that windbag would get in our way. Ever since his appointment as Head Invesitgator, all this business of being an Administration official has certainly gone to his head."

"He's only doing his job, son. His sole purpose is to protect the Landseer at all costs. Even," said Astronitus quickly before Sirien interrupted him, "if her…methods aren't agreeable by everyone. He was a valuable asset to the Solemn Hand, yes, but I don't think his loyalties have changed much. Fernius, too, noticed a change in Elwerth. But would you go against someone who has your very livelihood dangling from their fingers like a puppet?"

"If I knew it was right to do!" said Sirien.

"Listen, Sirien, you cannot hold a prejudice against him just because he decided to leave. He had every right to do it. He was not obligated to serve for the remainder of his life. You cannot hold that against him. That is not what a Pledge does."

"Watch me," hissed Sirien.

Percivine felt it a peculiar thing observing Sirien and Astronitus bicker. Such disagreements didn't happen often between them.

"I can't change your mind," said Astronitus. "However, I can tell you this: Fernius gave word about a meeting between Elwerth, Talus the Dark, and an unknown third party. Not sure who this party is and why they're to see Elwerth and Talus."

Sirien looked at his brother and everyone else in the room. "He told you that?" he said. "The Violet Veil Accord keeps opening doors, doesn't it?"

"Lately there have been rumors about Elwerth," said Astronitus. "Rumors that she secretly favors the efforts of the Argoms, and now that the King is…away…she has the power to do whatever she wants. I personally don't believe that claptrap about King Erelon and the entire Royal Family—saying they're on holiday and all that. I think Elwerth knows where the King's gone, but for gain says nothing."

A smile formed on Sirien's face. "Well," he said, "that is why I have created a plan…"

All attention focused on Sirien. Even Cosmera stopped preparing new bandages for him.

"Sorry?" said Astronitus.

"I will reveal more of that later," said Sirien. "When I am well enough, as you say, I will reveal what I intend to do once we have a meeting going."

"I don't like the sound of that," said Astronitus. "If it's another plan that might get you killed, then surely, I would have to compose more epitaphs…"

"Dad!" said Percivine aghast.

"You can never be too prepared, my boy," said Astronitus, and left the room.

"Any sense that he might lose family," said Cosmera, "your father will do things like that. It's been going on ever Merinni died. Bless his soul." She got up and followed suit.

"So, what's this big plan of yours?" asked Percivine.

"Impatient, are we?" said Sirien. "You'll find out when everybody else does."

Percivine had forgotten his brother's hot-headedness. After spending just a few moments with him, he realized Sirien had returned to his more stubborn and reckless state-of-mind.

"Seleborn," said Sirien, "now that my senses have returned, I'd like to share with you this…On my way to Mrs. Clavenhorn's, I passed by your home. It's still intact. A bit dusty, though. Mrs. Clavenhorn told me while I stayed in Bogsbury that she's been secretly tending to your garden, especially the Dern Tulips. You told me how much Filiiri liked them. I thought it was a very nice gesture from Mrs. Clavenhorn to do that."

Seleborn's upper lip curled stiffly. He found it hard to put on an elaborate smile. "Thank you. Nobody had suspicions about her doing this?"

"Not that I know of," said Sirien. "Told me that she'd go late at night, every other night, to soak the flowers and plants with water, so when the sun hit, it would be just right for them. As for the inside of your home, I don't think she's had luck getting in. You sealed it quite secure."

"I had to, you know that."

"Yes, yes, I'm not questioning your motives," said Sirien. "I would have asked Terrien to lend a hand in doing so, but his cowardice, and his position as Junior Landseer, has forbidden him from doing such things."

"How is Mrs. Clavenhorn, anyway?" asked Seleborn.

"Well, she's well," said Sirien in a bored voice. "Does the same thing, doesn't she? She recollected tales about our childhood. I didn't want to be rude, so I sat and patiently heard her speak. Kept talking about someone that went by the name of Hart. She didn't mention a first name, if you were going to ask. 'The next best after my husband,' she told me. She grows lonesome, however. But I'm sure we'll see her soon."

An interruption at the door prevented any further discussion.

"Come in," called Sirien.

The door opened, and in walked Nerod Nilius and Borak the Orc.

"Nerod! Borak!" said Sirien happily. "My, has it been a good while! So good to see the both of you!"

"A pleasure as always," said Borak.

"Likewise," said Sirien.

"Good to see you alive and in one piece, old friend," said Nerod. "I see Cosmera's touch all over your wounds."

"Most of it," said Sirien. "But I have my brother to thank for the complete healing of my chest wound."

"Really?" said Nerod. "Done with words and more into heals?"

Percivine was delighted by the congratulations he had been receiving. Cosmera, however, still did not fully approve the unorthodox manner by which Percivine helped his brother.

"Just left the Administration, did you?" Sirien asked Nerod.

"Went to the Gilden Service in Astronitus's stead, while he stayed here with you," said Nerod. "It was a bit trickier than usual, I'm afraid."

"Why?"

"Two Administration investigators: Arturus Grenden and Kalor Foggs."

"Those names sound familiar," said Sirien.

"Don't you remember?" Nerod said, sitting beside Sirien. "Just before you left for Maradine, I explained they snooped about the Museum. Well, I stumbled across them both discussing something very odd."

"What was it?" asked Sirien.

"I heard bits and pieces. Something of a plan going as it should. That he will be most pleased with this news."

That sentence reminded Percivine about what his father had said about Thiurwold. Was there a connection?

"Who the hell is 'he'?" asked Sirien, holding his chest where the gash was.

"Search me," said Nerod. "I suppose they didn't realize that I was there, until Investigator Squint shot them a greeting. It must've startled them. They quickly sped off."

"Cowardly warts," muttered Sirien, wishing all too well his want to confront Arturus Grenden.

"As I was preparing my things to leave and packaging the tomes your father and I discovered to bring back to the Depository, I closed the alcove we used and was abruptly halted by Grenden."

"He came back?" Sirien said, turning his neck abruptly to Nerod, a vein popping from it.

"Remembered me," said Nerod stiffly. "Asked if I had anything to share. I don't know what he's playing at, but whatever it is, it can't be good."

"I suspect he may know a little thing or two about the King," added Sirien.

"Possibly."

This was a bit riveting to Percivine. He'd never known that Sirien had great connections in places thought impenetrable. But he was wrong. Gah—his brother was as ever gallant as he'd always thought.

"Did you have any trouble getting here, Borak?" Sirien asked the quiet Orc.

Borak was a very different type of Orc, a friendlier, happier soul than the rest of his kin. It proved that not all Orcs agreed with the dark way of the Argoms, and why one should never generalize such things.

"I had a few wondering eyes upon me," said Borak, his large boots causing the room to rattle, "but once they saw me meet up with Nerod out in the courtyard of the Administration, a sense of easement flushed their faces."

"Good, good," said Sirien. "You haven't spoken to Marandir, have you?"

"Sadly, no," said Borak. "The last letter I received from was dated two months ago. I haven't gotten any word of him since. Negotiations with the Goblins must be going well. However small they are, they will not give in to just mere words. I'm sure he's giving it his best shot, though."

"A nice touch if we had the Goblins on our side," said Sirien, resting his head against the bed frame.

"You mustn't forget, Sirien," said Borak, sitting at the end of the bed, "that he goes there on direct orders from Elwerth. No one can know that it was our idea he suggest it to her."

"Thankfully no one knows the names of those in the Solemn Hand, but me," said Sirien. "To think what would happen if the Landseer discovered that her employees served not only her, but the Solemn Hand? I can picture her going berserk."

"She's not far off," joked Astronitus.

"Elwerth would condemn you all and raise you to the high rank of criminal like Percivine and I."

"We know of the risks, Sirien," said Nerod, clapping Sirien's left shoulder. "We proudly do it."

"We all would be condemned as criminals," Seleborn said. "Need I remind you that whoever helps Sirien or Percivine Ogthorne are criminals as just. We all have been branded treasonous by a government which we thought to be just."

Cosmera returned, looking annoyed.

"Give the man some room to breathe!" she grumbled, placing a meager drinking vessel on the nightstand. "We will all have time to reminisce and speak about Sirien's plan *after* he's well and ready. And *you*," she said, pointing a bony finger at Sirien, "I've told you to cease this excitement. Now drink the camadagrass tonic. It will calm your nerves. Your heart is slightly weak. You need to refrain to help build its strength back."

Cosmera shooed Borak and Nerod from Sirien's bed, so she could audit the wounds Sirien received on his arms and face.

"All right, all right," said Nerod, trying to stay clear of an irritable Cosmera. "Sirien, we'll be back. Just give us word when you're ready for us to gather."

"The man's fine, Cosmera!" said Borak, almost toppling back while also avoiding Cosmera. "I've never seen a healthier person in my life!"

"Yes, yes," she said loftily, "he's a true hero, now get moving—the both of you!"

"Good day to you all," said Nerod.

Nerod and Borak chuckled as they made their way out of Sirien's room. The door behind them shut.

"Cosmera, I highly doubt that was—" Sirien said.

"*Bite your tongue!!*" she spluttered at him. "I'm trying to do my job as your healer. You would think I'd know a thing or two of what's best for you, don't you agree?"

"Yes, but—"

"No buts!" said Cosmera. "If I see that you're fooling around with injuries like yours, *I will cure you completely of them, and inflict them back myself!* Do I make myself clear, Sirien Ogthorne?"

"As loud as ever," muttered Sirien.

Cosmera turned and glared at Percivine, Faruin, and Seleborn. None of them felt right making eye contact with her, almost like they'd be set ablaze with her anger. She roughly checked Sirien's dressings. They could hear Sirien goran as she hastily changed one of his wet dressings and applied a new one rather tightly, beyond comfort for Sirien. She gave him a once over and walked out, slamming the door that sent chills up their spines.

"I'll admit," said Sirien. "She a fine mender, but her temper needs …tempering."

"She has a point, though," said Faruin, ensuring it was safe to near Sirien. "She knows medicine, so I think you should listen to her, Sirien."

Sirien sighed. "Fine," he said. "I'll do as she says. I suppose I have no choice."

"I see you are doing better than when we first saw you," said Seleborn. "Within a few days, you should be ready to take your position as Leader of the Solemn Hand again."

"Here's hoping, Seleborn," said Sirien gloomily. He looked at Faruin and Seleborn. "Now that I think of it…I did not thank the both of you properly for protecting Percivine."

"We were happy to do it," said Faruin. "That's why you Pledged us."

Sirien put his hand in the air to make them stop talking. "No, no. A proper thank you is required, to make me feel better. You want me to feel better, don't you? It would certainly ease some of the pain I feel from these wounds."

"Well…all right…"

Percivine felt belittled, an emotion he's experiencing more and more as time went on. He got the feeling Sirien only knows him as a helpless child that needed guidance through his life. But he realized in minutes that if Faruin would not have emerged from the forest, he surely would have been killed by Bartholev and his Argoms, or, if Seleborn had not added his extra magical protection, he and Faruin could have been killed.

"You two shall be greatly rewarded for the protection that you've given my brother," said Sirien. "Once I'm well, I'll see to it personally that you move up and become senior members alongside my father, Cosmera, Pevarius, Thiurwold, Nerod, and I."

Faruin and Seleborn nodded in appreciation, and said nothing to alter Sirien's decision of them.

Percivine thought he could faint from all the hot air coming off Sirien's ego.

"I suppose if you don't mind," said Sirien, "I'll—"

Percivine gripped his forearm. The time has come for answers and Percivine refused to wait any longer.

"Brother, please let go."

"NO!" said Percivine, tightening his grip like one of Cosmera's ill-fitting bandages. "You're not going to keep this secret hidden from me any longer. *What do you plan to do?*"

After some hesitation, Sirien exhaled deeply, and muttered, "We're going to break into the Divination Administration."

CHAPTER NINE

SIRIEN'S PLAN

After a fortnight of recovery, the taller, more senior of the Ogthorne brothers was, at last, cured of his wounds. He was bustling about Headquarters, making preparations for his next meeting. Most days, he remained trapped within his bedroom, reviewing old notes and research, along with new evidence provided by Nerod Nilius and Trobius Stout having to do mostly about Estith Elwerth. Sirien, by request, wanted no disturbance when locked away in his chamber.

For the most part, Percivine was happy to be reunited with his brother, even as he remained frustrated with the lack of contact. Whenever Sirien requested something from his room, Percivine eagerly went to fetch whatever he needed, because the metallic stench of blood had finally lifted from Sirien's room, and retreated elsewhere.

Through Sirien's recovery, Percivine felt lonesome at times. Astronitus would leave regularly every day at the Eighth Hour, and return at the Fifth; Seleborn would take leaves randomly and would refuse to tell them where he went; Faruin usually wondered off to the market, or would travel to the River of Jerdane to catch the evenings supper, and Sirien would remain shut up in his room. He found visits from Cosmera to be nice, but realistically only came to check on Sirien's health.

One warm evening, Percivine sat in a wooden chair overlooking the garden behind the cottage. He admired seven statues at the very center of the garden, all neatly placed in a circle. He reminisced quietly about recent events that he'd partaken in, and wondered if he would ever again witness such dramatic upheaval.

It was half-past the Fourth Hour of the Third Day, meaning his father was due to return soon. That would mean, in turn, imminent supper. He got up from his seat, took one last look at the statues, and dashed inside the abode. A voluptuous aroma found him. The smell danced gently into his nose, but soon couldn't be enjoyed.

"*How much more do you need to hear, Handolan?*" snapped Faruin, suddenly. "I have constantly told you I don't need this overreach of yours!"

"Faruin—this is what he wanted."

"You dare speak of him? *Where were you when he died?* Where were you after he died?"

"I need to know you'll be safe." The Omitay realized it was no longer just him and Faruin in the Ogthorne kitchen. "I will make my leave, then. Good night, Mr. Ogthorne."

"Night," said Percivine delicately.

Faruin let his head drop fiercely and exhaled deeply.

"I'm sorry you were privy to that display," said Faruin, raising his head.

"No need. Is everything—?"

"Just fine. I assume you're hungry. But we can't eat just yet."

Percivine knew he shouldn't be grinning after Faruin's ordeal with Handolan, however, he found it arduous not to. He eyeballed Faruin filling various bowls with spiced pork, Elvic bread, and an assortment of vegetables.

Not fish, he thought. *Thank the Pantheon of Gylranor.*

"Still no sign of Seleborn, then?" Percivine said, stuffing his face full of Elvic bread.

"Thought I said we mustn't eat yet?" said Faruin.

"Must've slipped my mind," said Percivine, slowly and awkwardly placing the bread down.

"Anyway…he's been away for almost four hours. I don't know what he's up to, but whatever it is, I'm sure it's beneficial in one way or another."

"You *always* look on the better side of things, don't you?"

"Someone has to," said Faruin. "All right, supper's ready. We'll just wait for Astronitus to return. He's due back any moment now. The Fifth

Hour approaches. I wouldn't fill myself with so much bread." He had caught Percivine lifting the bread again. "You won't have room for any of this fine pork that I've so willingly made for us."

Percivine dropped the piece of bread. "Fine. Can I ask you something?" He wiped the crumbs that had fallen on his chest. "It's been biting at me since we recounted our stories to one another."

"Sure," said Faruin, wiping his hands with a rag. "What's on your mind?"

"Seleborn mentioned that he had moved from Mjorsten to Borgsbury, thus he had a home to go to. I have this one. Where exactly have you stayed since your exile from Ni'shorus?"

The question seemed to dawn on Faruin. "Let me be frank. Each time either you or Seleborn mentions of exile, it irritates me. I told you once before that I am on the run, not in exile, still wanted by my Elvic brethren. So, if you don't mind…I'm wanted as much as a criminal as you are, Perci."

"Apologies," said Percivine.

"Once they had apprehended me, I was dragged off to the Citadel. You wouldn't believe the filth I had to share a cell with. Some rogue Elf that had brutally murdered his wife and three children just for the tiniest reason of disobeying his orders on dinner. Yes, I was threatened, but I knew it was the ordinary way of life in there. Five days later, that idiot I shared a cell with tried to escape. He almost made it, until one of the guards caught wind of him and killed him on the spot. I could not make the same mistakes he did, so I waited a few days revising my plan for escape.

"I had not received a new cellmate. They thought me too dangerous. Thought I would kill the next one like I 'had Dedrinus.' I laughed at their stupidity…If they knew…At the Ninth Hour of each night, a guard would go to each cell and deliver very disgusting food. I saw that as my chance. Usually, they put one arm in the cell to lay the tray down. The very second he put the tray down, I grabbed the guard's hand, and twisted it."

"The guard didn't squirm?" asked Percivine suspiciously. "I would have thought he would alert the others."

"Ah," said Faruin, "that's the exciting part since any magic is subdued within the cells of the Citadel. The very moment I grabbed his hand, he pulled it back with tremendous force. That's all I needed…Lme explain to you how they open cell doors. With the simplest touch from their hand, they can open the magically sealed door, which works to only recognize the genetic material of the officials. Now that I had drenched my hand in his genetic essence, I touched the door. As I had thought: it worked."

"Doesn't seem like a well-rounded system," said Percivine.

"Why?" said Faruin, taken aback. "What's the matter with it?"

"That means anyone could do it. It sounds far too easy to remain locked up in that place."

"Trust me," said Faruin, leaning against the counter. "I'm no scientist, but anyone with a bit of common sense would know that the slightest bit of genetic essence like sweat would unlock the cell. Those other convicts are far too stupid to ever think of something like that. Their brain cells have deteriorated over the course of their lives spent there. They simply wouldn't lift a finger to detach themselves from what they've become so accustomed to. I spent only days there. I was not yet harmed by prison life.

"At the start start of the Argom War in 5D 492, Elvic patrols were light on the River of Jerdane, so once I managed my escape I made my way south down the river and into Nell."

"I assume you transformed yourself just in case?" said Percivine.

"Oh yes," said Faruin. "As you know well I'm an expert runecaster, so that was the first step I took in order to make my escape perfect. For the next year, I worked on a farm in the countryside. The owner was an elderly gentleman who lived with his darling wife. They were very warm and welcoming—generally speaking, Elves wouldn't do menial labor like that for a Neledar.

"Jump forward five years to the winter month of Moon's Favoring that I met your brother. He recognized me almost instantly! I was rather shocked so naturally I denied it, but your brother…I don't know how he did it. He persuaded me that he would not tell a soul. He knew of my innocence, and he'd heard about my previous post as Assistant Elf of Beautification. He flattered me with his interest. Told me they were looking to fill the spot of a recently deceased member. Sirien explained that the Solemn Hand would provide me with the best protection I could ever hope to receive, and he was right. I have not had one complaint since. Your brother saved me from ever being caught, and I owe him my life for that."

Percivine did not expect for Faruin to reveal exactly what had happened the day he escaped and onward. Admittedly, he'd always wondered how exactly Faruin had managed to escape such a fortified prison.

Percivine picked up another helping of bread. This time not caring whether he should eat or not.

"Put it down!" snapped Faruin. "Can't you ever stop acting upon your gut? Your father should be home soon! *Wait!*"

"I've waited long enough," said Percivine sourly.

Faruin drew in breath. "I'm sorry, Perci. I knew speaking of it would bring this out in me."

"It's all right, Faruin. I should not have provoked you to tell me about it."

"It's my fault," said Faruin. "You asked me about where I stayed since I escaped, not all the details in between."

The hour was getting late, and Seleborn and Astronitus were nowhere to be found. Percivine's stomach grumbled loudly. He picked at the bread only, as to prevent any further escalations with Faruin. Faruin, too, grew impatient. Every evening he cooked the meal, and had to be kept waiting. He had an eyebrow-raising notion that Astronitus and Seleborn secretly took turns showing up late to each meal just to spite him.

"And you still don't know where Seleborn goes off to?" asked Percivine.

"Not a clue," said Faruin, picking up an empty pot. "I did once overhear him Orbing someone. Sounded like a man. Mentioned something about the Enviro District, but that's all."

"Maybe that's where he's been going all these days!" said Percivine loudly.

Came a cold voice behind them: "Yeah…maybe that's where he's gone…"

Percivine whipped around. Faruin dropped the pot on his foot and cried out in pain. Seleborn stood behind them, arms crossed and glaring at them both.

"S-Seleborn!" exclaimed Percivine. "H-have y-you been standing there the whole time? We didn't even hear you come in!"

"No," he said. "I just managed to hear that last part. You two really are a piece of work. Did it ever occur to you that my mentioning of the Enviro District was simply *just that*?"

Neither replied.

"Well I see you've already begun to eat without me," said Seleborn, glaring at the half-empty basket of bread.

"Can you blame us?" said Faruin, recovering from the dropped pot, which he tossed into the sink. "We've been waiting for you and Astronitus to return. We can only wait for so long before we become famished. We can't wait for you all the time. We're not here to serve you as you please."

Still glaring at Faruin, Percivine interjected and asked Seleborn, "Did you see my father on your way here?"

"Your—? Oh—your father!" The crossness lifted in Seleborn's voice. "I did, actually."

"Where?"

"Outside Headquarters."

"*What?*" The news struck Percivine straight across the face. He'd been wondering and starving for his father, and this whole time he'd been outside. "How long's he been there?"

"I don't know," said Seleborn. "I've just arrived."

"What's he doing out there?" said Percivine, flushed.

"Speaking to your neighbors."

"Elnius Bash…What for?"

"Dunno," said Seleborn. "As I walked past I overheard them talking about some odd stuff happening at the Duke of Greater Anloth's old summer manor down the road."

"I know…that place," said Percivine darkly. "Sirien and I would wander ourselves to it and play in it, when the King's son went away." Percivine paused to catch his breath, at the same time Seleborn loudly cleared his throat. "Once, late at night, I could swear I saw three figures leaving from the back of the manor, but when I told Sirien about it, he thought I was just probably exhausted. I was, though."

Faruin fixed Seleborn a plate full of food, before any further anger fell from his mouth. Percivine helped himself to a second serving of spiced pork and potato-stuffed cabbage leaves, punctuating it all with a loud belch.

"Is your brother not going to eat?" Faruin asked, preparing to store the leftover food, since neither Astronitus nor Sirien had come.

"You know he's been working on that plan of his," said Percivine. "He's got no time to eat."

"Food fuels the brain," said Faruin. "I would think you of all know that."

Percivine and Seleborn helped Faruin store the remaining articles of food when, a heavy voice called out to them, and said, "Don't even think of putting it away! I'm starved!"

The lanky appearance of Astronitus Ogthorne stood at the kitchen's archway, holding his stomach and gesturing for Faruin to bring out the food.

"We were beginning to wonder if you were ever going to come, Astronitus," said Faruin, opening the containers of food. "We've been waiting for hours."

Astronitus walked in and sat between Percivine and Seleborn. He grabbed the plate Faruin had fixed.

"I do apologize for that, Faruin," said Astronitus, grabbing an eating utensil. "I was off work rather late. I spent most of my day examining and taking notes with Nerod on that Mage tome. Then had to make a run for the Museum of Nell. Didn't help that I caught Arturus Grenden snooping about the Museum. *Yet again.* Incidentally, he's there every time we are."

"Still on that, is he?" said Seleborn.

"It's worse than ever. I've been told Fernius has given him full jurisdiction of the Museum, but I don't believe a word of it. No warrant was shown. Fernius may be a strict follower of the rules, but he knows the procedures and laws of the land. Grenden, not once, showed me the proper documentation to act as he did, nor has Dillory at Felefor."

"Had no idea they intruded there, also" said Percivine. "Why do they focus so much on your workspaces?"

"I think they're trying to uncover information about the Solemn Hand," said Astronitus, before scarfing down a mouthful of spiced pork. "Must be easy for Dillory, especially, since the Felefor Depository is rather small and about a shop away from the local investigative post."

"What's the Solemn Hand got do with anything?" said Sirien Ogthorne in his raspy speech.

Everyone turned around to see Sirien standing there, pale and sunken-eyed. "Well?"

"Son, how long have you been there?"

"Long enough," said Sirien.

"Good to see you getting out of your cave," said Astronitus.

But Sirien did not laugh. He grew impatient that his father did not say anything to his question.

"Are you going to tell me?"

"Yeah, what's this all about, Dad?" said Percivine.

Astronitus pushed his plate aside, as if he'd lost his appetite. "You mustn't disembowel me because of this. It's a rumor, a mere rumor."

Percivine had never seen his father splutter so nervously before; a Neledar of his stature; a Neledarian man who could normally hold his emotions.

"As you may or may not know," Astronitus began, "I'm rather good friends with one of Fernius's Assistant Investigators, Irinea Squint. She keeps me updated about the day-to-day activity of the Sanction Service. If Fernius found this out, she would certainly be out of the job. This does not leave the kitchen. Landseer Elwerth has been fed information that we are conspiring against her, secretly giving off valuable information to the Argoms. To think we would *ever* be so kind to the Argoms."

"Parsite of a Neledar," said Sirien, with a crazed look. "First the warrants, and now this muck about us working hand-in-hand with the Argoms! Stupid woman! But after today's meeting, things will change."

"Don't act so surprised, brother," said Percivine. "You know she's been out for us since our separation in the forest."

"Like I said, Sirien, it's only a rumor," said Astronitus.

"I doubt that now!" snarled Sirien, banging his fist against the frame of the archway. "I overheard you say that Grenden bloke snooping around your office as I walked down the staircase. It can't be a rumor if they are acting on it."

"Something is not right," said Seleborn. "Why would she think we'd want to help them? It doesn't make any sense. That would mean Bartholev is on our side, and we know he isn't."

"Yeah, he almost killed me—twice!" said Percivine.

"Bartholev works for Elwerth," said Seleborn. "How could—? It doesn't fit, does it? So, we must be aligned with Bartholev, who aligns himself with

Elwerth, who thinks we plan to strike against her? This equation has no solution. I definitely think she has no idea what she's doing."

"Your theory works well to a certain extent," said Faruin.

"Oh?"

"I don't believe Elwerth knows that Bartholev works for their side. No one exactly knows about Bartholev, do they? He's always been very secretive, hasn't he? Usually people end up dead from him, and therefore cannot reveal him."

"Yes," said Seleborn, remembering what Bartholev did to his wife. "But there are those of us who remember him killing those we loved, and those of us" —he tilted his head toward Percivine and back— "who managed to escape from his grasp.

"However," he added, "I am beginning to wonder how Elwerth could ever have approved his appointment of—? For what Service does he actually work for?"

"I could shed some light on the matter," Astronitus said. "He works in the Sanction Service, in a sub-ward called the Intelligence Service. It was newly created shortly after the Violet Veil Accord went into effect. Bartholev was selected to work for the Administration by Talus the Dark.

"I suspect Elwerth hadn't heard of Bartholev before, and was convinced his qualifications were outstanding or rubbish."

"He is virtually unknown to most of the world," said Astronitus, "while, to us, who know the severity of his actions, remains infamous."

"We're going to stop them," said Sirien, gazing down at the wooden floorboards. "We're going to stop Bartholeve, stop Elwerth…The time is here. No going back now."

"What do you have in mind, son?" said Astronitus, a bit unclear what Sirien's words meant.

"I have devised the perfect plan. But I won't reveal its contents just yet, for there are still a few things I must revise before my plan can take full effect. I have already given word to Nerod to begin preparing the arrangements for our next meeting."

Four days had come and gone, and Percivine could not stop thinking about what his brother had said about breaking and entering the Divination Administration. What did he have in store for them? Percivine was beginning to wonder if his brother was more for stopping the Argoms dead in their tracks, or a revolutionary trying to overthrow a corrupt government.

He could be both, said the voice in Percivine's head.

The day of the new meeting arrived with a jolt. Sirien grew anxious awaiting the arrival of the Solemn Hand. Percivine could see that his brother really wanted to detail the rest of his plan with anyone.

Percivine stood in the gardens, looking at the seven statues from a distance. A gentle breeze came over the scene; it was a different sort of breeze, carrying with it a feeling of change. Not even the smell from the kitchen could overpower him today. Faruin helped Astronitus and Cosmera prepare an abundance of food for the meeting. Seleborn had taken one of his mysterious departures and returned within two hours.

"They are arriving," said Seleborn to him through one of the open windows.

Percivine made his way inside to hear Cosmera Rodriys squawking at Sirien.

"…over excite yourself," she said, waving a stalk of celery as she spoke. "You may have healed from those wounds, but they have weakened you."

"I'm fine, Cosmera," said Sirien. "I've told you countless times."

"I'm not so sure," she said. "Look at those sunken eyes, those dark rings. Your skin is as pale as an apparition. You look a bit peaky. Has this Neledar been eating, Astronitus?"

"Yes," Astronitus lied.

"I hope he hasn't been locked away in that room of his," said Cosmera.

Percivine never realized how much Cosmera reminded him of his mother. He remembered his mother feeling the same way about the infinite hours Sirien would spend in his room, always pretending to be an adventurer, his playthings followers of his.

"Percivine, make sure to get the door when you hear a knocking," said his father. "We're going to head to the dining area and lay out the nourishment."

"Not to worry, Dad," said Sirien, "Nerod and Trobius have already begun."

"They're here?" said Astronitus. "I didn't hear them come in."

The next few moments were boring for Percivine. He sat at the front of the hallway, opening the door and greeting the several members of the

Solemn Hand as they walked in. Luckily for him, Seleborn showed pity and stayed with him, while Faruin helped take the food to the long table in the hall.

"All right," said Seleborn, closing the door after Twy'leden Paros. "We're just missing Linaus and the twins."

"What about Thiurwold?" asked Percivine.

"I don't think he's going to show. Didn't you see the look on Dunn's face as he walked in? Looks like they may have had another row."

A knock came at the door. Percivine reached for the door, but before he could turn the knob the door opened, nearly bumping him on the nose. Linaus Olvea walked in.

"Hullo, Linaus," said Seleborn.

"Hi."

"The meeting's to start soon. We're just waiting for Viri'el and Vaureth."

Linaus snorted. "Figures they'd be late."

He looked coldly at Percivine and made his way to into the hall.

"Is he always that dark?" Percivine asked, trying to rid himself of the shiver Linaus sent up his spine.

"His dedicated work has been about creating potent potions and poisons. Botany has been his life study, and becoming an alchemist has helped him bring together what he knew and evolve his line of expertise. His alchemical laboratory has him breathing in fumes all day. I'm sure some of those fumes are a bit more than harmful than others. You can't blame the Neledar for being a bit drab."

Percivine knew next to nothing of the botanical world, so Seleborn's rebuttal, *or* excuse, made a little sense.

"Good afternoon," said Viri'el, taking it upon herself to open the door. "I can hear much noise and talk coming from the hall. Am I to assume we are the last to arrive?"

"Yes, you are," said Seleborn.

"We apologize for our late arrival," said Vaureth. "We had to intervene to help a poor Orc being beaten. These drunken Neledar assumed the Orcen man took pride in the Argom Influence."

"It's a soothing feeling knowing that not all Orcs are in accordance with the shameful ways of the Argoms," said Viri'el.

"I'm sure Borak will be pleased to hear that you helped out that Orc," said Seleborn.

"It's a soothing feeling knowing that not all Orcs agree with the despicable ways of the Argoms," said Viri'el.

"I'm sure Borak will be pleased to hear that you helped out that orc," said Seleborn.

Arriving from down the hall, Faruin saw Viri'el and Vaureth. Vaureth glowered at him.

"Hullo, Faruin," she said kindly.

Faruin breathed heavily through his nose and said "Hullo" back at her. He continued to stare at Viri'el.

Vaureth cleared his throat, and said frowning at Faruin, "Yes—well, I think we best get in there before Sirien drags us by our pointed ears."

Percivine, Faruin, and Seleborn followed Vaureth and Viri'el inside the hall, where they were greeted by Sirien, who stood at the front of the long table.

"Vaureth! Viri'el! I was beginning to wonder whether we should begin without the both of you! Come—take your seats! There's" —He pointed over to two seats next to Pevarius Garcinius— "two seats right next to Pevarius. And you three at the very end near Dunn!"

They took their seats in their designated areas, awaiting Sirien's words. To Percivine's point of view, Sirien looked lost for words, for he remained in silence, possibly looking at his reflection in the table's polished maple wood.

"I implore you all," Sirien spoke, slowly lifting his gaze at the Solemn Hand, "that we must now, more than ever, join together to apprehend the dark forces that are currently at work. As you know, I've been devising a secret plan for days on how to resolve this problem. I have been receiving intelligence from a crucial and reliable source from within the Administration. Now—as for the contents of this riveting plan, I shall reveal momentarily. I must, at once, take the time to inform you all of the tragedy that's brewing within the Divination Administration. Landseer Elwerth seeks to have us arrested, executed, if possible, for conspiracy and treason against Nell."

Whispers broke out among the Solemn Hand.

"And now," said Sirien, "she hoists a man whom we know is not who he says he is—Bartholev. As my source informs me, Bartholev delivers these outlandish lies to the Argom at Elwerth's side, and implants them within her mind." He turned to Percivine. "Your escape from Marandine Forest really had an affect on Bartholev, Percivine."

"Elwerths tainted Nell's government with Argom influence," Sirien continued placing his knuckles from both hands flat on the table, "which we cannot allow for the sake of further embarrassment. Furthermore, I suspect Bartholev isn't the only one operating within the Administration. According to a reliable source of mine, there are a couple others who seem supportive of the Argoms' ways—Arturus Grenden and Kalor Foggs. They must be silenced, though preferably not killed. They take their orders from Bartholev, so we can assume the orders are not just."

More whispers erupted in the dining room. Percivine leaned over and whispered something himself to Seleborn.

"Is he sure about this?" he asked him.

"If Sirien's speaking about it," said Seleborn, "then I'm sure he's certain about it."

"Recently," Sirien said, "it has also come to my attention that they have been parading about offices in the Administration without proper documentation. With insistence from Bartholev, Elwerth has been granting permission to the searches, surpassing Fernius's power to block the searches."

"I too experienced their meddlesome behavior not two days ago," said Pevarius Garcinius, stomping his staff.

"That is why they must be brought at an end," said Sirien, loudening his voice. "As I have told my brother, we must, and will, break into the Administration. My source is ready at a moment's notice, as are we."

Many eyebrows rose, some stunned, some in what looked more like skepticism. Percivine himself could not deny his excitement about this whole ordeal. Months ago he nearly died, and now was to head into the heart of danger.

"In a week's time, we are to make our way to the Divination Administration—I have a feeling that they will know we are coming. That is why we are to split into three groups each having a party leader. I've created the groups, and you must remain with them at all times, each performing a specific task."

"Sirien, this—you can't be serious," said Trobius Stout, standing up to show his objection.

"I know some of you do not believe in this, but I assure you all, only good will come from this," said Sirien. "Now more than ever, we must act together. We cannot let a grounded Landseer wage a personal war against us, when the enemy looms so close. Now, if I may—"

"Isn't there another way?" asked Cosmera Rodriys.

"None, I'm afraid," said Sirien. "This plan has been carefully researched and thought out. You are here because of the unique expertise you each bring. I would not have have spoken about my plan, if I knew there was room for failure. Now, if I can continue…The groups are as follows: Group one will consist of myself, Percivine, Faruin, Seleborn, and Nerod. Group two will be led by my father. Viri'el, Pevarius, Linaus, Twy'leden—that's yours. The last group will consist of Cosmera as lead group member, followed by Borak, Vaureth, Dunn, and Trobius."

"Grea'," muttered Dunngarunax Galon, praying that a mug of Morgs Ale would pop into his grip, "we know our groups, but wha' exactly are we to be doin'?"

"I will get to that my dear Dunn," said Sirien. "Arriving at the Administration District of Elbynshire won't be a problem. Getting inside is what will be difficult. More than likely, Argoms will be guarding the gates into the District, and any and all Diviports. We'll have to surpass them. I know Faruin has a newfound mastery of transformation, and it is his and Twy'leden's skills we will use. I was thinking a couple of pots, then we smash them. Does that answer your question, Dunn? Trobius, I hope this settles your objections."

"Brilliant!" exclaimed Trobius. "But can't we just kill the lot? If this were reciprocated, they'd show no mercy is sparing us."

"Who's really going to question a couple of broken pots by the gates?" said Sirien, walking around the table. "To avoid any unwanted attention, those will suffice for now, and once that is taken care of we will strike! Those of us in group one will leave one day in advance. On our way, we'll need to make a stop off in Borgsbury. I'd like to pay Terrien Waterborn a small visit. He's an old friend of ours."

"Could work," said Pevarius.

"As Oroseer, I'm sure he can Transport us to Elbynshire. I don't think he has forgotten where his *true* loyalties lie."

"And you're certain he will approve of this?" said Borak, his hands resting on his oval gut.

"Not everything is dwindled in certainty, Borak," said Sirien coolly. "But I think with the proper negotiation tools, he'll be more than happy to oblige my request."

"Why not just have Terrien transport us to the Administration itself?" asked Faruin.

"A clever question!" Sirien had shouted it behind Faruin, which caused Percivime to jump a little. "It would be unwise of us to all appear in the District when it will be heavily guarded by Argoms. Just at the gates will be fine."

"As long as you're sure," said Borak, sounding unconvinced.

"I am. Now then," there was a happy rise in Sirien's voice, "after we have gained entry, group two will patrol the Administration grounds, while group three makes their way to the Main Courtyard which lies in front of the Diet Chambers. Here lies the Diet of Nell and the Landseer's office and that of her immediate staff. Lastly, my group will make its way to the Chambers. I'm sure we'll be halted, so expect any delays."

All remained silent on the matter, trying their best to appreciate Sirien's plan of action.

"Do you believe you're going to have success with Terrien, Sirien?" asked Vaureth. "I've heard tell he's somewhat of an alarmist."

"Yes, I do. I'm certain we'll be successful with Terrien; once we are, he'll show us his personal Diviport."

"Can you explain again why Pevarius or I can't simply use our portable Diviports?" said Trobius, waving the little device around his right wrist.

"That's how Bartholev disappeared after our encounter with him at the Temple!" said Percivine, pointing a finger at it. "How do they work?"

"Simple, really," said Pevarius, moving his wrist forward. "These are given to Administration employees only. Anywhere one might be, with a simple push of this button, they'll instantly be taken to their respective departments or offices within the Divination Administration. The same works in reverse: it'll take us to our homes respectively."

"In layman's terms," said Trobius, "one goes from home to work and work to home."

"This couldn't be part of the plan?" Percivine asked Sirien.

"I thought about it," said Sirien, rubbing the scruffy bed of hair on his face with his thumb and index finger. "Can't risk it. Who knows if those are being tracked? Would rather avoid the risk. Which is why we need Terrien. The Seers of the Land supposedly get their own permanent Diviport installed after their appointments, according to your friend Verilius Lish, right, Pev?"

"Correct," said Pevarius, removing his wrist from the table."

"So, once we've safely arrived to the gates of the District, I'll Orb each of the group leaders, and have them portaled there at once."

"And if you are unsuccessful?" said Twy'leden Paros. "What then?"

"For your sakes, you best hope I'm not," said Sirien coldly. "But if the situation were to arise, then it appears we will have to travel by foot, and my plan will have to begin several days before the initial date."

No one liked the sound of that. To travel by foot would mean they would be far too exhausted to even carry out such an elaborate plan. Percivine looked at his brother and was surprised to see Sirien's firm, confident manner. He expected not to fail.

"Are there any questions?"

No one said a word.

"So, everyone understands, then?"

"I have a question," said the low voice of Linaus Olvea.

"By all means, Linaus," said Sirien. "What's your question?"

"Once we manage to enter the Administration District," he said, "how exactly are groups one and three to get into the Diet Chambers without any proper government issued identification?"

"I'm glad you asked," said Sirien eagerly. "Once we arrive, and the grounds are secure, Faruin and Twy'leden will perform temporary transformations on each one of us. Group two will not need it for they will not step into the Chambers. Once groups one and three are securely past the security gate, we will remove our disguises. We are operating late at night, so there will not be many to stop us and recognize us until we reach the top floor of the Chambers. And as for identification, we are to make eleven other Identification Cards from Pevarius's and Trobius's models. Trobius, if you would be so kind to bring the components needed to make them."

"Right," said Trobius, clearly still skeptical about the whole thing.

"Good, good," said Sirien. "Does that answer your question Linaus?"

"Indeed," said Linaus.

"We shall reconvene this meeting in thirty minutes," said Sirien. "Please help yourselves to the wondrous grel steaks Faruin and my father have prepared. And help yourselves to the fabulous wine and ale Dunn and Twy'leden have provided."

Percivine quickly got up, grabbed a plate, and started piling on large amounts of grel meat, churned potatoes, corn, and other assortment of vegetables. Grels are carnivorous, evolved forms of the common bull, who have been known to have horrific temperaments. Percivine also helped himself to three soft biscuits. Trying ever so hard to balance his plate in one hand, he struggled with the other to pour ale into one of the pints provided, until Viri'el intervened and poured it for him. He thanked her, and rushed back to his seat to begin stuffing his face.

"Careful, lad," said Dunn, grabbing the seat next to him, his maggedium arm pulsating brightly. "If ye continue eatin' like tha' ye might suffocate."

Percivine looked blankly at Dunn, and slowly swallowed the remaining bits of food in his mouth.

"See? Isn' tha' better?"

"Yes," said Percivine, who really did not think so. There was much more on his plate that he wished he could devour without being criticized. "How are you, Dunn?"

"I'm all righ'," said the Dwarf, pouring down his ale.

Faruin and Seleborn now took their seats on each side of Percivine and Dunn.

"You finished that ale rather fast," said Seleborn. "I hope you can remember everything Sirien has talked about."

"Bah!" said Dunn heavily. "I can an' will!"

"Does Thiurwold know we had a meeting today?" said Faruin.

"Don' talk to me abou' tha' blundering idiot!" said Dunn. Cosmera and Nerod, who were in deep conversation, stopped and looked at him.

"Care to tell us what occurred between you both?" said Faruin, cutting apart the large piece of meat.

"I'll tell ye wha' happened! Thiurwold is too caught up with all this government business. He thinks himself too noble an' far too grand to attend these meetings. I can' stand it when 'e does tha'! I've told him countless times tha' for the benefit of the Solemn Hand he should come!

Still, he insists that the Solemn Hand is going awry, an' that I should not associate meself with Sirien an' everything the Hand stands for."

Seleborn cleared his throat. "He seemed well aware of the dangers of being in the Hand in the last meeting Sirien held before his disappearance."

"Oh, lad," mumbled Dunn, "times 'ave certainly changed, 'aven't they? I don' really care anymore if me cousin wants to show or not. Personally, I think Sirien should ban him from any remaining Solemn Hand activity! Be rid of that egotistical pest, once an' for all!"

"Don't be so hard on him, Dunn," said Seleborn, "I'm sure being Minister of War is something stress—"

"Givin' him the benefit of the doubt, are we?" croaked Dunn. "I've been doin' tha' for quite some time now, and I'm sick of it!" Wanting to prevent others from being inquisitive, he lowered his voice dramatically. "There's somethin' else..." he leaned in closer to them. "The previous nigh', I had gotten up from bed for a late nightcap...As I stumbled past Thiurwold's room, he had been Orbing someone..."

"*Who?*" they asked.

"Tha' I do not know. I could hear the voice on the other end of the Orb saying that the 'the plan shall soon unfold.' Tha's all I could really come to know. As you see, I was still a bit under the ol' juice."

"Plan, you say?" asked Percivine, remembering a distinct conversation with Astronitus.

"I dunno the rest," said Dunn. "Thiurwold stopped an' heard stumbling about outside. He asked me wha' I heard an' I said nothing. I think 'e smelled the ale on me breath and closed the door tight, and tha' was the end o' tha.'"

"Must be War Ministry business," said Seleborn hopefully.

"I don' think so," said Dunn. "You can' mistake his tone."

"If there's a plot, then surely we would've known it," said Faruin.

"Thiurwold is no fool," said Dunn weakly.

"You should report this to Sirien," said Faruin. "He ought to know about this. It doesn't sound like Thiurwold should be left unnoticed."

"We can't count the votes before they are cast, Faruin," said Seleborn. "Besides, I don't think it's easy, is it, reporting one of your own family members?"

"For the time bein'," said Dunn, "I'll keep a close eye on me cousin."

What was Thiurwold up to? This was not the first time Percivine had heard disturbing news about Thiurwold. Astronitus and Linaus shared their own suspicions about Thiurwold, but Percivine felt it best to wait until concrete evidence presented itself.

"If I could have your attention, please!" Sirien announced. The room quieted. "I hoped everyone has enjoyed this delivcious meal and drink provided. Now, I hope you all have had time to discuss the plan amongst yourselves while eating. I know it's a risky business what we plan to do, but if we succeed in doing so, then this world may yet live to see another day.

"You must remember, however, not to mention what you've heard in this room today, not to a single soul! I'm sure it would be rather unpleasant to have the investigators knocking on your front door, waking up the whole town. I urge each and everyone one of you to act with the finest grace you can conjure. This mission that we are to embark on is not for the faint-hearted, so if you have any problems, personal problems, then I suggest you come and speak with me, so the proper arrangements can be made to further accommodate you and your situation.

"I further digress by telling you that, in a week's time, we will fight to restore the honor that many of those who live in Eradell have lost! If you die, your loss will certainly have not been in vain, I can assure you that. But remember this: you die to make this place a better world, for your family and friends and those destined to walk this world.

"I have one last bit to tell you lot. Once you see yourself face to face with those beasts, show them the same mercy they have showed your brethren! They deserve it and more! They will come at you with all they've got! They don't care whether they hurt you! Remember, kill them with the utmost brute force you can relish upon them!

"You may now," finished Sirien, breathing heavily, heart racing, "help yourselves to more food and drink."

Percivine was happy to hear that.

CHAPTER TEN

Cowards and Symbols

Percivine could see the anxiety in his brother's demeanor. All sound being muffled, palms moist, knees wanting to buckle, heart stampeding like a herd of grels—these were all too familiar sensations for Percivine. Sirien wanted to begin the first steps of his plan, but they were still four days away from beginning—his group, especially.

In the meantime, Percivine eased his own anxiety by taking trips with Faruin to Frodrir's market square. He was not as fascinated by the market as he had been by Unin'shai's Trade Province. There was a dull and rustic look, given off by the market's meek appearance.

Faruin headed off to the local butcher shop for the evening's dinner, and Percivine wandered the several small shops and booths. He passed a little corner shop selling many magical remedies and herbs. Soon, he found himself approaching a stand selling something familiar he'd seen only once before.

"Those instruments," said an all-too-familiar voice, "will help modernize the way—" The Elf stopped dead cold in his sentence. "I know you! You're that Neledar back in Unin'shai who didn't buy one of my conductors!"

"I—what are you doing here?" said Percivine.

"Trying to make a living," said the Elf hoarsely.

"Are you Ya'ril?

"Intriguing! How did you know?"

"You've propped a sign here."

This is something Percivine can't recall noticing last time. Ya'ril looked down at the wooden placard in front of his conductors that read *Ya'ril's Magical Instruments and Oddities.*

"So I have!"

"Do I assume that you haven't sold anymore?"

"Not one," said Ya'ril, with downcast eyes. "I've still just only sold the one I told you about. I closed shop and decided I might have a better chance working here."

"And are the results more sufficient?" Percivine asked.

Ya'ril shrugged. "Unfortunately, business is as bone dry here as it was in the Trade Province."

Percivine noticed a tremor in Ya'ril's eyes. The story Ya'ril spoke left out some truth and Percivine was going to find out, one way or another. Why he cared so much about knowing the real reason, he had no clue, but he knew it was something worrisome.

"Are you sure you wouldn't want to buy one of my conductors? It's a lovely fall day to purchase one."

"I'm sure," said Percivine politely. "I've come with a friend."

"Where is your friend?"

"He's at the butcher shop getting our evening's ingredients. And—I don't think he would want to purchase your conductors either. I'm sorry."

Ya'ril sighed. "Very well. Have a good—"

"*Why are you really here?*"

The question seemed to hit Ya'ril square in the face, leaving him quite dumbfounded. He opened his mouth to speak, but no words came out. The question had utterly bewildered him. He was not expecting it. He stared blankly at Percivine.

"I don't suppose that's any of your business, is it?" said Ya'ril, in the same rude tone Percivine gave him earlier.

"Is that how you treat potential customers?" said Percivine slyly.

"Potential?" said Ya'ril, with a snort. "I've tried *twice* to have you buy one of my conductors, and both times you have refused!"

"I know you're lying!" said Percivine. "Something happened that made you come here of all places! What was it?"

Ya'ril trembled a little at the vicious look Percivine gave him.

"*All right! All right!*" he spluttered, placing the conductor in his hand down. "Around the same day you came to my stand, I'd overheard a disturbing conversation about how an owner of an eatery had been harassed and nearly killed by a devilish grey-skinned being! It wasn't until some mysterious person had intervened and helped the poor owner escape. *But*…that wasn't the only thing I had heard! Someone had mentioned that the same man had himself a squander with some Elves near the Temple of the Stars. People were growing worried that they might be his next victims, so naturally, I decided to close my stand, and make a run for it before he came after me!"

"Why on Gylranor would he come after you?" asked Percivine. It was typical of Bartholev, causing an uproar wherever he stepped. He did not need a further explanation as to who the person was. Clearly the evidence Ya'ril spoke of was enough.

"I don't know, do I?"

"The only reason Bartholev went after that eatery owner was because he thought the Elf knew valuable information about Percivine Og—"

Just then, Percivine realized the error of his ways.

The Elf stood gazing at him in great suspicion. "How would you know that was reason? And the fellow you just named…It was him that terrorized us."

"I—I had heard that that was the reason," he said, before Ya'ril said anything else. "I—I could be wrong."

"Yes…well," said Ya'ril, still eyeing Percivine curiously. "I'll go back when things quiet down." Ya'ril looked down to something that only he could see. He then looked up to Percivine, and back to whatever it was he glanced at. "You know, Percivine Ogthorne—"

Percivine's eyes bulged. How did this Elf know who he was?

"—I would take great care in where I go, and what I do. You are aware, I'm sure, that there are warrants out for you. I wouldn't be so calm about what I do and where I go without being transformed. I urge you great caution."

"I don't know who the hell you think *you* are," said Percivine coarsely, "but I would advise you to not make such presumptions about someone you don't even know!"

Ya'ril raised the thing he was looking at: a parchment, imprinted with with Percivine's and Sirien's faces.

"*This*," he said, "is how I know."

There was absolutely no point in arguing—he was caught. Ya'ril knew, or had known, about his presence since Unin'shai. There was just no point at all.

"Must've been you at the Temple of the Stars," said Ya'ril, hopeful for Percivine to confirm. Then came no speech from Percivine. "But don't *you* worry," he continued quietly, "I won't tell a soul. I don't believe this town to be so harmed by the government's wrath just yet." With a more pompous air, he said, "We Elves know things, and we will help those who would benefit from it.

"Now," continued Ya'ril "if you would kindly move along, for there may be a potential customer wanting to browse my fine assortment of conductors. Good day to you, *kind* sir."

Shocked, Percivine could barely move. When he eventually did leave the stand, he was still trying to figure out what had just happened. This entire time, he'd believed he was secure. No wonder why Bartholev and the Elvic guards outside Unin'shai had given him a most suspicious look.

He continued wandering the market square like a mindless zombie. Ya'ril had surprised him with everything that he knew. Paranoia now stirred in him. Who else might have noticed him? He quickly went to the butcher shop, where he found Faruin first in line, awaiting meats.

"Where have you been?" Faruin asked. To the clerk, he said, "One pound of your finest brisket, please."

The butcher shop owner cut the meat in front of them, and lifted it up. "How's that?"

"Fine, that's fine," said Faruin.

The owner wrapped the brisket in thin parchment and handed it to Faruin. Faruin paid the man, and they made their way out of the shop.

"Let's hurry home," said Percivine.

"What's your rush?"

"I—I'm rather hungry, you know," said Percivine, frantically making sure no eyes watched him. "You know how violent my stomach gets when it craves food."

Faruin chuckled. "Oh yes. I forgot you're the only person I know who has a stomach that can cause bloodshed."

"Right," said Percivine. "Let us leave!"

Faruin made the meal more happily than others. Astronitus, Seleborn, and Sirien were present this time. For once, they could enjoy a happy meal together.

"You're home rather early, Dad," said Sirien.

"It was a very short day," said Astronitus, removing his mustard-yellow bracers. "Well, for me, anyway. We discovered an old map of Bren within the contents of the tome. Bren is, as you know, the only city of Beled Ruun, the hidden Valley of Mages. It's said Beled Ruun lies somewhere deep in the Helin Mountains."

"I thought there were no others maps of this place besides the Atlas?" asked Percivine.

"There aren't," said Faruin, who knew more on the matter. "The Atlas details Beled Ruun in its entirety, the Obelisk's location, and the alternate passage into it following the destruction of the Green Grotto. The map they found seems to depict Bren and Bren only."

"Its markings are rather old and faint," said Astronitus, placing a parchment of research notes in front of him, "so we had to dip the map in a solution that darkened the map's features. What we saw—amazing! Bren is a wonder to see—a great walled metropolis, almost like Unin'shai, and at the very center, a magnificent, gleaming tower. I suspect that's where they channeled the power of Ruric's Heart, to control and hone its elemental abilities."

"How do you suppose that such artifacts like these are found spread across Eradell?" asked Seleborn, not familiar very well with Mage lore than what his Warlock order teaches, and it's not much.

"Probably almost the same as what had happened to the tablet during the Battle of Esid," said Astronitus. "History states that before the ancient Mage Deconus fell, he cast a piece of the Atlas far across Eradell using the earth, that place now confirmed as Ni'shorus. But there are little records to turn to, in the vast timeline of ours. We are nowhere near its discovery than we are of getting rid of the Argoms. Nerod stayed behind to further examine the map. I shrugged to leave. I urged him to be careful in case those smelling investigators roam about."

"I know Nerod," said Sirien. "He can handle them."

"I should certainly hope so," said Astronitus.

"You didn't have any trouble as you left?" said Faruin.

"Nah," said Astronitus. "I did stumble across Fernius who seemed on edge. We didn't speak to each other. He glanced at me, and took off."

They finished dinner early that evening. Seleborn and Astronitus decided to head to the gardens to smoke a bit of garoherb before calling it a night. Faruin remained in the kitchen cleaning up before he went to bed. Upon Sirien's request, Percivine had followed him up to his room.

"That Faruin really outdoes himself in the kitchen, doesn't he?" said Sirien, taking a seat behind a polished wooden desk surrounded by bookshelves. A marble bust on a column stood before the study window.

"Yes," said Percivine. "The best cook since Mum."

"How are you holding?" asked Sirien.

"Better," replied Percivine.

"I know we really haven't communicated since my accident," said Sirien. "I've been a tosspot the last several days."

"You have," agreed Percivine.

"But you need to understand that what I'm doing is for the better, for the benefit of every single living creature on Gylranor."

"I do understand," said Percivine. "I wish you wouldn't shut out me and dad so much, though."

"I don't intend to intentionally," said Sirien. "I nearly arrived at the point, where I wanted to extract the hair off my scalp! I was going mad trying excessively to get the plan right down to the very last detail. It was extraneous work, mind you."

"Dad worries about you," said Percivine. "He dreads what you do, risking your life each and every day leading the Hand. I can see it in his eyes."

"He knows what I am and what I do," said Sirien, leaning back on the chair and locking his fingers over his head. "He should know that by now."

"You could, *at least*, be a bit more sympathetic to him. He hasn't been the same since mum died. How do you expect him to feel at the thought of losing someone else that he loves?"

"I—" Sirien could not express words. He's been so involved with the Solemn Hand's dealings, that he was aloof over the stresses he gave Astronitus, but it was to make for a better world. "I don't mean to make Father feel that way."

"Well, you do," said Percivine coldly.

"He won't have to any longer! We're going to carry out the plan together!"

"Aren't you forgetting the group leads that will remain on the grounds?" said Percivine. "You've shunned him, yet again."

"I chose him to lead the group, because his spellcraft abilities are some of the sharpest I've come to know."

Percivine rolled his eyes. "Or perhaps you worry that something worse will happen to an old Neledar like him."

"*Look*," said Sirien, "I didn't bring you up here so we could argue!"

"Then why have you brought me?"

"Because—because—"

"Because what?"

"Because I've missed you brother!" cried Sirien. His eyes moistened. "I've missed having you by my side, like when we were children! I feared I would never see you again after our split in Maradine!"

Sirien grabbed his brother and squeezed him so tight that Percivine was afraid his eyes would erupt from their sockets. Surprised but delighted that Sirien was showing emotion, Percivine hugged his brother back enthusiastically.

They separated.

"We've hardly spoken to each other since I returned," said Sirien, wiping his eyes. "I don't know what's gotten over me. This is highly unusual."

Percivine laughed.

"They're called *feelings*," said Percivine. "They're what Neledar feel. It's a mortal sensation."

Percivine remained in a bit of shock. The pressures of infiltrating the Divination Administration and the worries of death might be too vast for one to take on. He probably feared losing Percivine during the fight. Or his father.

"I can see mum in you all the time," said Sirien. "She was strong-willed on the inside, with a soft exterior. I always valued that in her. And now I see that she's left that bit of her with you. As for myself—I have Dad's hotheadedness and haste behavior to do things. I don't always fancy being like dad."

For the remainder of the day until the very next morning, Percivine and Sirien spent the rest of the day reminiscing about memories past such as their little journeys to Da'thanis's tomb, being scolded by Mrs. Clavenhorn for tugging at Averwyn Dibble's hair, or poking the little flamefrogs, a class of amphibian whose bellies glow like lights at night, in the gardens.

On the day of their departure, all three groups gathered in the hall to await further instruction by Sirien.

"Today we embark on one the greatest missions the Solemn Hand has ever faced," said Sirien to the crowd of members. "If you are to fall, then it will have been for the honor to free the world from the dark grasp the Argoms have among us.

"My group leaves today. I have entrusted the safeness of my family's home to Nerod and Cosmera, under the prerequisite permission of my father, of course. I know you will do your best in protecting our Headquarters."

"You will not worry with us," said Nerod.

"Faruin has prepared breakfasts for us to enjoy as one before we depart. Help yourselves and enjoy."

"You look a little worried, dad," said Percivine to Astronitus, who picked up a piece of buttered bread.

"I'm fine, son," said the worried father. "I couldn't sleep well, that's all."

"Why not?"

"Er—stuff…"

"Stuff?" said Percivine. "What sort of 'stuff'?"

"My, you certainly are sticking your nose in deeply today."

Percivine should have expected this sort of response by his father. It reminded him too fondly of how Sirien would have responded to a similar question. He progressed no further. He nodded stiffly at his father and went to helping himself grandly to the spectacular array of hog's bacon, fried eggs, Dwarvic dried beans in a tangy sauce, cow's milk, and dardenfrut, bumpy-skinned fruit with a wet, sweet blue filling.

After Percivine filled his plate, he went and took a lonely seat at the very end of the table. For some odd reason he never seems to enjoy a meal at peace, and he wanted to do so before they left…for it could be the very last he ever ate.

The Percivine from several months ago would have hidden in his bed, he thought.

Best of luck, said the voice. *You're going to need it.*
Thanks…

Just as he was about to fill his mouth full of food for a third time Faruin, Seleborn, and Trobius Stout approached him.

Well there goes that, he muttered in thought.

He reluctantly dropped his fork into the plate, and smiled sardonically at them.

"We thought you would like some company," said a happy Trobius.

"Did you?" said Percivine sarcastically. "I would like some."

"Good," said Trobius.

"Why have you seated yourself so far?" asked Seleborn.

"I thought it would be nice to sit this far," said Percivine.

"You must be excited that you venture off today!" said Trobius, stuffing down his food. "I was originally part to be of your group, but Sirien thought it would be best if my talents were used instead in Cosmera's group. Keep the plan together, you know?"

"I—er—yeah, I'm rather pleased," Percivine said.

"Good man!" said Trobius. "Hopefully your meeting with Terrien goes well."

"Why wouldn't it?" asked Percivine.

"Well—I shouldn't be saying anything—he is a bit of a—of a coward. Since his appointment as Oroseer, his mind has been at a constant war over whose works are for the greater good, those of the Solemn Hand or of the Administration. He wouldn't want to risk losing everything if they found out his part in the Hand, but he doesn't want to betray those whom he calls friends.

"He's a good person," Trobius continued. "His heart's in the right place, but his mind isn't. I'm sure your brother can put a good word or two in that chaotic mind of his."

The feeling of a chaotic mind resonated with Percivine, his mind having a voice of its own. One that he cannot control very well.

They finished their meals and waited for Sirien to speak. He addressed them soon enough, and everyone quieted.

"You all know the parts to play," he said loudly. His Wayorb illuminated itself in bright orange. He picked it up and answered.

"Ready when you are," said the voice of a woman.

The portal opened. Sirien called off to his group, and one by one they entered. Percivine was the last.

"Take care," said Astronitus to his younger son. "We'll see you in two days."

In the flash, his father, Headquarters, and the rest of the Solemn Hand were gone. Percivine now stood in front of what appeared to be a familiar cottage. An old woman in short, wavy, white hair beamed at them as they arrived. She dusted her dark brown pantaloons and her hands before embracing Sirien.

"Thank you, Mrs. Clavenhorn," said Sirien, greeting the old woman with a hug.

"'Clamantia', please," said Clamantia Clavenhorn. With mounting joy, she said, "Oh! Percivine! It's been years!"

There had been no expectation to revisit with his old caretaker. Mrs. Clavenhorn stood before Percivine with open arms. He went to her, and they hugged like Sirien before him. An odd scent of flowers entered Percivine's nose.

"Good heavens, how you've grown!" she said, releasing him. "Don't mind my appearance. Been tending to the Dern Tulips."

Percivine caught sight of the Dern Tulip bulbs. These were a type of tulip with no stem to observe.

Percivine now remembered the cottage from his youth: the same vine-covered archway, the wooden perimeter fence, and the river babbling in the backyard. He also remembered staying several nights with Mrs. Clavenhorn, while his mother and father were away at work.

This too was an emotional trip for Seleborn. His home was only one cottage away from Mrs. Clavenhorn's on the opposite side of the road.

"Seleborn!" said Mrs. Clavenhorn. "Seleborn!" —she hugged him tight— "It's been so long. How are you?"

"I'm well, older and bent, but well."

"You're not a day older, my boy!" she said cheerfully.

"Clamantia," said Sirien, "this is" —Sirien directed her to Nerod— "Nerod Nilius." Sirien placed a hand on Faruin's shoulder next. "Last, and most certainly not least, is Faruin Abrandil."

"Ah, good pleasure to meet the both of you," said Mrs. Clavenhorn cheerily.

"The pleasure is mine, madam," said Nerod Nilius, taking a short bow.

"Very good," said Faruin.

"Seleborn," she said, "you'll be happy to know that I've taken quite a look after your home. I've prevented those nasty spiders' webs and dust from forming. I've also taken the liberty of refreshing your garden with brand new vegetation."

"I can't thank you again, Clamantia," said Seleborn, "for everything that you've done since Filiiri past. Please allow me to reimburse you for your time."

"I'll have none of it!" said Mrs. Clavenhorn, shaking her head, eyes closed. "You saved my life that day, and I am forever in your debt. "I see a sense of urgency within you, but how about we all go in and have a cup of tea? Yes? Might relax those nerves."

"That sounds lovely, Clamantia," Sirien said, "but—"

"Nonsense!" she said. "You've earned the right to relax a little before you head off and do those dangerous things."

"Yes, well—all right, *one* cup, then," said Sirien.

Sirien and everybody else passed through the cottage door. When it was only Percivine and Seleborn left, Mrs. Clavenhorn stretched an arm out to halt Seleborn, resulting in Percivine bumping into Seleborn's backside.

"I'm sure you would like to see your home," she said kindly. "Go on. I'll tell them that that's where you'll be. You've earned it."

Seleborn nodded. "Thank you," he said, and turned around and, at last, headed toward home.

"Percivine in!" she said. "No need to wait for me. At my age it will take me a while to get there."

"You're as young as I remember, Clamantia," said Sirien.

"Flattery won't get you an extra serving of tea, Sirien," she said with a laugh.

She opened the door to reveal a living area with comfy looking couches, a table at the center, a fireplace overlooking the room, and a doorway leading to what seemed like a kitchen. Percivine remembered the area being smaller.

They nestled themselves on the couches, and waited for their tea. A teapot and four teacups hovered through the doorway over to Mrs. Clavenhorn. The teapot poured its contents into the four cups, and each of the cups with their own coasters placed themselves gently into each of their laps, waiting to be grabbed by their handles before their magic faded away.

Percivine nearly gagged after inhaling his first sip. The taste was so disgusting he wanted to scrape the top layer of his tongue right off. He gently and painstakingly swallowed the rest of the hot liquid still in his mouth. He saw that neither Sirien nor Nerod nor Faruin appeared to be enjoying it either. Nerod coughed as he swallowed the tea. Faruin gritted his teeth as the tea went down his throat, and Sirien created a bit of a hiccup after gulping his mouthful.

"Scrumptious, isn't it?" she said, pouring the entire cup in with one swallow.

"Delicious," said Sirien.

"So…er…what sort of tea is this?" said Nerod.

"A brew I concocted myself," said Mrs. Clavenhorn proudly. "The original form of tea I use is called Agreous Tea, and my special ingredient that gives is it its wonderful taste—whiskey!"

Their eyes bulged. Sirien closed his eyes as more of the liquid burned its way down his throat.

"Splendid," said Nerod, clearing out his throat.

"Are you trying to get us drunk before we leave, Clamantia?" said Sirien, holding the outer parts of his throat.

"No, of course not!" she said. "I thought you could use a little something to give you confidence!"

"Oh…" said Sirien, massaging his throat. "I think we have all the confidence we—"

"Finish up!" she called.

They reluctantly finished their cups of tea. A warm feeling spread through Percivine's body. He found himself to be smiling for no apparent reason. It rather seemed that the tea was more parts whiskey than tea.

"Have another go," she said.

"No!" said Sirien. "I mean—no thank you, Clamantia. It was delicious, but we cannot perform well if our mind aren't sharp."

"Very well," she said. "More for me."

And she drank another cupful in one try.

"Where has Seleborn gone?" Faruin asked the others.

"Home," said Mrs. Clavenhorn. "You didn't expect him to return to Borgsbury and not go back, did you?"

"It's rather dangerous, though," said Sirien, setting aside his cup and coaster.

"Ever since the day that stupid shapeshifter attacked me, this village has seen no trouble from those blasted Argoms. So, there's no harm in Seleborn heading off. Anyway," she said, pouring another cup's worth of tea, "how is Astronitus these days? Haven't spoken much since Merinni died."

"Good, he's good," said Sirien.

"Happy to hear," said Mrs. Clavenhorn. "I'm elated to know he's been holding good grip of himself since that tragedy."

Percivine didn't like how openly people he'd just met spoke about his mother's death. Nonetheless, he is in Mrs. Clavenhorn's home, and it would be rude if he spoke out against her in it.

Sirien rose to his feet. "We really have to go, Clamantia. We have a day to persuade Terrien, or else the plan will fail."

"Already?" she said. "Just one more, perhaps?"

"I'm sorry, but we really must get a move on. The day slips away."

"Very well," said Mrs. Clavenhorn. "Need I remind you where Terrien lives?"

"No thank you," said Sirien. "We know."

She nodded. "Best of luck to you all and your endeavors. May the Primals be with you always. Take this blessing with you."

They thanked her for everything she did. They hurried out the door after Sirien and down the road, passing Seleborn's home, where they could see no sign of him. They soon arrived at a slightly bigger cottage than Seleborn's. As expected, the cottage sat next to the River of Zanbros.

There was no archway, and fewer flowers than Mrs. Clavenhorn's front yard. Everything about the cottage looked rather plain. It almost seemed that no effort or love had been put into it.

They marched up the yellow grass-covered cobblestone walkway. Nerod obliged Sirien by knocking first on the door. There came no reply…They waited a few seconds before Sirien knocked a second time.

Still no answer.

"Is there anyone home?" Sirien called out.

Nothing.

"Nerod, Faruin, check the windows," said Sirien. "Tell me if you spot anything."

Faruin and Nerod each took a window on both sides of the door and peered through them, but saw nothing.

"I know for certain this is Terrien's home," Sirien told them, analyzing the door. "If you look up there on top of the door, you'll notice the symbol for the Divination Administration."

They looked up to see the symbol depicted: a design that held a circle on top, with a triangle underneath that had an inwardly bent base. A vertical line divided the circle in half, creating the *D* for Divination, and a horizontal line swept through the top half of the triangle, creating the letter *A* for Administration.

"He isn't home," said Faruin.

"He has to be," said Nerod, attempting to spot any movement from within the homestead. "Aolean Twench works with Trobius in the Archival Service and told him Terrien was to be on a holiday at home for the week. Odd time for a getaway."

"Maybe Terrien's decided to take his holiday elsewhere," said Faruin. "Probably knew we were coming, and wanted to avoid any situation possible."

Sirien looked down for a moment, and began to think. His eyes rested the doorknob. He knew the trick: he would have to break into the house of the Oroseer of Nell!

"Are you insane or completely stupid?" said Percivine. "That's a horrible idea."

"Your brother's right, Sirien," said Nerod. "We can't afford to bring any unwanted attention to ourselves."

But it seemed that Sirien had not put any attention to them. He grabbed the knob and began wiggling it around.

"Don't you dare come in this house!" said a nervous, stammering voice. "I—I'm warning you! I will have you thrown into Nerwold!"

"Then open the damn door!" said Sirien, banging on it with his left palm.

"Look," said Terrien Waterborn's feeble voice behind the door, "I told you last week I don't know why Landseer Elwerth is allowing the Argoms to roam Administration grounds! *I just don't know!*"

"What?" said Sirien. "Terrien you idiot! It's Sirien!"

"*What the devil?*" spluttered Terrien. "What's the idea on scaring me half to death?"

"If you open the door, then I can explain everything to you."

There was a moment of silence.

"Terrien?"

They could hear the crackling of locks being removed The door flew open, and a tall, ghostly-looking Neledar with orange hair stood before them, saying, "Get inside! Quickly!"

He popped his head out and scanned the area.

"What the hell are you doing here, Sirien?" said Terrien crossly. "I thought I told you—"

"I know what you told me," intercut Sirien. "I don't need a reminder. We've come on account that we need your help."

"I am no longer a part of the Solemn Hand. I really wish you'd understand that I don't want to be pestered about those issues any longer."

"Pestered?" jeered Sirien. "You didn't think so when you were a member."

"Well, times have changed…I can't be harboring a—a—"

Sirien crossed his arms. "What was that you were about to say? Oh yeah, a 'criminal.'"

"I don't say I like it, but it's the truth!" snarled Terrien. "I've changed."

"Not for the better," muttered Sirien.

"If you've come to badger me about the path I've chosen, then I'll have no choice but to personally throw you out myself!"

"You act for a corrupted government! I know where your heart lies! Your loyalties have not changed, for one thing!"

"How do you know where my heart lies? Where my loyalties lie? Last I checked, you're not Terrien Waterborn, *I am!*"

Terrien and Sirien glared at one another. Percivine, Faruin, and Nerod each backed out of the line of fire.

"And how *dare* you insult the government I work for? You speak treasonous words, man! I have the right mind to lock you away!"

"This government hasn't been the same since the Violet Veil Accord's signing," mocked Sirien. "If you can't see what a terrible thing that idiotic woman is doing, then you are truly lost!"

"I've had enough! I want you and all your imputent friends out of my house! GET THE HELL OUT! NOW!"

Sirien pushed Terrien straight to the floor. He sharply turned and stormed out the door. Everyone followed hastily behind him.

"We don't need him!" said Sirien as he walked back to the main road. "We can get into the Administration on our own!"

Percivine knew they couldn't, but didn't dare question his brother in such a state.

They continued down the road until they bumped into Seleborn, who had just locked the front gate to his cottage.

"How did it go?" he asked.

Percivine nervously shook his head at Seleborn.

"Let me tell you—" Sirien began heatedly.

"Wait! Wait!"

Terrien Waterborn caught up to them, a light pant in his breathing.

"Hold there!" he said, exhaling, as if the next words were going to be painful. "I-I didn't mean to lash out at you that way. I apologize for my savage behavior. I deserved that shove. I've been under a lot of pressure lately from Elwerth. I didn't mean to take it out on you. Let's go back to my cottage."

"Are you *sure?*" said Sirien, unsure of how convinced he felt.

The party followed Terrien back to his cottage. This time he was friendlier, and offered them a drink.

"No thanks," said Sirien. "Clamantia gave us plenty to drink earlier."

"I should have known she had something to do with your being here," said Terrien. He threw himself into a chair, and gave a face that looked like he wanted to sulk. "So, what's all this about?"

Behind Terrien was a door that sported the same Administration symbol as the front door.

"What's behind that door?" asked Nerod.

"My personal study," said Terrien.

"Terrien," said Sirien. "I'm afraid we haven't come to chat."

"No, I'm afraid you haven't, have you?"

"Sorry," said Faruin.

Terrien rubbed both of his eyes and sighed. "You're up to something dangerous again, aren't you?"

"Precisely," said Sirien. "I have devised a plan that the Solemn Hand is ready to initiate."

Terrien stood up straight from his sulking posture and listened thoroughly to what his old acquaintance had to say.

"—three groups, each of which have a special task…Faruin and Twy'leden to transform us…My group will head off to the top floor of the Diet Chambers to finally confront that idiotic woman…Everything will be put right—"

Terrien looked sick. His face grew an incredible expression. All the color had drained from his body.

"—that is what we intend to do," finished Sirien.

Terrien blinked, and stared at Sirien vacantly. Sirien turned to Nerod, who merely shrugged. He too did not understand what Terrien was doing.

"Terrien?" said Nerod. "Are you all right?"

"*How do you expect me to react to THAT?*" Terrien screeched. "*Do you realize that has been the most sedicious statement I have ever heard in my life? It would be completely dishonest, and a betrayal of my country, if I do not have you all arrested for such a treasonous idea!*"

"Maybe it was a mistake telling him," said Seleborn, rubbing his thumb on Ruric's Necklace.

"A *mistake?*" said Terrien, making angry motions with his hands. "No, no, you have done the right thing by informing me of the illegality of your action!"

"But you won't…" said Sirien coolly.

"I won't, won't I?" said Terrien.

"I don't think you will."

"And what makes you so sure I won't?"

"Because you're too much of a coward to ever betray those who took you in, and called you their friend," said Sirien.

"I—you—don't dare to presume!" snapped Terrien.

"Then why haven't you?" said Sirien.

"Well—I was about—*you're right!* I won't do it—I can't!" burst Terrien. "I may not be a part of your Solemn Hand anymore, but I know the Pledge I took, and I could never betray the trust of those that cared so deeply for me."

"Good," said Sirien. "It was high time that you finally reveal where your true loyalties lay! You know that absurd woman is making a mockery of Nell and her government. She needs to be put to an end! We want to stop her, but we cannot hope to dream of doing so if you do not oblige to us, and aid us in our cause, Terrien."

Terrien's right foot began to tremble. He knew the Landseer was out of control, that she was performing actions the previous Landseers would never have dared. Worst of all, she had allowed the Argoms to take refuge upon Administration grounds, and that was a complete disgrace.

He rose to his feet, at last. Without a word, he turned to the door with the Administration symbol, and it opened it slowly. As the door opened, a bright blue glow shone out from it.

"Is that your Diviport?" asked Percivine.

"Yes," said Terrien. "I would explain to you what they are, but I can see you've been across one before. There are bigger ones at the Administration we use to travel from Service to Service with. Each employee, however, has their own portable Diviport. Only high-ranking officials of the Divination Administration have these permanent ones installed. This is how I travel back and to from the Administration to my home. The Supreme Council of Elves and the Dwarvic Uln Seat also use a similar system. These special portals were created by our friends to the west." He grinned. "Whatever will they come up with next?"

CHAPTER ELEVEN

THE DIVINATION ADMINISTRATION

"Well, what are you waiting for?" Terrien told them. "Are you going to enter the portal, or are you just going to stand and stare at it?"

"I should have asked," said Sirien, "could you possibly have us teleported near the gates to the Administration District?"

"I don't see why not?" said Terrien. "There is a Diviport in the guard's office adjacent to the gate's wall."

"Thank you, Terrien."

None of them seemed eager to move, until at last Sirien said, "I'm simply astonished, that's all."

"About?"

"In a matter of moments, we could change the course of the world."

"Not like that, you're not," said Terrien. "Now, if you would kindly oblige me by you getting through the damned portal!"

Faruin was the first to enter the portal. Seleborn followed, then Nerod; Percivine was about to set a foot inside, but noticed his brother's hesitation.

"Aren't you coming, Sirien?" he asked him.

"In a moment," Sirien said. "You go on."

Percivine always took orders from Sirien. This time, however, was different. He did not budge.

"Not without you, I'm not," he said sternly.

"What are you waiting for?" said Terrien, now becoming impatient.

"I just would like to thank you for this," said Sirien, regretting having shoved Terrien earlier. "Without your help, none of this is to be possible. Also—"

But Terrien waved him off. "There is no need to thank me. I do know where my loyalties lie, and I could not betray them. I know that woman is making a mockery of how grand the Administration used to be when Eloran Pinshot governed as Landseer. I want to make this world a better place just as much as you do. Now get on. I won't tell you again."

Sirien nodded, jumped right into the portal. Terrien followed behind Percivine.

As Terrien had promised, they were now in a small, dark guard box that was empty for the evening. Sirien peeked through the moonlit window to observe if there were any passersby. The scene was clear, and he silently turned the knob on the door. As he'd stated previously, the entrance to the District was being watched over by two menacing Argoms, who appeared quite bored at their posts, conversing among one another.

"When's the next shift change?" said the Argom on the right, poking at a couple of grey pots beside them with her polearm.

"In about an hour," said the Argom with brass bracers on his wrist and a brace on his scaly tail.

"Not fast enough."

"Anymore onion bread?"

The Argom nearest the pots, glanced in them, and said, "No. You've gone through it all."

The sun was beginning to set. It was at this pristine moment that Faruin used a simple spell to change his appearance, as well as Sirien's. Faruin thought runes would be too noticeable. Faruin became a Neledar with blue eyes and yellow hair. Sirien disguised himself as an Elf with pierced ears and purple eyes. They headed to the gate, while Percivine, Seleborn, Terrien, and Nerod waited discreetly behind shrubbery.

The two Argoms readied their spears.

"Halt," said the woman Argom, pointing her weapon in Percivine's direction. "What business have you here?"

"We are simply here to attend to the flower beds," said Sirien quietly. "Not a crime, is it?"

"We shall be the judges of that. Where are your tools?"

"In the sheds, near Daraman's Park."

"As workers, you should know those grounds are closed past curfew."

"It's a likely story," said the Argom decorated in bracers. "You will not be allowed entry until you present us with the necessary identification."

"Ah, yes, identification," said Sirien smugly. "Yes, we shall at once hand you our—"

In a sudden flash of white light, the Argoms were rendered voiceless, causing them to fall and crash on the pots, shattering them into many shards.

"That was easier than I expected," said Sirien, a giant smirk on his face.

"Mustn't get ahead of ourselves," said Percivine rushing over to them.

"Now we must move forward," said Sirien.

"I still can't fathom all this," said Seleborn in disgust. "To have these degenerates walking freely amongst us."

"The latter thought is common amongst many of us," said Terrien. "Now, what was that other plan of yours again?"

"Oh—oh right!" said Sirien. "I must Orb my father."

He withdrew his Wayorb. Within seconds his father answered.

"Sirien, is that you?" said Astronitus.

"Yes, dad."

"Did that cowardly wart of Terrien finally give way?"

"Yes, he did," said Terrien. "But I don't know about cowardly wart, Astronitus."

"Terrien! My good Neledar! How are you?"

Embarrassed at the insult he lunged at Terrien, Astronitus scrambled to prevent any further cheek from leaving the hole in his face that was his mouth.

"Swell," said Terrien coldly.

Before any argument could be made, Sirien opened the portal to allow the remaining two groups to reconvene with them. In a matter of moments, the remaining Solemn Hand members were soon in full ranks, awaiting further instruction.

"All right," said Sirien, "now that we're all here, Faruin, and Twy'leden's aid, will now transform you to appear as Administration workers. Looks like I was wrong—not many Argoms in sight. That is excellent."

Faruin and Twy'leden soon began casting temporary transformations on each one of them. Those not of Neledarian descent were changed completely to reassemble a Neledar, while native Neledars only had their faces warped a degree or two.

"Quickly take your Administration IDs," said Sirien, passing them grey cards with the help of Pevarius Garcinius.

Terrien was amazed at how much time Sirien had put into every detail down to its finest threads.

The sun had almost gone down, which would help Sirien's plan. He ordered that group two spread throughout on the main street of the Administration District, preferably a couple near Daraman's Park and another couple near the Archival Service building, which is draped in two long canvas banners, each with the seal of the Divination Administration.

As they got closer to the Main Courtyard, more Argoms began to appear before their eyes.

"There appears to be about twelve of them patrolling the grounds," said Sirien, eyeing the Solemn Hand's second group. "They should be able to get them without causing any alarm."

Groups one and three waited patiently and silently behind the walls of the Archival Service building. Along the center of the main street were long rows of flower beds with trees evenly spread out in them. Across the beds, Percivine saw the opening that led to Daraman's Park, and to his horror, two Argoms approaching it and Astronitus. He began to panic, his heart beating like a wooden drum. Astronitus somehow sensed his son watching him, so he put an index finger over his closed mouth to ensure Percivine made no attempt to startle the Argoms. What Percivine witnessed next caused his stomach to churn. Astronitus severed the Argoms' heads swiftly and with as less noise as possible.

Knowing the other Argoms would so notice the lingering Argom heads, Linaus Olvea and Twy'leden ran past Astronitus and the dead Argoms to where four tothers stood conversing with one another, no less than one hundred feet away. Percivine saw them attack those Argoms with less brutality, only knocking them out cold using conjured battle hammers.

"They're really moronic creatures, aren't they?" Percivine whispered to his brother, still reeling from the dead Argoms. "I can't imagine this is really who Elwerth wants as protection."

Percivine next witnessed Viri'el and Vaureth chasing after two

Argoms, while a third nearly escaped from their grasp. Luckily, Vaureth shot a bolt of red magic that burst through the escaping Argom.

The final three Argoms stood guarding the entrance to the Diet Chambers. Pevarius and Astronitus quietly ran to them and lifted the Argoms into the air. Within a couple seconds, the dangling Argoms were launched miles and miles into the night sky, disappearing somewhere unknown. They signaled to the rest that remained hidden.

"There it is!" said Sirien. "*GO!*"

Everyone sprinted past the working fountain towards the entrance to the Diet Chambers. Percivine looked back beyond the fountain of a man and woman, the man dressed in robes and the woman carved to be wearing a tabard over a tunic and breeches, to ensure they were not followed. Once they reached the entryway, Terrien slowly walked up to a shining lens on the right door that resembled half a blue jewel.

From the lens, a hologram projected itself about three inches outward. A Neledar's bald head with a long nose spoke.

"Identification," said the hologram.

Terrien withdrew an identification card from inside his tunic and placed it directly in front of the hologram's eyes. A light emitted from the hologram's eyes, scanning his card.

"Terrien Waterborn, Oroseer of Nell," said the hologram. "Yes. Welcome back."

"Thank you, SB-19" said Terrien. "I've brought guests with me."

"Indeed," said the hologram, inspecting the lot. "How many exactly?"

"Fifteen."

"And do they have proper identification?"

"I believe so, yes," said Terrien.

"I will need at least one of them to scan their cards in order to grant access for entry."

"I will show it mine," said Pevarius.

Pevarius withdrew his personal card, and held it up in the same position as Terried had. The same scanning process took place, and the hologram said, "Pevarius Garcinius, Undersecretary to Ambassador Dibble. Welcome."

Sirien was rather pleased that he had actual Administration

employees in the Hand, for the ones that were duplicated might not have worked the scanning process, and that would surely have foiled his plan.

"I am happy to inform you, Oroseer," said the hologram, "that the Dwarvic Minister of War has graced us with his presence this evening."

Terrien frowned. "What for?"

Percivine shot a glance at Dunn, who was fuming. Astronitus looked at Linaus.

Must be the unknown party Fernius tipped my dad about, thought Percivine. *The very same who was to meet with Elwerth and Talus.*

I believe so, said the other voice in his mind. *Why would Dunn's cousin be here tonight? What is the purpose? I'm not sure what good would come from this.*

The projection even laid its eyes suspiciously on them, but it had no choice to answer Terrien's inquiries.

"Landseer Elwerth and her advisor Talus are to hold a special meeting with the Minister of War. I suspect it to be some sort of peace negotiation."

"Wha' a lark," hissed Dunngarunax Galon.

"You have successfully passed the scanning process," said the hologram. "You may now enter at your leisure."

They heard an unlocking noise. Group two remained outside. Terrien pushed open one of the doors to find a dark lobby full of chairs, and a central, unoccupied receptionist's desk. On either side of the desk two hallways led down corridors full of offices.

"Where is everybody?" asked Seleborn.

"Gone for the night," said Terrien.

"Terrien," said Sirien, "remember what we discussed back at your home. Group three must be elevated to the middle floor, if the plan is to succeed."

"Yes, yes," said Terrien. "I remember. Are you quite certain the other group can maintain a good lookout outside?"

"They're the best," said Astronitus. "I would trust them with my life."

"Very well," said Terrien. "I will lead group three up to the second and third floors. Astronitus, I am sure you can position them where you like, since you spend a lot of time here at the Administration."

"That I can do!"

"I shall meet you on the top floor, then," Terrien called to Sirien, as he led group three down the corridor on the desk's left side.

"I hope Dunn doesn't do anything rash knowing his cousin is here," said Seleborn.

"That would put an end to your plan, Sirien," said Faruin.

"He knows what he has to do," said Sirien assuredly. "He wouldn't dare do anything to disrupt what we've worked hard on for so long. Now come on. We have to get to the top floor."

Sirien decided to take the opposite corridor. They almost reached a lift that would take them to the top floor when a cold voice spoke out to them: "And where do you think you're going?"

A tall, black Neledar, missing a pointed lobe on his right ear, with coarse brown hair appeared behind them.

"It's Fernius!" Sirien whispered. "No sudden movements!"

Chills crawled up Percivine's spine. He could feel he was closest to the mysterious figure.

"I *said*,where you do you think you're going?"

"To the top floor," said Sirien.

"What business do you have up there?" said Fernius Phinean. "Landseer Elwerth has an important meeting tonight. No one should be here."

"We were not informed," said Sirien.

"But *surely*," said Phinean, "anyone who *is* anyone would know that she sent out a memo to each individual official. I don't see how none of you could remember."

"It was hardly of any use to us who work in the Standard Living Service," said Nerod Nilius hotly.

"Well, it's hardly any use for you to go to the top floor, right? You've strayed far from your offices, which lie nearest to the gates of the District," said Phinean, curling his upper lip. "Imagine my thought when I discovered you five going up there on my rounds. Come on. Let's go to my office."

"As Head Investigator," said Seleborn, "isn't your office outside of the Chambers, on the right of the Main Courtyard?"

"We of the Sanction Service have a small, private office located here in the Chambers for instances just like this one."

Phinean guided them onto a spherical disc. Without gears and other works like that of the Dwarves, the platform hovered its way to the top floor, passing through translucent barriers on each floor. Those barriers served to protect anyone from falling should they step onto the opening when the lift isn't there. They exited the lift, into a many-doored room shaped like an octagon. Two larger wooden doors stood directly across from the entrance to the lift, an Administration symbol over them.

"That's where Elwerth must be!" whispered Sirien to his brother. "Her main staff must also have offices up here!"

"Quiet," said Phinean. "You will not disturb these proceedings."

Phinean opened the door that read "Sanction" on it. Inside were glassy offices, with seats outside each of them, and a cast iron table in the middle of the room. A door behind the table opened. A red-haired Neledarian woman walked right towards them.

"Fernius?" she said, folding the parchments in her hand, wearing a badge that read "Irinea Squint." "What are you—?"

"Not now, Irinea," said Phinean, "I've just apprehended these five before they could disturb the Landseer's meeting."

"Why would they want to do that?" said Irinea.

"Exactly what I'd like to know," said Phinean.

"We work for the Administration," said Nerod. "You can check our badges if you'd like."

"I don't recall seeing you five before, and where is it you said you work from?"

"The Standard Living Service," said Sirien. "We had to make sure the Landseer's office meets with current health regulations."

"But why do it at night?" asked Phinean. "Surely, you could have done—"

"The Landseer is far too busy to be disturbed during the day," said Sirien. "They won't allow us near her office."

"You could have requisitioned a permit from our main offices," said Phinean.

"And be turned away by the likes of you?" said Seleborn.

"You must abide by the laws or face the consequences," said Phinean.

Percivine noticed Irinea looking at him curiously. What was she staring at? He did not know, but rather wished she did not eye him so.

"You will wait here until I figure out what to—"

His voice suddenly broke. He, too, was staring at them the way Irinea had been at Percivine. "What the hell is happening?" he asked Irinea, who did not know what to say.

"What?" said Sirien.

"Your—your faces are—are—changing! Impostors!" cried Phinean. "Who are—? Oh…for the love of Gylranor…It *had* to be you! It just had to be *you!*"

The conjured disguises Faruin and Twy'leden had cast on them had worn because transformation magic isn't over when the user decides it to be. These types of magicks are only temporary. How long one can remained transformed is dependent on how experienced the spellcaster is using this skill.

"Your—your face was sort of—spiraling," Irinea said to Percivine. "That's why I couldn't help but look at you. I'm not well-versed in transformation magic, but I think it was a good cast."

Percivine's cheeks turned a bright pink from this foolish encounter.

"Hullo, Fernius," said Sirien, stepping from behind Nerod.

"I should have known you would have stuck your nose in here!"

"Fernius, care to explain?" asked Irinea Squint.

"You know who this is, Irinea!" said Phinean, exasperated. "The man the Administration wants! And look" —he looked right at Percivine— "his brother's here too! My, this certainly is a good day for us!

"Health regulations—ha!—what a load of dung! Should have known from the start that you were impostors. But how you got in still baffles me. How did you do it?"

"That's our concern only," said Seleborn.

"Like hell it is," said Phinean. "Tell me. Now."

"No," said Faruin.

Percivine noticed Phinean looking at Sirien. His brother merely returned the gesture.

"Do you realize that I could have you locked away in a moment's notice?" said Phinean calmly. "I would think you wouldn't want to disrupt whatever it is you're doing."

"We're not telling you," said Sirien. "You know how the Hand works being an ex-member and all."

This really seemed to catch Phinean by surprise, for he was now fuming.

"I do not care what you think or say about the Hand—"

"Get off it, Fernius," said Sirien. "Don't you see what's happening? That maniacal woman is walking hand-in-hand with the enemy. Does that not bother you? I never thought the government of Nell could sink so low…She has just proved that…Why would she want our arrest? We strike only against the Argoms, but as of late, she's made us out to be the *real* enemy of Nell."

"I—she is not—how—?"

"You know she's doing no good. And where exactly is the King? It's his kingdom after all, not hers! I think she's done him out, and wants to grab the Throne for herself!"

"The—the king is on h-holiday!"

"So she says," said Sirien. "He's been on holiday too long."

"I think he is right, Fernius," said Irinea.

One of Phinean's eyes twitched, wanting her to stay silent on the matter. He had not at all expected her questioning. How could she speak against him, *him*, her superior, her mentor in the Sanction Service?

"Irinea, you can't tell me you believe this lot?"

"I neither accept nor deny his claim," she said bravely. "But it is odd, isn't it? I mean where is King Erelon? He's been away for weeks, and without a word to no one. And look at what those two idiots, Grenden and Foggs, have been doing lately—snooping around areas that aren't even within the Administration District. That breaks the Code of Privacy of this government's constitution. I know they've been prying upon the Museum of Nell and the Depository in Frodrir, and without warrants I might add."

"Correct!" Nerod pointed out, being a worker of the Felefor.

"So, you have chosen your side?" asked Phinean.

Irinea blinked, looking perplexed. "I, Irinea Squint, have pledged allegiance to my King, and to support the rights and goods of the Nellian government, and I will not betray either of them. So…yes, I have chosen the *right* side. I implore that you do the same, Fernius, for when this is all over, and you've decided not to act, you will be severely punished for your acting against the very same oath you took."

"Well, Fernius?" said a voice behind them all.

Everyone jumped slightly. They turned to face Terrien Waterborn. No one had anticipated him to show up so soon after their split. Even Phinean seemed shocked.

"O-Oroseer, what are you—?" Phinean straightened his stuttering voice. "What brings you here at this hour?"

"Wanted to see what side you've chosen."

Everyone tried not to smile. Percivine knew if anyone could make Phinean quiver in his wake, it would be those who stood above him.

"Oroseer, I—this is most unorthodox!"

"Just answer the damn question already!" said Sirien. "We've not finished yet."

"What plan?" Phinean said. "Oh, I see! Oroseer, you let them in, didn't you? Although it is not my place to say, I am disappointed."

"You watch your mouth, *Phinean*," said Terrien. "I am the Oroseer, and I do whatever I well please!"

Percivine knew that Terrien's use of Fernius last name was something Phinean should not take so lightly.

"Need I remind you who you're speaking to? I could have you sacked at this very moment if I wanted, and have Irinea replace you."

"Terrien, you wouldn't," Phinean said, but he wasn't so sure.

That seemed to shake some sense into Phinean. The pressure was building. All eyes lay upon his dull, brown eyes. He almost seemed to wince at this painstaking situation.

"Just watch me."

Before Phinean could form any answer, the knob to the Service began to turn, and voices could be heard just outside.

"I know I heard something, Kalor," said one voice.

"Well then open it."

"What do you think I'm trying to do, you idiot?" snapped the voice. "They've locked the door on us!"

"Arturus and Kalor!" said Irinea.

"I heard someone speak!" said Arturus Grenden from behind the door. "Stand aside, Kalor, I'm going to blast open the door!"

"Don't!" shrieked Kalor Foggs. "Landseer Elwerth and Lord Talus are with—"

"*Shut your stupid mouth!*" said Grenden, trying to avoid being heard by Elwerth.

Terrien turned and began walking towards the door. He signaled everyone to keep quiet until they were safely inside the Services lounge. He unlocked the door.

"It's unlocked," said Foggs.

Terrien swung open the door, and, with unprecedented strength, grabbed the two Neledar by their tabard-covered tunics and pulled them into the office. He threw them both to the floor. He sealed the door with a bit of Magic, denying them any chance of escape.

"L-Landseer?" said Foggs, the wider Neledar of the two who were just pulled in. "What are you doing here?"

Both Grenden and Foggs didn't notice the array of other people in the room. They were too focused on the one man that had nearly subdued them. Arturus Grenden, the smaller between them, wiped the sweat from his crooked brown nose. As he tried to pick himself up, his eyes fixated on one individual in particular.

"Look, it's Sirien Ogthorne! Irinea, get him!"

But Irinea made no such move. Dumbstruck, Grenden pushed his head back.

"Did you not hear me, Irinea? Arrest him!"

"No," she said.

"Are you disoberying an order?"

"I no longer take orders from you," said Irinea happily.

"Fernius, are you hearing this?" said Grenden, raising his torso while his legs remained stretched out in front of him. "Have her arrested, along with each and every other person in this room!"

Phinean made no move, either. He hesitated in his spot. He watched everyone's eyes, especially Sirien's and Terrien's. He walked to where Terrien stood and looked down at both Grenden and Foggs. He moved his wrists, and suddenly Grenden and Foggs found themselves pinned against one of the olive-colored walls in the Service.

"Have you lost your mind?" said Grenden, struggling to break free of the magical bonds. "Release me, I say! *NOW!* I will have your head for this, Fernius!"

"First, you'd have to break free of my bind," said Phinean coolly. "But I don't think you will."

This came as a shock to everyone in the room. Up to this point

Phinean has been rather cold and almost indifferent to what occurs. Perhaps Irinea's surprise bravery to fight for the good of things inspired him to do the same.

"I will ask you, Arturus," said Terrien in a calm voice, but Percivine knew he was no happier than a dead person. "What is the true purpose of that session?"

Grended spat directly at Terrien's face. This heated him to a full extent. Terrien grabbed Grenden by the throat to choke him.

"No!" said Sirien. "Terrien, you mustn't—!"

"*Back away!*" Terrien said. "He's mine! *Don't you ever, EVER, do that again, do you hear me?*"

Grenden made no effort to repent. He would rather die than share anything with the likes of Terrien.

"Arturus…"

The voice seemed to illuminate him. He looked over to Irinea Squint, who had stepped forward. Still trying to breathe, he looked at her in a very amorous way.

"Landseer," said Irinea, "please release him…for the moment."

Terrien loosened his grip. Grenden was able to catch his breath, while Foggs could only gawk at Grenden.

"Please answer them, Arturus," said Irinea. "You've already gotten yourself in deep. You've nowhere to go."

Grenden continued staring at this beautiful woman. With a heavy swallow, and a loud sigh, he spoke.

"This government has stepped its foot in shite! Dog shite!! Ever since that woman took office, she's made a mockery of things. The Argoms are coming…I suspect you've brought your lot, then, have you, Ogthorne?"

"I have," said Sirien.

"So, you're not going to tell us what they're talking about in there, then?" said Terrien.

"No, I don't believe I am," said Grenden.

"And what about you, Kalor?"

The other Neeldar, who had accompanied Grenden up to the room, had remained rather quiet since their elevation to the wall.

Foggs shook a bit. He seemed clearly nervous.

"I—I—"

"You say one word to these *filths*, and you'll be dealt with severe extremeties," said Grenden to his colleague.

This made Foggs shake more.

"*Silence!*" said Terrien. "You keep that mouth of yours shut!" He formed a fist and plunged it hard into the side of Grenden's face. "Yeah, that should do it."

"Well, Kalor?" said Phinean.

"I can't— I won't—you cannot force me to!"

"Very well," said Terrien irritably. "You leave us no choice, but to leave you pinned to the wall until we can decide what to do with you two. I will need someone to stay here, and keep watch over them."

"I can do that," said Phinean.

"So can I," said Irinea graciously.

"Thank you," said Terrien. "Keep a close eye on them, especially Arturus. Once this is all over, we'll have them thrown into Nerwold—"

A thundering rumbled underfoot. Everyone scrambled to the window where they could see several lights of magic, trying to make out who conjured them, flying in every direction. The barrage of magic chipped away at the grand fountain down in the Main Courtyard.

"They've come!" said Seleborn.

Percivine quickly turned to his brother, and said, "Sirien, we must go down, and help them! They'll be outnumbered!"

"We—we're so close—they can handle it!"

Percivine could not believe his ears.

"SIRIEN!" he said. "WE NEED TO GO DOWN AND HELP THEM!"

"Percivine's right, Sirien," said Nerod earnestly. "The Landseer will need to wait. It would not be in our best honor if we don't supply some relief to the others."

"All right!" said Sirien. They are so close…so close. If only they could just burst into the Landseer's meeting, but the safety of his Solemn Hand came first. "We'll reconvene downstairs. Can one of you stay here with Fernius and Irinea should they require assistance?"

His group valiantly offered their service, but Sirien requested that Nerod stay, and provide the extra help.

"We can use the back entrance of this room to make our way down below," said Terrien. To the remaining three, he said, "Good luck to you all.".

They shuffled towards the office Irinea had come from. They scurried to a bookcase at the back of the office and removed it, revealing a vaguely visible door. Terrien tapped the door gently, and it opened.

"This door is only used in emergency cases," said Terrien. "It links to each of the three floors—the Chamber Level, Lobby Level, and Landseerial Level."

"I think this is as good as any, don't you think?" agreed Sirien, as they made their way down the dusty staircase that seemed unused in years.

They reached the second floor. Sirien had to stop to warn Cosmera Rodriys about the changed plan.

"Cosmera, there you are?" Sirien called out.

Cosmera came running right to them, from a corridor she'd been patrolling.

"Sirien!" she called. "You can't be finished already, can you?"

"No, there's been a change of plan—"

"Cosmera," said Trobius Stout, running up to them. "Did you hear all that commo—? Sirien! You can't be done already!"

"We're not!" said Sirien anxiously.

"Sirien, we have to go!" said Terrien.

"Right—look, have Dunn, Borak, and Vaureth stay on the third floor! It looks like some Argoms have made their way to the Main Courtyard and are attacking my dad's group. We're heading down there now to offer aid!"

"*What?*" croaked Cosmera. "Let us come!"

"No! You must stay here! We cannot let the plan crumble at an instant!"

"Where's Nerod?" asked Trobius.

"He's upstairs with Fernius. We've caught Grenden and Foggs. Nerod stayed behind to give extra protection in case something arises."

"Then off you go!" said Cosmera.

They clambered back into the wall, where they'd appeared earlier and jumped over two steps to make their way down quicker. Percivine almost tripped in the process, but Faruin caught him just in time before he smacked his face into the stone steps.

Once they reached the Lobby Level, they ran to the door where the same hologram appeared.

"Oroseer," it said, "there's something going on out there."

"I know," said Terrien.

The hologram looked at the group of people that followed behind, and they were not the same people who'd entered earlier.

"Where are—?"

"There's no time to explain! Let us through!"

"Certainly, if you wish it, but," said the hologram, "this isn't usual procedure, I could get replaced—"

"You won't!" said Terrien. "I'll make sure of it! Now let us through!"

SB-19 said no more and opened the door. Already smoke and smut filled the air. In the haze of combat, they split, and began casting their own magical attacks to the Argoms. Beneath the dirty air, they could see the tails of the Argoms, swaying, giving away their position from within the thick haze.

Percivine and Faruin quickly ran to Viri'el, now battling three very large Argoms on her own. She managed to slam one of them to the floor, his skull falling like a heavy rock. The other Argom managed to run off.

"*Come back here!*" yelled Seleborn and disappeared into the haze of battle.

"Seleborn!" cried Faruin, but it was no good. Seleborn could not hear any longer.

"Glad to see you here!" she told them. "They won't stop!"

"Let me get that one for you!" said Faruin. He summoned a yellow rune that formed a rope around the Argom's neck, squeezing tightly until the gasping Argom fell still.

"There you are," he said.

She thanked Faruin, turned to Percivine and said, "Have you seen my brother? Is he all right?"

"Look out!" called Percivine. He quickly grabbed Faruin and Viri'el by their arms and pulled them ferociously to the ground. Using the bodies of the two unconscious Argoms Viri'el silenced as shields, they protected themselves from the onslaught of icy magic directed at them, many bolts missing them by centimeters. "Yeah," he said covering his head, "Cosmera said he was on the top floor. He should be all right."

"Ah, a relief to hear," she said, covering her own head.

"Where did they come from?" said Faruin, a set of red runes creating a negating shield like the one in Maradine Forest. "How did they know we'd be here?"

They got up from the ground and nearly bumped heads with Sirien and Astronitus, who were running and shielding themselves from Argoms coming in several directions.

"A vision picked at me," said Viri'el, casting a blocking spell to protect them as they made their way to Linaus, who battled two Argoms at the very end of the Diet Chambers building. "I saw blood and dead bodies everywhere on the floor. That's when I realized they were coming. Before I could warn Astronitus, it was too late. Our rounds became interrupted when out of nowhere an explosion occurred at the fountain, sending bits of marble flying everywhere. That's when we saw a parade of Argoms rushing right toward us. Naturally, we attacked before they could begin theirs!"

Percivine, Faruin, and Viri'el lunged to their side to avoid an oncoming Argom tail. With just enough time Viri'el sliced the Argom's tail right off using a cutting curse.

"Are you two all right?" she asked them.

"Better now that you saved us!" said Faruin, blood dripping from his left eyebrow.

"Get them! *Get them!* GET THEM!" the Argoms shouted, running to them.

Percivine launched himself to the side again, to avoid being plastered to the floor. The Argoms stumbled about in the haze. They found themselves being bombarded by magical attacks. They fell one after the other to the ground, making a loud *thumping* noise.

They heard a scream coming from the flower beds embedded in the main street of the District. An Argom had floored Linaus amongst the flowers with her tail. A blue beam of magic cast yards away.

"Thank you," said Linaus being held up by Faruin and Viri'el "I don't think I could have managed any longer if you hadn't shown up!"

"Are you hurt?" asked Percivine.

"A small limp. Nothing to worry about!"

He bowed his head in gratitude, then ran off in his capacity to get his next would-be-victim.

In all this commotion, how can Elwerth, Thiurwold, or Talus the Dark not even bother to find out what is happening outside?

They continued running all over the Main Courtyard crouching so they would not be hit by any of the Argoms' spells. They came across Pevarius who, it seemed, had just finished with his Argoms, who were doused in flame and screaming in agony.

"Serves you right!" they heard him tell the Argoms, as they approached him, his staff ready to perform spellcraft again. "Burn! Burn until your flesh becomes nothing more than charred remains of filth!"

"How did they get into this state?" Faruin asked.

"Oh—a bit of tricky magic, if I do say so myself," said Pevarius Garcinius. "I certainly hope this teaches them a thing or two about what they've done to us for so long now!" He stopped, astonished to see Percivine and Faruin before him. "Shouldn't you two be with Sirien?"

Percivine spoke. "We saw the Argoms attacking you all from Fernius's window, and Sirien decided it would be best to come lend a hand in warding them off." Even though it was his persistence that had made Sirien budge, he felt that Pevarius didn't need to know any of that.

"It's a good thing to," said Pevarius, throwing himself to the floor to dodge an incoming attack, "that—you arrived. We're quite good, your father and I, at magic, but there are simply" —he dodged another— "too many of them for a group of five to deal with!"

Pevarius crouched his head a third time and sped off to a couple of Argoms that stood shooting attacks in all directions by the destroyed fountain.

One after the other the Argoms fell, even as they kept pouring in. The Solemn Hand was growing outnumbered. There were ten Argoms for one member of the Hand, and those numbers were far worse than Sirien had hoped for.

"There's too many of them!" said Percivine, lunging himself at an Argom who had grabbed hold of Viri'el. Both he and Faruin kicked and slammed into the Argom, until finally Faruin picked up a heavy chunk of marble and sent it crashing into the Argom's skull.

"There you are," he said. "I thought it almost had you."

"Thank you, again, to the both of you," said Viri'el.

From a distance Percivine could see the Administration's bronze doors opening. Several figures emerged, casting their own spells. Who were they? Percivine finally caught a glimpse of one of them: Borak, wielding a silver sword and slicing through any Argoms that came his way.

"I knew there were perks to being a blacksmith!" he said out loud.

Though they endured cuts, bruises, and the occasional blood drip, none from the Solemn Hand were incredibly wounded until Percivine, Faruin, and Viri'el found Seleborn on the floor, overseen by Dunngarunax Galon who was *very* pleased to them.

"What's happened to him?" said Percivine.

"They've broken my nose!" said Seleborn in a nasally voice. Blood smeared his face. "It hurts like hell! Aaargh!"

"I got 'ere jus' in time, eh?" said Dunn. "I managed to fend some off! Could've killed the lad! Ye three go off! I can fix his nose!"

They wasted no time in doing so. No quicker had they left Seleborn and Dunn than Twy'leden and Borak pummeled a couple more Argoms to the ground, and casting spells directly to their heads to fell them. Percivine saw his father and Sirien still back-to-back, shooting away at the Argoms. They ran to the edge of the Main Courtyard near the lake beside it, where they could see Cosmera being ambushed.

In a sudden burst of familiar pain, Percivine dropped to the floor. An Argom, some distance away, had managed to hit his leg—the chilling, icy feel almost burning his leg. Everything seemed to muffle, to cancel out itself around him. The pain grew more intense; he panted; he sweated; his breathing overtaking any other sort of noise. He was back in Maradine Forest, Tharacar standing over him ready to perform the killing blow.

You need to break from this, said the voice in Percivine's head.

Percivine's vision focused, and over him stood Faruin.

"Go on without me!" he called to them.

"We would never do that!" said Faruin. He hastily summoned an orange rune that melted the painful ice from Percivine's leg, leaving a very red mark where it had been, stinging a bit still. They picked him up, and soon were off to aid Cosmera.

"Nonsense," said Cosmera, "I can handle myself!"

Yet they helped her finish the three Argoms, then ran back to the center of the Main Courtyard to continue resisting the Argoms still pouring in They needed more help. Suddenly, when all else seemed to be failing, they heard a horn blow. Out of the depths of the woods surrounding the Administration District, Neledarian soldiers marched in. Now, it seemed, the Argoms were the outnumbered ones.

"Attack at your own will!" cried an officer, dressed in heavy, patted armor, a glinting sword in her right hand.

More swords danced in front of Percivine's eyes, and bolts and jets of magic by combat sorcerers dashed over his head striking at the enemy gracefully, while of these attacks managed to graze Percivine's left shoulder.

"Where did that come from?"

They looked all around. Finally, to their horror, they saw who was attacking them. It could not be…It just could not be…

Probably can't see through all this, thought Percivine.

Sirien was attacking them.

"Stop! Stop!" said Percivine. "It's me! Your brother, Sirien!"

But Sirien did not listen or seem to care. He continued lashing out at them. Percivine did not want to attack his brother. But then something really extraordinary happened: A curse hit Sirien on the left side of his torso, exploding, and sending him flying, crashing into an unsuspecting Argom. The curse came from none other than Sirien.

"What the—?" said Percivine.

"That's not me!" Sirien shouted. "It's Murgoy, the shapeshifter! Found Dunn attending to Seleborn not long ago, and Seleborn witnessed him attacking you just now! He's the one who killed Filiiri! He thought he could fool you by taking my appearance. I don't think he knew I was here!"

"Thank the gods!" said Percivine.

"I would *never* betray those I love," said Sirien.

"Is Seleborn going to be fine?" said Viri'el. "What happened to him?"

"An Argom broke his nose," said Faruin.

They fell back to through the mess where Seleborn and Dunn were. They could now see the first casualties for their side. Neledarian soldiers had fallen over dead Argoms. The smell of blood now filled the smokey air. It was a dreadful picture—Percivine had never seen so much blood and innards at one time. His stomach churned.

At last, beneath the chaos, they reached Seleborn and Dunn casting their spells, the exhaustion covering their expressions. Blood still covered Seleborn's mouth and clothes, but his nose did not seem to be sticking out oddly anymore.

"Sirien!" said Dunn. "Good to see ye back, lad!"

"Same, Dunn!" said Sirien. "Seleborn, I didn't get a chance to ask you earlier if you were well. All better?"

"Yeah, loads," said Seleborn. "I hope Murgoy breathed his last breath!"

"Not sure if he's dead, but I certainly sent him flying into the disorder."

Disappointment filled Seleborn's face. Percivine can't forget the tears Seleborn shed when he shared the story of his wife's death, so he can understand why Seleborn looked and felt this way. Nonetheless, Seleborn couldn't be more thankful to Sirien for fending off Murgoy.

Wanting a shift in subject, Seleborn said, "Dunn fixed my nose right up! Have you been taking private lessons from Cosmera?"

Dunn laughed. "Nah," he said cheerfully, swinging a mace at an Argom coming to them. "I figured it wasn' tha' hard to perform one, do I did!"

"If you'll excuse me," said Viri'el. "I must go and look for my brother!"

"I saw him not too long ago," said Sirien, "fighting alongside Linaus near the back of the Diet Chambers structure!"

She nodded, and sped off.

"We need to keep moving!" said Sirien.

They gathered themselves and went no further, stopped by Bartholev, smiling hungrily.

"Well, well, well," said his oily voice.

CHAPTER TWELVE

TALUS THE DARK

"I see you blasted away my dear help," said Bartholev, looking at the pathetic sight of Murgoy trying to get up. "Useless. Worthless. I should have known he would be incapable of dealing with you."

"It's just like you, isn't it?" said Seleborn, stepping forward. "Never could face us by yourself. Always had to send others to do your dirty work. Such a coward, you are."

Bartholev laughed deviously. "Seleborn Alveroth…It's been a long time. Tell me, how's your *darling* wife?"

A spark of pure, white anger seethed through his veins. With his full might, he cast a curse of purple magic at Bartholev that narrowly missed his right shoulder by inches.

"It seems it was a mistake to trust my help to warm you up. Mere failures. But today, I will prove my worth to Lord Talus, and vanquish your very existence."

The sounds and echoes of an ongoing battle raged all around them, but still, not one attack seemed to have carried in their direction.

"What a joke," Sirien spat.

"Ah, Sirien Ogthorne! And look—Percivine Ogthorne! Today is certainly rewarding. Both Ogthorne brothers together, again! Not going to abandon little Percivine here, are you Sirien? You almost let me kill him last time."

"I think," said Sirien, "that this time we will kill you. I will enjoy every bit of it."

Bartholev laughed again. "So, Percivine, you got lucky at the Temple of the Stars, didn't you? Had poor Twy'leden use up all his strength on me. Something you would never be able to do. Oh yes," he added, looking upon their confused faces, "I knew it was you three with him that day."

"But why didn't you stop us, then?" said Faruin. "Surely, you would have been rewarded by a higher power if you had gotten us."

"There is no doubt I would have," said Bartholev, "but I had more important matters to attend to."

"That is a lie!" said Percivine.

"Lie, is it?" said Bartholev, raising an eyebrow. "What makes *you* so sure?"

"On my last day in Unin'shai, I'd stumbled across you and the owner of that small eatery at the end of the Province! Why on Gylranor would he know where I was?"

Percivine seemed to have lost Bartholev for a moment, but soon caught up.

"*You saw, did you?*"

"I did," said Percivine.

"I knew that idiot was lying! I had asked around. I came up to some oaf, selling some stupid inventions called conductors…Modern, *indeed*…When I asked him about you he seemed to know something, but he just grew nervous, and sped off. I tailed him for a few moments, until he went to the eatery, and had spoken something to the owner. I saw that seller rush out of the Province. That's when I figured he must've told him something about you!"

This now made complete sense to Percivine. So, that was the reason for the Ya'ril's departure from Unin'shai. He'd known the whole time it was him. Percivine felt the greatest of gratitude for him, not mentioning a word about him to Bartholev.

"I still do not understand why you didn't have us arrested in Unin'shai," said Percivine.

"There is much you don't understand," said Bartholev. "Why have you arrested when I could personally deal with you myself? Where's the enjoyment in that? Lord Talus had gotten word from a reliable source of ours about the missing part of the Atlas being found."

"So, it's true…" said Faruin.

"Of course, it is! We were sent to investigate, and that is why I left you alone…for the time being. But there was something more. Something far worthier. That wrinkled old Elf possessed something greater than any map or magical property in this world: foresight. Lord Talus wanted it. I wanted it. *He* desires it. Dedrinus thought he could win. I showed him. Pity, what a waste. Now but a disgusting memory. I had other orders to carry out. But it was no success, the same way we had had no success at the University of Elvic Magic."

"You were there?" said Faruin horridly. He could feel something he never felt before. His anger had risen to near dangerous levels and knew it would be foolish to let this man continue to live.

"Well, of course, I was there, as were two of Lord Talus's chief lieutenants, Murac and, you've already had the pleasure of meeting Murgoy. Murgoy so kindly and quietly took care of that Etwood, that our investigation went without a whim. With him dead, that would leave the rest of you to focus more on his death than your insistence of locating the lost fragment of the map. And it worked, didn't it? We were undisturbed, and what with the blame going around. Poor you, Faruin. Blamed for Murgoy's killing. Such a pity…"

"Your satisfying death will justify my exile," said Faruin calmly.

Like Seleborn, he took all the might he had and and attempted to cast the blue beam from a rune at Bartholev. He missed, as well, Bartholev deflecting it back at them, causing them to get out of the way.

"These inept tactics really need to stop," said Bartholev lazily. "It nearly destroys the pleasure of victory."

"And what about the Imbartus and Sendrik murders?" said Sirien. "They had no reason to be murdered!"

"Oh," said Bartholev, his lips curling up, "I had every reason to kill them. You see, Avalon Imbartus served as Head of the Mediation Service, and I had discovered Avalon secretly writing to the other nations about the, how did he put it, 'treachery Elwerth has committed by giving aid to the Argoms.' I told Lord Talus upon my discovery, and he ordered the immediate execution of Avalon."

"You filth!" said Sirien. "He deserved nothing of the sort! What about Shelina? She had nothing to do with this!"

"She had every bit to do with it, as Avalon did," said Bartholev. "Upon Avalon's approval, she sparked together an obscure meeting with the other Heads to have Landseer Elwerth ousted from office. We couldn't let that happen. Elwerth was to create friendly ties with the

Argoms and us, and we could not let *anyone* interfere with such a pact, with the Master's plan! It would make the world a better place—"

Master? thought Percivine. *Lord Talus?*

I don't think so, said the voice. *I think they follow commands from another power…Percivine, it's time to act.*

Percivine plummeted his body against Batholev's. Bartholev struggled to break loose of the tight grasp on his arms. As their bodies shook, something caught Percivine's eyes: a small, rolled parchment fell from a small pocket on the side of Bartholev's robes. Without pondering it, Percivine reached for it, until Bartholev became aware and started hitting Percivine in the stomach. He thrashed his head against Percivine's, sending him reeling onto his back. Percivine's eyes slowly watched as Bartholev prepared to stick a dagger in him. It drew near…Bartholev was toppled by Sirien. Bartholev swung his leg and struck Sirien right on the side of his head.

"It will take more than that to kill me!" spat Bartholev, blood dripping from his mouth. "Do you not see how perfect this world will be once we take it over?"

"A better place for the Argoms, not for the rest of us!" said Seleborn.

"For everyone!" said Bartholev. "And how can I forget about the lovely Solemn Hand? My source told me about you all. I relayed everyting to Elwerth about you, Sirien, and your Solemn Hand. She agreed that your organization would have to be removed or face criminal charges. That is why we searched for you in Maradine Forest. Your poor father, I had meant to kill him, not just harm his shoulder. I would have thought a man of your stature would have understood what a threatning letter looked liked. I should have expected it, of course. Sirien Ogthorne—always too eager for glory and doesn't listen to the advice of others."

"It was you!" said Sirien.

"Yes, me, all me," said Bartholev. "I will do it again if I have to! Wait—I misspoke, I'm going to kill you tonight, so there won't be another time to do it!"

"But it appears that you have failed," said Percivine.

Bartholev stared blankly at Percivine, and said, "Failed, have I?"

"Yes," said Percivine, "because there are five of us, and one of you."

The Argoms had to have known that Bartholev was in the center of the battle. That was likely why no attacks had been made in their area since Bartholev appeared.

"I have not failed anything!" snapped Bartholev. "You are all here! I will kill you all! You have evaded me for the last time! *Die*!"

Bartholev took a few steps back and began projecting bolts of yellow, stinging bolts from both hands. A couple of these bolts struck Faruin and Percivine making them crouch in pain. The others moved out of the way, other spells now coming from all directions. Argoms entered the gray to guard Bartholev and help ward off the Solemn Hand.

"Murgoy, you waste! Get your arse over here!"

The shapeshifter appeared again, but in his natural form of an Argom. Murgoy swept away soldiers with his tail and stormed right at Sirien, the Argom falling over after Sirien dodged him. Faruin, having recollected himself from Bartholev's earlier spell, and Dunn ran at Murgoy and helped to restrain him, so he could remain pinned to the ground. Murgoy managed to escape by smacking Dunn behind the head with his tail. He broke free of their ranks and headed towards the Diet Chambers doors.

"After him!" shouted Dunn, a bit wobbly from the heavy blow to his head.

"No! Leave him!" said Sirien. "He's of no importance now! Go after Bartholev!"

Bartholev sent explosive spells at them, each missing his attacks by a small margin. At last, Bartholev was hit in his right arm by one of Percivine's punching spells, a transparent spell of grey.

"You think that will weaken me?" Bartholev said, straightening himself. "Think again!"

He hit Percivine square in the chest. The next moments were critical: Percivine awoke in midair, hurling backwards. The impact of the fall would not end well for him. Bartholev's offensive magic is too powerful. He closed his eyes to brace for the crash. Percivine never met the floor. His flying body froze where it remained and gently lowered itself to the ground. Seleborn conjured a floating spell that forbade Percivine from falling to his agony. Bartholev saw this and grew infuriated. He rushed towards Seleborn, who slammed a fist right into his mouth, breaking two teeth.

Bartholev spat blood to the ground. "You will not win!"

"We shall see about that—"

Seleborn stopped cold where he was. He stared at Bartholev. This seemed to confuse Bartholev. Seleborn closed his eyes and began chant something under his breath. A glowing white circle formed in between them both.

Bartholev took a couple steps back. "What is this? What are you doing?"

A glowing odd shape began to form in front of Seleborn.

"What is he doing?" Percivine asked Faruin.

The glowing shape formed a tail, a small horn sticking from the center of its forehead, clawed talons, and caramel skin. The creature's black eyes watching Bartholev.

"Ah, yes, a Warlock's true weapon," said Bartholev. "Welcome to this spectacle, Netherid."

Percivine could hardly mistake the shakiness in Bartholev's voice.

Seleborn summoned a Netherid, a similar creature in appearance to that of an Argom but slightly larger, and which lived in the Nethermire, the Dark Primal's underworld. He had used his abilities as a Warlock and dabbled in Netheriditry, the use of Netheridic Arts, to summon it.

"What is your bidding, Seleborn?" the Netherid asked.

Everyone, including several soldiers and Argoms who'd stopped fighting one another to witness the event, were in such amazement they almost forgot what they were doing. Percivine could not believe this. He only heard tales of times past when Netherids roamed this world in previous wars. An actual Netherid stood before his eyes, more devilish than he could have imagined.

"Andronus, kill that man," said Seleborn, pointing at a frightened Bartholev.

"As you command," said Andronus.

"Stand away, filthy Netherid!" said Bartholev. "I said stand away!"

Andronus paid no attention to this, and slowly walked towards the man of grey.

"I said *stand away!*"

Andronus, obviously, wasn't going to abide, and continued walking, closing in on the assassin. Bartholev now shot forceful spells at the Netherid, but it seemed not to affect it. Andronus finally stopped. He hissed and raised his arms. Andronus widened his black eyes. Andronus brought down his arms, extending them to a great length. The heavy hands gripped Bartholev on both sides, his arms stuck under Andronus's might, unable to move them freely to defend himself. In seconds Andronus tore Bartholev in half. Unmoved, Andronus dropped both halves of Bartholev on the ground.

Don't think I'll ever get used to stuff like that, thought Percivine, feeling lightheaded.

"If that is all, I would like to return to the Grey Void," Andronus said to Seleborn. "Urian Bartholev is finished."

"You may."

With the same white glow, the Netherid vanished.

Bartholev's halves bled profusely, his entrails scattered where they shouldn't be. Silence hovered over the battlefield momentarily, many Neledarian warriors disturbed having witness such a slaughter. Realizing where they were again, a warrior attacked an Argom, reigniting the fight.

"We must make our way back to the Chambers!" said Terrien, running up to them. "I've already warned Astronitus and Cosmera, and the groups are making their way back down the structure! The soldiers can handle the Argoms out here!"

They quickly made their way through the battle, dodging anything headed their way.

"Identifi—"

"There's no time!" Terrien told SB-19. "I order you to—let—us—in!"

"I'm programmed to—"

"SHUT IT!" said Terrien.

The hologram disappeared, and at once the bronze doors flung open. It was a lot quieter in the lobby. Only the faint sounds of the outside could now be heard.

"Everyone all here?" asked Sirien, frantically inspecting everyone to make sure no one remained outside in combat.

"We need to head back to the original plan," said Astronitus Ogthorne, his face covered in black dust.

"Right," said Sirien. "Since group two is no longer needed outside, you make sure no one enters the Chambers. Group three you head back to the second and third floors. Group one—we go to the top! This time we will face the piece of scum, Talus the Dark!"

They ventured back to the same transport disc that took them to the top floor the first time. Without any interruptions they made their way quickly to the floor. As they exited the lift, an eery silence fell upon them. There was no one to be heard. They ran to the Ward. Nerod Nilius quickly greeted them.

"What happened down there? A lot of you are covered in blood!"

"It's worse than we thought," said Sirien. "Hundreds and hundreds of Argoms keep pouring from all sides of the Courtyard."

Irinea placed a hand over her mouth. Phinean remained calm, watching Grenden and Foggs closely.

"We were surely outnumbered," said Sirien, "but thankfully those soldiers appeared. How did they get there, though?"

"I can answer that," said Phinean. "I knew something like this was capable by those foul vermin. All the Heads have a private means of communication—"

"But you're not a Head, Fernius," Sirien cut in.

Phinean ignored this.

"—amongst one another. I quickly alerted Mr. Baine, Head of the Armed Service, and told him what was happening. Irinea, Nerod, and I were able to see the dark creatures flooding the area, so immediately I requested he send reinforcements. He responded almost within minutes after alerting General Pinch. Pinch sent nearly four hundred soldiers from his ranks to come help us. Pinch, himself, couldn't make the journey, for they were currently in combat with a force of Argoms at Bolhana."

"Thank you, Fernius," said Sirien. "Without your help, none of this could have been possible."

Phinean pressed his lips together. "There is no need to thank me. It is my civil duty to do what's right."

They could hear laughter in the back.

"You think it's funny, do you?" said Sirien heatedly.

Grenden did not say a word.

Sirien walked up to Grenden and punched him square in the stomach. Grenden let out a gasp for air, but quickly recollected himself, and returned to his crazed smile.

"We need to get in," said Sirien to the others. "Come—"

Grended laughed again. Sirien glared at him.

"Want another beating?" he asked.

"You fool," said Grenden. "There's no way of entering the Landseer's Chamber."

"*Oh?*"

"Lord Talus made sure to seal it with very protective magic. He wants no one to disrupt them."

"Talus made the seal?" said Seleborn.

"Yes," said Grenden.

"Where's the Landseer's private guard?" asked Irinea.

"Disposed of," said Kalor Foggs.

"Makes sense now," said Nerod Nilius. "Since our arrival, I haven't seen the Solerel Guard. Where've they gone? And come to think of it I haven't seen her Support Staff for ages, either."

"Like Kalor said," said Grenden, "they've been *disposed* of. Nuisances, they were. Always so close to the Landseer. Never could let any of us get closer than ten feet when addressing her. That soon had to change. Lord Talus gave the order of their immediate expulsion."

"*Lord* Talus gave the order?" repeated Sirien. "Who is *Lord* Talus to be giving the orders to Landseer Elwerth? And the Solerel Guard? Had them thrown back to the Sect of Solerel, did she?"

Grenden merely chuckled.

"*Good gods!*" said Sirien shockingly. "Things now are clearer to me!"

"What things?" asked Percivine.

"All those horrific things Elwerth has done…It's not her doing!"

Grenden chuckled no more. A stern expression now clouded his face.

"Care to elaborate?" said an already perplexed Percivine.

"Don't you see, brother? Elwerth isn't herself! She hasn't been herself since the Violet Veil Accord was decreed. She would not have done it willingly. She's being controlled by another…Someone who's always close by to the Landseer."

"*Bartholev!*"

"No…" said Nerod. "The one we're after, Talus. We were wrong about Bartholev. Though he has played a major part in all this, he is not capable of such trickery. He surely would have used it on you or Faruin in Maradine."

"Yes, it all makes perfect sense," said Sirien, staring at the floor. "He's a Minthrys, Percivine, those who can subdue someone with their own thoughts—

Am I being controlled by one? Percivine said to the voice. *Is someone governing my thoughts?*

No, said the voice. *My reactions to your thoughts are a mirrored effect.*

"Once one breaks through, they can command the poor victim to do their every bidding. I should have known from the start that Talus is a very capable Minthrys. With him, safely indulged within her mind, he was able to brand us official enemies of Nell, thus resulting in warrants for our arrest. Second, he forced her to allow Nell to give sanctum to the Argoms, and lastly, with Talus the Dark's control over Elwerth, he was able to impose the ridiculous rules that havoced the Divination Adminsitration and the appointments of his followers, especially Bartholev."

Percivine's eyes nearly jumped clear from their sockets. It all fits together: No other group had the voice to publicly denounce the statutes and limitations the Violet Veil Accord had imposed on the people of Nell. Talus—*an Argom*—had been responsible for much of the downfall of Nell.

"Faruin, Seleborn," said Percivine, cutting off his brother. "This is what the sprite meant: '*From within the forms of government, there is the one who seeks power in bold, to rage, to havoc, to destroy…Not until a hero comes along to break the hold.*'"

Faruin and Seleborn found it hard to believe that Percivine had quoted the sprite in every word he had told them since he spent most of their earlier travels complaining and moaning.

"You're right, Perci!" said Faruin. "Talus has been working from within the government of Nell all this time, and he *is* seeking power!"

"The sprite was right all along," said Seleborn.

Sirien, a little confused, took back his turn to speak, and shot a look at Grenden.

"By the way," he said, giving the same smile to Grenden that Grenden had given to him, "you'll be *happy* to know that Bartholev is dead."

"Y-you—you lie!" snarled Grenden.

"Actually, I don't," said Sirien. "Ripped in half, I'm afraid. Our friend

Seleborn and his Netherid counterpart here did us the favor of ridding this world of his malice. Thank you, again, Seleborn."

"Happy to do it," said Seleborn.

"You will pay!" said Grenden. "Once I am free from these bonds you will wish you would never have been born!"

"With or without your bonds," said Seleborn, "I would not fear the likes of you."

"Well, Terrien, there you are," said Sirien, turning his palm upwards and directing it at Grenden. "What do you think?"

Irinea Squint, having not much experience being an investigator, never dreamt someone could deduce so much in so little time. Phinean remained quiet, lips pressed together.

"It—it does make absolute sense," said Terrien. "I don't think your Master, Talus the Dark, is going to be very happy with the information you've given us."

"We've discovered what has been happening," said Sirien. "You will be punished, I'm sure."

"G-given?" said Grenden. "I didn't tell you filths anything! Lord Talus is my superior, yes, but he is certainly not the one I call 'Master.'"

Heads raised in an alarmed state. No one except Percivine had realized "Master" was the title of another.

"What d'you mean?" said Terrien. "Then who—?"

Grenden spat. "Do you honestly think I would tell you?" he said. "I'm no fool."

"Oh, right," said Nerod, "you're a complete arsehole."

Everyone burst into laughter. There was no mistake in Percivine's eyes Grenden fumed at the insult. Grenden flailed in his bonds, wishing so severely that he could rip Nerod's head off.

Terrien marched quietly up to Grenden and Foggs. Phinean and Irinea followed behind him.

"You are to tell us what exactly the purpose of tonight's meeting is," said Terrien. "What business does the Minister of War have here? What are the contents?"

"You *really* are foolish," said Grenden. "Haven't you learned anything? I will not speak. No matter what you do to me, we will not speak a word."

"Fine," said Terrien, "if you won't tell us, I'm sure you won't have a problem in telling me what you've done to Fioriul Prons and Ignius Malhavius. You remember them, don't you? The Landseer's Support Staff."

This time Grenden seemed at ease, and was more than happy to explain what had happened to them both.

"We knew those two wouldn't approve of Landseer Elwerth's decisions. Although, Fioriul almost seemed tempted to. As her highest-ranking advisors, they surely would have *advised* against her decisions, and above all, against Lord Talus and the Argoms."

"*Where are they?*" demanded Terrien, growing impatient.

"Locked away!" said Grenden.

"Where?"

"Nerwold Hold."

"You gargoyle!" said Terrien. "They will die there if we don't help them!"

"I know," said Grenden icily. "*That's* the idea. You'll have a hard time getting to them, though. Dillory and Hendlen are personally guarding their cell. No one will get past them."

"Yes, I'm sure, if they put up the same fight *you did*," said Percivine, "we won't be able to get to them."

Faruin, Seleborn, and Nerod sniggered.

"Laugh all you want," said Grenden. "Once the meeting is over, there will be no stopping us!"

This made Percivine feel that the meeting, so called, was indeed no such meeting. Something bigger and darker was at work there. And who exactly was this "Master"? Why is Thiurwold here? What's the purpose? He could not be there to prove Astronitus' and Linaus's theories about him, could he? Farfetched it seemed. How exactly were they to enter the Chamber if it was magically sealed? All these questions raddled his brain.

Sirien's patience, having waned extensively, left him no other choice. He slammed open the Service door, disregarding the shouts of "Sirien wait!" from his brother and the rest. He stomped heavily towards the large doors of Landseer Elwerth's office. He clenched his fist and slammed it hard onto the magically protected doors. Before he realized, he was thrown back, spots of white appearing in his vision. He fell to the floor.

A faint sound echoed and grew louder. Percivine and Astronitus knelt beside Sirien tyring to wake him up.

"Sirien! Sirien!"

Sirien moaned with pain. His head throbbed. He tried to get up, but could not.

"Now we know how powerful that seal is," said Phinean. "The seal must also whisp away any sound from the other side. I think the seal not only covers the door, but the whole office. That is why no one's come out from there. They've heard nothing."

"There must be a way to penetrate it," said Seleborn.

"Yes, but what?"

"I'm all right. I'm all right," said Sirien, shaking his head to focus. "Help me up, Percivine."

Percivine lifted his brother to his feet, Sirien swaying where he stood. An immense pain at the back of head knocked roughly at his skull.

"You should have waited," said Percivine.

"We need to think of a way to get in," said Faruin.

Before any collaboration could be made, they heard the clanking of the lift.

"Someone's coming!" said Irinea. "Quick! We must get back inside!"

They hurried back to the office, where they dimmed the spheres giving off light. Terrien cracked open the door and peered through it. Percivine stood at an angle just enough so he could also see outside. Faruin and Seleborn clamped their hands over Grenden's and Foggs's mouths. The lift stopped. Someone was certainly there. They heard footsteps.

It can't be her, thought Percivine.

Viri'el walked towards the Landseer's office.

"What do you see?" whispered Seleborn.

"Shh!"

Viri'el stopped and looked all around her. She was Viri'el no more. It was Murgoy! The shapeshifter that had managed to treat his wounds from the battle. But that had been over an hour ago; what had taken him so long to reach the top floor? Percivine drew nearer to Terrien. They watched closely as Murgoy walked to the doors. He raised a hand. At the simple touch of his finger to the door, he was able to open them, and walk in.

"Well?" said Sirien, holding the back of his head. "What did you see? Who was it?"

"Viri'el…"

Percivine turned his head to watch Faruin, who could only look in horror, his grip slowly losing slack over Kalor's mouth.

"Are you sure?" said Faruin.

Everyone was able to breathe again. Relief swept over them rather. It would have been an awful extremity, and an inconvenience, to find out that one of their own would betray them like that.

"He managed to escape your groups, Sirien," said Terrien. "Pretended to be one of them so he could get past without any trouble."

"But what's he barely doing up here?" said Seleborn. "He should have been in the office by now."

"Did you see how he got in?" said Sirien.

"Yes," said Terrien, looking at Grenden. "It was easier than we thought."

"How so?" said Nerod.

"The magical seal, it seems, was created using dark magic. The creator, someone who dabbles in dark sorcery, is one who could enter the domain. So, anyone who follows these dark ways is able and allowed to gain entry."

"Where are we to get—?" Sirien stopped. There were two in the same room who followed these dark ways. "Well," he said, "looks like we'll have to use Arturus. Maybe Kalor?"

"Don't you dare touch me!" snapped Grenden, biting Faruin's hand.

"You rotten rat!" cried Faruin, holding his hand. Grenden's teeth managed to puncture his skin. Irinea ran to a drawer and pulled out Healing Powder, which she sprinkled on the wound.

After seeing Faruin's hand, Seleborn removed his from Kalor's mouth and instead placed a conjured barrier in its place.

"You'll regret this!"

"Arturus has given us most of the trouble," said Phinean. "Why don't we use him?"

"Sounds like an idea," said Sirien. "Very well. We will use Arturus to get us in."

"Son of a bitch!" said Grenden.

"Faruin," said Sirien, "would you mind summoning a rune to shut him up? I've had quite enough of his big mouth."

"It will be my pleasure," said Faruin. He stepped back, and, with a turning of his wrist, a white rune appeared. The rune lifted off the ground and sort of thinned itself as it made its way to Grenden, who struggled to break free. The rune stuck itself over Grenden's mouth.

"You've got to teach me that some day," said Seleborn, rather impressed.

Phinean and Irinea cautiously removed the magical bonds holding Grenden to the wall. They brought him down, each holding one of Grenden's arms. Binding his feet, they dragged him out of the Sanction room to Elwerth's doors.

"Well, Arturus," said Terrien, "forgive me for not thanking you for all that you've done."

Grenden tried to scream maniacally. Phinean and Irinea were have difficulty keeping Grenden still, he trying to turn over so that his large belly would squash Irinea. Percivine rushed over and took hold of Grenden's hand. Still squirming where he lay, Grenden's hand had been up and with a simple touch of the finger, opened the doors. The remaining Solemn Hand members were now at the door, ready to combat the minions behind it.

"Irinea, can you stay with him?" Phinean asked.

"Yes," she said. "I'll make sure he doesn't get anywhere."

She created a bond around his hands, and let him fall to the ground.

The doors creaked opened. There they were…Estith Elwerth, Landseer of Nell and Talus the Dark, leader of the Argoms. Percivine couldn't see Thiurwold anywhere.

"Ah," said Talus the Dark. His tail peeping from behind his official green Divination Administration robes while his clawed feet at the bottom of his robes moved towards Percivine and Phinean. "How kind of Arturus to let you in to our domain. Murgoy, Murac, please bring our guests further this way."

Unbeknownst to the Solemn Hand, Murgoy and Murac, the other of Talus's chief Argoms with a missing tail and canine tooth waited quietly behind them. Murac and Murgoy pointed them in the direction of Talus the Dark, down the way full of columns, to where he and Elwerth stood in front of a marble, grey desk.

Was Thiurwold's presence merely a ruse?

Can't know exactly, the voice replied.

"Welcome," said Talus the Dark, his darkened teeth showing as he produced a wide smile. "To what do I owe this pleasure?"

"To us," said Sirien. "We should have known it was not Bartholev, but you, who was manipulating Elwerth."

"Can't believe it took you this long to realize?" said Talus, laughing. "He was my peon, like the rest of them, useless now that he's dead. But you are too late! The ritual has already begun."

"Ritual? What ritual?" said Sirien, being pushed to walk.

"The ritual to summon the Master from the Nethermire."

"You're not the 'Master' Arturus and Kalor were referring to, then?" said Seleborn.

"There is one above me—" said Talus in a gentle voice. "Master Haraxas, brother of Karxas, the Netherid who failed to conquer this world last time. Lord Haraxas's return is inevitable."

"You won't get away with this!" said Percivine.

"But I already have," said Talus indifferently. "Once my offering here sacrifices herself, the ritual will be complete, and no one will be able to stop us!"

"You worm," scowled Terrien.

"That…really…hurt," said Talus mockingly. "By the way, Seleborn, I was rather impressed the way you killed one of my best lieutenants. I now know he was weak, and incapable of handling the simplest of tasks. Murgoy said he spotted you through a window…summoning a Netherid, was it? I will, however, have to return the favor for Bartholev's killing. Sound fair?"

"How does that sound for you?" said Seleborn.

"Highly unlikely," said Talus.

"We'll see about that," said Sirien.

"You will die the very way your putrid mother died," said Talus, "with nothing to live for."

"Don't you *dare* talk about my mother, you load of bat droppings!" said Sirien. "She had all the worth to live for, unlike you! Who knows nothing of what it means to be alive!"

Behind Percivine he heard the whispers between Murgoy and Murac, arguing over something probably that wouldn't please Talus.

"L-lord Talus," said Murac.

"What is it? I'm rather occupied."

Talus the Dark's voice almost seemed to make Murac shudder.

"M-Murgoy here has just informed me that Bolhana has been lost to the resistance. Our forces were completely destroyed, and the very few Argoms remaining have retreated to Nerwold Hold."

"Bah!" said Talus. "That makes no difference to me. A worthless city of worthless souls. Once the Master returns, we will be able to fully execute his ultimate plan!"

Sirien whispered something to the others, while Murgoy, Murac, and Talus the Dark conversed.

"We must do it," Sirien told them. "With them out of the way, it will make it all the easier."

"Silence!" spat Talus. "Do not speak among yourselves! If you have something to say, then I'm sure we would all like to hear it!"

No one said a word.

"Not going to speak, are you? Very well. You—*come here!*"

Estith Elwerth, who had remained quiet this entire time, walked over to Talus in a trance, her greasy black and white hair covering her purple skin, a color not common amongst Neledar. She gazed into nothingness and followed his orders, wordlessly.

"Prepare yourselves for the sacri—"

"*Now!*" said Sirien.

The Solemn Hand split apart to allow Terrien a clear shot of the two Argoms in the back. Murgoy was thrown back against the doors and Murac against a column, where he slid unconscious to the floor, by a blast of orange light from Terrien's fingertips.

Talus only laughed and ridiculed them. "Is that really all you can muster?"

A wall of fiery ice formed itself in front of him. Making a pushing notion with his pointy-nailed hands, the wall swept across the room to the Solemn Hand. The wall shattered as the result of Sirien's bashing counterspell.

"Fools!" he roared. "You will not prevent me from using her body to summon Haraxas! Murgoy! Murac! Get up, insolent parasites!"

Neither Murgoy nor Murac made any sort of movement. They had been damaged, and rather significantly.

"No less," said Talus. "I can finish you myself! Attack!"

Estith Elwerth produced small jumping lightning strikes that crawled on the polished rock floor, as Talus launched the signature move of an Argom: icy bolts.

"Don't attack, Elwerth!" Terrien shouted at them, as he and the rest of the Hand retreated towards the doors to avoid the lightning spell. "She's innocent, remember that! Only use defensive spells against her!"

"No," said Sirien, "I've got a better idea! Cosmera once told me about a dark magic that attacks the body from within, a rare spell that only few magical users can perform. If the spell works the way she explained it, then I could use it to push out Talus's mind prison."

"Are you referring to sangrinus magic?" asked Percivine. "Sirien, that's illegal in Nell!"

"JUST DO IT!" called Terrien, the lightning conjury a couple feet away from their own.

Sirien decided to have a go at it. Still hiding behind the column, Percivine watched Sirien close his eyes. Sirien's body jolted briefly. There was no visible magic. He struggled to maintain it.

"Mind control—is—too—strong!" he shouted, yet he was not about to forfeit.

"You—are—finished!" Sirien roared.

Talus the Dark let out a deafening shout. Elwerth regained her own consciousness for a second before falling, hitting the floor with a loud thump.

"We must get to her," said Terrien to Phinean.

"What have you done? *What have you done?*"

"A bit of wizardry that you will never come to know," shouted Sirien. "I penetrated her body so I could push you from her mind, for good!"

Talus let out another screeching roar. They covered their ears in pain.

The relentless Argom now began to shoot spells menacingly the same way Bartholev had done down in the Main Courtyard. They ducked and covered whenever an icy attack came close to them, debris and dust from the columns covering their heads. Talus mainly focused his attention to Sirien, now being supported by Terrien and Nerod. Phinean dragged Elwerth's unconscious body to a part of the office Talus wasn't focused on dispersing with deadly bolts.

Percivine, Faruin, and Seleborn ran past Talus, who noticed them but soon returned in his attempts to thwart Sirien and Terrien. The three now attacked him from behind, lashing out at him with every bit of strength they could. Percivine casted a curse, which sent little meteor-like formations down upon Talus, popping as they touched the Argom's head. Sirien and Terrien and Nerod made their way to Percivine, Faruin, and Seleborn to help them fend Talus off, now that he was a little disoriented from the curse Percivine used. Phinean casually sent spells every so often at Talus, while shielding the Landseer's body.

"You cannot win!"

Talus screeched something awful from his sharp-toothed mouth and sent them flying against one of the walls. Talus proved himself to be a very worthy combatant, but his patience grew as thin as air.

"*I have had enough! INTRODUCE YOURSELVES TO DEATH!*"

CHAPTER THIRTEEN

A GREAT FRIENDSHIP

Talus the Dark stood at the center of the office with what appeared to be some sort of off-white magic aura enshrouding his body. They knew this could not be good. They quickly gathered themselves and decided to make a run for the doors.

"HA!" said Talus. "You can try to escape!"

The aura unleashed itself, cascading frosty bolts raining down on them. They did their best dodging these bolts and went straight through the office doors, destroying the platform. They could now hear the cries coming from the outside.

"What's all this?" shrieked Irinea Squint, peering in through the newly formed hole in the wall. She can see Talus standing at the center and laughing crazily as they tried to avoid his attacks.

"Stay with Grenden!" shouted Phinean, holding Elwerth. "Do not take your eye off of him!"

She made no rebuttal, just returned to Grenden who squirmed on the floor. She dragged him a little closer to the hole, so she could get a better view of the fight.

"We have to stop him!" said Seleborn.

"Yes, but how?" said Percivine.

No one knew how exactly they were going to put an end to this monstrous being. Talus continued his attacks. Dust and debris rained from all corners of the office.

Among the rioting noise, there was a woman's scream. Percivine and Seleborn rushed to the hole in the wall. Through it Irinea lay gasping on the floor.

"Irinea, what's happened?" asked Seleborn, through the hole.

Grenden was gone. Irinea had been left with a gash by her eye. The door to the Sanction room had been broken into.

Irinea staggered to say anything. With a shaking arm, she gathered what strength she had left and caused the wooden doors to crack and crumble with invisible sorcery.

Seleborn tended to Irinea while Percivine rushed over to the investigators' room. Kalor Foggs was nowhere to be found, either. His bonds had been cut, but by who? And why?

"He's gone, Kalor's gone!" Percivine called to Seleborn, who was helping Irinea against the wall.

"What did you see, Irinea? Who did this to you?"

"I had my back turned," she said slowly. "I should—should have been aware of what was behind m-me. I felt an agonizing sting across my face. I couldn't see their face very clearly. It was covered by a hood. As I lay on the f-floor, I saw the figure rush into our room, and cut Kalor free. The three r-ran off."

"Whoever it was," said Percivine, "knew it was a good chance to grab them while we were occupied with Talus."

"Which we still are!" said Seleborn, almost forgetting the ongoing battle just across the Sanction room.

They rushed back to Elwerth's office. Talus did not show any sign of tiring, however the rest were.

"He's gaining on us," said Nerod Nilius, who'd been hit on the side of his stomach.

"Had enough yet?" Talus called out. "I can go at this all day…but I would rather not. You're wasting my time." He looked over to Phinean and Elwerth. "Stand aside. She is mine."

"You'll have to kill me first," said Phinean, making no hesitation to protect the Landseer.

"If death is what you desire, then I will give it to—"

Talus the Dark did not finish his words. He had been thrown straight to the back of the office, causing another hole in the wall. Astronitus Ogthorne had appeared surrounded by his group.

"Dad!" shouted Sirien. "Was that you?"

"We would have been here sooner, but the Diviport has been smashed. Cosmera told us of the secret passageway you spoke to her out of earlier. We used that, and now we're here. Luckily, I got to you in time before any *real* damage could have been made."

"Thanks, Dad, but he's escaped," said Percivine.

"He may have," said Sirien, "but all is not lost. We prevented his finishing of the ritual, and the prevention of Elwerth's death."

"Don't forget his plans working here in the Administration just might be over," added Seleborn. "Is the battle over down there?"

"Gods no," said Astronitus. "Shall we?"

"I'll stay with the Landseer," said Phinean.

They used the secret passageway, and slowly made their way to the Lobby Level. The Chambers' bronze doors had been severely damaged. As they approached the hologram projector, SB-19 said, "There's no point now, is there? You may come and go as you please. I've had enough for one day."

They pushed their way out into the battlefield. Each went into their own direction. Percivine, Faruin, and Seleborn stood together, forcing away Argoms that came offensively close to them.

Talus was nowhere to be found, and neither were Grenden and Foggs. They saw that Murgoy and Murac had awoken, and now made their way to leave. They chased after them but were too late.

As he made his desertion from the scene, Talus shouted to his fellow Argoms, "Continue the fight! Don't let these disgusting Neledar triumph over you!"

And with that, Talus disappeared behind the Diet Chambers building.

"Let him be!" said Percivine. "Seleborn, listen to me!"

The rage in Seleborn's eyes were plain as day to Percivine. He knew Seleborn wanted ever so badly to annihilate the being that had taken his wife, but he knew Percivine spoke truth. Reasoning to pursue Talus would be fruitless, at this moment him being too far. Besides, the matter of fending off the remaining Argoms before them still exists.

The bloody battle waged on for what felt like an age to Percivine. Night fell. They only had the light from the spells to decipher who was Argom and who was not. After one final blow, the soldiers and the Solemn Hand managed to make the Argoms retreat for their lives, hollering threats after them. The Argom Influence was over, Bolhana had been retaken, and Landseer Elwerth no longer remained controlled by Talus's powers.

Sirien had a quick word with the commanding officer before they began clearing away the dead Argoms to burn.

"Mr. Baine and General Pinch," said the officer of broken armor, "will be pleased to know that tonight was a success. We must get going. We march to Baladin Fortress."

"The best of luck to you," said Sirien. "We'll help you retrieve your dead."

"And you as—I can see you've done well for yourselves. Thank you."

The commanding officer bowed, and rallied his warriors to prepare departure for Ni'shorus to assist the Elves at Baladin.

The warriors placed the wounded and dead into wooden wagons for transport. The remaining soldiers dispersed through the gate of the District, and from openings on the District walls created by the battle.

As much as Percivine hated dealing with dead Argoms, the District must be returned to as it were before the battle. Cosmera insisted they use magic, instead of moving the bodies themselves physically.

Vaureth and Nerod used hover spells to lift the bodies. Before that, Borak stabbed the bodies with his sword to ensure they were indeed dead. They put the corpses into a mountainous pile and lit it on fire. The smoke lifting into the air from the dead Argoms was a sign of victory that all of Nell would know.

Irinea limped to them through the broken bronze doors, blood dripping from the gash she sustained earlier.

"Landseer Elwerth has come around," she said. "She would like to speak with you."

"Go on, son," said Astronitus to Sirien. "The rest of us will stay down here and finish up. Take your brother with you."

Percivine and Sirien followed Irinea through the mess, through the secret passageway, and up to the top floor. Irinea went ahead. Slowly stepping past the broken doors to Elwerth's office, they saw Phinean talking to a body laid on a floating bed.

"They're here, Landseer," said Irinea.

"Bring…them to me," said the faint voice of Estith Elwerth, a weak finger signaling them in.

"Come," Irinea called to them.

They quietly walked down the carpet surrounded by the many columns. Brick and rubble lay everywhere.

A heavy breathing escaped the wrinkly mouth of Elwerth. Her black hair with streaks of white in it hung from the sides of the bed. Some of the purpleness of her skin faded.

They were greeted by Elwerth's green eyes. Estith Elwerth forced herself upright. She wanted to speak clearer to them.

"You're weak, Landseer," said Phinean. "Lay back down, please."

"Nonsense," said Elwerth. "If I want to speak with them this way, then so be it."

Phinean said not a word, and moved out of the way.

"So…" she said. "I see you've made a mess of things. It's going to take ages to repair the damage done."

Was this her way of thanking them? If it was, then Percivine would rather much see dead Argoms burning.

Elwerth beamed. "However, your boldness and bravery have, undoubtedly, saved my life," she said thankfully. "The Head Investigator here has informed me of your plan, Sirien Ogthorne. I daresay you acted with the utmost illegality that it is simply a crime speaking to you, *but*, yet again, I must remind myself all that you did to rescue my life. I see no reason to dawdle on the matter any longer. Right, Fernius?"

The shrunken, hunched investigator said nothing, but agreed with the Landseer.

"I thank you with the greatest praise I can possibly give," Elwerth said, struggling to keep her stature firm. "Thank you."

"It was not I, alone, that saved you, Landseer," said Sirien. "I had help. Every and each member of the Solemn Hand helped me. Not to forget the aid Fernius Phinean and Irinea Squint so bravely gave."

"Ah," said Elwerth. "Fernius failed to mention that he had partaken in any of this."

Phinean cleared his throat.

"You will all be generously rewarded," said Elwerth, "once I have spoken to King Erelon. I think I should see the King right away. But your faces…tell me otherwise. What has happened to our monarch?"

"Landseer," said Sirien, "the King…the King has been on a forced…extended holiday…"

"The King's got to be somewhere," she said. "How is this possible?"

"We had rather remained on the hope that you, Landseer, knew of his whereabouts," said Sirien. "It is futile of us to have thought that."

"I don't know anything," said Elwerth, a little more aware of her surroundings. "When I was under that Minthrys's control, I wasn't aware of what I was doing, was I?"

"I suppose not," said Sirien.

"Where are Fioriul and Ignius? So much to do, so much to do. I have a lot to speak with them about. They should be here next to me." Elwerth examined their sullen, silent expressions. "Don't tell me they've disappeared, as well?"

They nodded.

"They disappeared months ago," said Percivine. "Some recent information revealed they are currently entombed in Nerwold Hold."

"We have much more to tell," said Sirien. With every ounce of strength she possessed, she heard everything Sirien had to tell from the Violet Veil Accord to the Argom Influence and everything in between. In grave tones, he explained Grenden's and Fogg's betrayal, alongside Darus Dillory and Tenaius Hendlen, who were guarding the cells of Elwerth's In and Out Secretaries. "Those are the names of who we know. There could be several more still among these ranks."

Elwerth seemed appalled that the Service, dutied to keep control of the law of Nell, had concealed so much darkness.

"Fernius," said Elwerth, "have an envoy sent to Nerwold to free my Staff and to have those two arrested."

"I don't know about arresting, Landseer," said Sirien. "I'm sure by the time the envoy reaches the Hold they will have become aware of what's happened."

"Very well," she said.

"Now, Landseer, we have told you everything we know so far. You must tell us everything you remember can remember prior to Talus's control," said Seleborn. "What is the last memory you hold?"

"The last...Let's see...Well," she said, rubbing her head, "the last thing I did *on my own*...Oh yes—I remember now! I left Avalon Imbartus' office. He's the Head of the Mediation Service, you know? We had discussed Ambassador Dibble's envoy to the Goblin Empire of Zal'man...But no...there was something else...Right! I had taken a walk to Daraman's Park, like I normally do with Iwyn...She had gone and—and Vulryc came about...Now that we're talking about this, I'd like a word with them. Fernius, would you go and fetch them for me?"

"Er—Landseer, Mr. Imbartus died a few weeks ago," said Phinean.

"He and Vulryc were murdered. And Iwyn disappeared years ago, not a trace of hers to be found."

"I'm—I'm so sorry to hear that," said Elwerth. "Iwyn was so young, so full of life and Avalon—a good man he was, as was Vulryc. How did Mr. Imbartus die?"

"You had made an appointment of a one Bartholev, who was nothing more than a murderer for *their side*, and his orders were to kill the man. Shelina Sendrik of the Service suffered the same fate."

"It seems many died, while that vile creature had me controlled," said Elwerth.

"Afraid so, Landseer," said Sirien.

Percivine heard a hissing noise. He looked back to see a man with long black hair pointing at Irinea.

"Irinea," whispered Percivine, "I think he wants a word."

Irinea left the room without a noise. All Percivine could hear was the faint whispers between the two like Murgoy's and Murac's previously.

"After the meeting, everything seemed to go dark," said Elwerth. "I can make out slight occurrences when it seemed I had regained my senses, but nothing in between until now. It all seemed like a bad dream."

"A nightmare," said Sirien. "The worst isn't over, however, Landseer. The Violet Veil Accord with the Argoms must be rescinded. You must implore the House to terminate that abomination. They will still have protections here in Nell, while the treaty is in effect."

"I will attend to that immediately! Make no mistake," she added. "The war will continue to send them back to the holes they slithered out from!"

"Might I suggest something a bit more lenient?" said Sirien.

"What do you have in mind?" asked Elwerth, rubbing the temples of her head. The effects of the Minthrys still dwelt.

"The retraction of the treaty will compel whatever remaining Argoms to flee back to Argoth, as I'm sure most are doing right now, where I suspect the Orcs—*and* others—will be waiting on them. They will return. When? We haven't the slightest, but from what I can theorize they are not going to waste anytime configuring a new plan of assault. We are not at peace, Landseer, therefore, you must dub this moment until we fight again as the Recelacrum—a term of my making; a recess from warfare for the time being."

"Very well," said Elwerth. "As my Out Secretary is indisposed momentarily, someone must write this down on parchment so that the Recelacrum begins officially."

"Might I suggest the reinstatement of the Solerel's Guards," said Sirien.

"The Solerel Guard?" said Elwerth. "Where've they gone?"

"That we do not know, Landseer," said Percivine.

"Might've been banished back to the Arxinium at the Dothdir Crescent…" said Sirien.

"Landseer, also," said Phinean, "I highly recommend you disband and remove the Intelligence Service from our ranks."

"The Intelligence Service?" said Elwerth.

"Yes, the Intelligence Service was created by Talus the Dark to hunt and silence enemies of his administration. He implanted Bartholev as its head, and this gave him unlimited, unsupervised power."

"Disgusting," said Elwerth. "And you said he was responsible for the killings?"

"Yes," said Sirien. "Our friend Seleborn, in his outstanding grasp of the Warlock arts, disposed of that rat."

"A Warlock?" said Elwerth. "I have never met a real Warlock before. There kind is rather scarce around here."

"He was happy to oblige us," said Percivine.

Irinea burst into view. "Landseer, most wondrous news has arrived!"

"Well, what is it girl, don't keep us waiting!"

"Cowin has just informed me that the search party you requested have reached Nerwold. They have located the cell holding your Support Staff. They're being released now!"

"Wonderful," said Elwerth. "What of the other two?"

"Dillory and Hendlen are nowhere to be found," said Irinea. "There's more, as well. The search party came across a few other individuals. Seems this 'holiday' of the Royal Family's was really a dark, cold, wet cell. Near the Warden's office in the dungeons."

"The King will be furious with," said Elwerth. "Might even have me removed from office."

"Isn't that for the Diet of Nell to decide?" said Sirien. "Besides there's more than enough proof that it wasn't your doing."

"The Diet approves those elected by the people. The King has the authority to remove any from office, though it doesn't happen very often."

"I'm sure he'll understand once it is explained to him that you were not acting on your own accord, but from another's," said Sirien.

"I'll deal with that later," said Elwerth. "Now, if there's anything I can do for you all, just name it."

"There are a few things if you don't mind, Landseer," said Sirien.

"Not at all!" she said happily. "Name it."

"Though we are no military organization," said Sirien modestly, "I would like to continue the operation of the Solemn Hand, without interference."

She stalled.

"Yes, yes, all right," she said hesitantly. "We will not stick our nose in it. But beware: you must still adhere to the laws of the land. Once I have my government back in order, the investigators will return to their normal, standardized practices. Any form of crime will be punished."

"Understood," said Sirien, "and lastly, we request the removal of all charges set upon us by the Administration. We have never worked against the Administration, and would like our records to be kept that way."

"There is no worry to that claim," said Elwerth. "The criminal charges imposed upon you under Talus's government are nonexistent. He therefore no longer serves this post, thus declaring you all exonerated of any previous charges."

Elwerth had saved up enough energy to finally stand on her two feet. She almost fell with the first step, but was saved by the hand of Fernius Phinean. Her head felt light, and she was dazed from it all. She looked all round her to see the awful mess left by the battle. She next looked out a window from her office, and saw the Main Courtyard had also been left in a complete sunder.

"We have a lot of work to do," said Elwerth. "Once Fioriul and Ignius return, we will have to get started right away. I should like to get to know them. Fernius, have the Heads of the Architectural and Gilden Services meet me here in my office at once. The Divination Administration has to be restored to its former glory. Like Landseer Eloran Pinshot once said,

'Good impressions are not only met from within, but how they appear on the outside.' He speaks the truth."

"Right away, Landseer," said Phinean. He bowed slightly to Sirien and the rest, then disappeared through the gaping hole in the wall.

Elwerth turned to Percivine and Sirien. She nodded at them in appreciation.

"I will request to the Treasury Service to reward each member of the Solemn Hand a fair amount of zarks."

"That—that is not necessary, Landseer," said Sirien. "What I asked is all that we need. There is no need—"

"Don't be daft," she said. "Take it. You've earned it."

"That is most generous," said Sirien. "Thank you. Landseer, can I ask one last favor?"

"By all means."

"I would like, for the time being, that our efforts of the Solemn Hand be kept in secret alongside no interference. We'll put our name in the local registrar if we must, but we don't want the Solemn Hand to be mentioned in the parchments, at all."

"Might be a bit difficult," said Elwerth. "After tonight's events, I do not think anyone is going to be absolutely quiet about it." She paused shortly. "And this is your desire?"

"Yes."

"You will be left alone, but your first and only mention will have to appear in tomorrow's morning edition," said Elwerth, as Sirien shrugged. "Now, if you'll excuse yourselves. I have a terrible lot to do now that I've returned. The next few weeks are going to be…interesting, but it has to be done. Oh, and if you happen to see my Oroseer down below, do send him up, will you? Good d—"

"Forgive me," said Percivine, "but I feel I must also ask of you something, Landseer."

Elwerth sat herself down on the floating bed. Percivine swallowed anxiously.

"I have a friend…a friend down there waiting. He's helped much with the reclaiming of the Administration. Goes by Faruin Abrandil. He's been in exile from Ni'shorus for very long and is tied to a heinous crime of which he never committed. Might you, in all your grace, write or speak with the

Triumvirate on his behalf? They'll listen to you rather than anyone else."

"Let me see what I can do," Elwerth said displaying a wrinkly grin.

Irinea offered to escort them to the bottom floor. Terrien and Astronitus waited for them by the hologram projector.

"How was it?" asked Terrien. "How is the Landseer?"

"Splendid, actually," said Percivine. "She's far healthier than she has been in months. Sadly, the same cannot be said about her face."

Irinea tried her hardest not to let out a giggle.

"Good," said Terrien.

"Terrien, the Landseer would like to see you in her office," said Irinea.

"Thank you, Irinea," said Terrien. He turned to Sirien. "Well, I will see you soon, *and*, I would like to inform you that I am to resume my duties with the Solemn Hand—if you'll have me back."

"Of course," said Sirien, encompassing Terrien with a hug.

Terrien smiled and headed off to a secret passageway behind the reception desk.

"Well," said Astronitus Ogthorne, "looks like our work is finished for the moment."

"Looks like it," said Sirien. "Although, we do have a minor problem."

"And what is that?" said Astronitus.

"How the hell are we going to get home?" said Sirien. "I did create an elusive plan, but I failed to include in the plan a way for us to head to Frodrir."

Astronitus laughed. "Not to worry, my boy. Before you called us here, I spoke to Elnius about securing our way home."

"Elnius Bash?" said Sirien. "Haven't heard that name in some time. Surprised he'd lend us aid."

"It took a bit of persuasion to do it," said Astronitus, "but I managed. You see, we are rather good friends, him and I. When we are ready, I will Orb him."

They walked past the broken bronze doors, only to be met by the rest of the Solemn Hand, surrounding them with cheers and whistles of victory.

"Well done, Sirien, well done!" said Cosmera Rodriys.

"Your plan worked!" said Trobius Stout. No one had noticed the small flash in his left hand. "How about we have ourselves a drink? Or two maybe?"

"I agree with the lad," said Dunngarunax Galon. "Did ye see me cousin inside?"

"I'm afraid not, Dunn," said Sirien.

"It was odd," said Seleborn. "We had been informed that Thiurwold would be in meeting. When we arrived at the top floor he was nowhere to be seen."

"Tha's odd," said Dunn, thinking out loud. "I wonder wha' on Gylranor he would be doin' there…of all places…"

Percivine caught a glimpse of Astronitus and Linaus vaguely looking to the other. They knew something had gone wrong with the plan. None of them said a word. They did not want to stir up any hard feelings from Dunn.

"I will see 'im when I arrive back at home, then," said Dunn.

"I'm afraid will we have to hold off on the celebrations, Trobius," said Sirien. "The Argoms have yet to be completely erased from Nell. We have a lot of work to do. For when they attack again, we will be prepared."

"Ah, how about just one?" asked Trobius in high hopes.

"All right, *one*," said Sirien, grabbing the small flask of bourbon from Trobius.

The sounds of their victory cries muffled the voice jumping into Percivine's ear that Astronitus spoke with through his Wayorb.

"Are we ready?" called Astronitus to the jolly members of the Solemn Hand.

One by one they stepped into the portal that just formed itself through the Wayorb. Percivine, Faruin, Seleborn, Sirien, and Astronitus were the last ones to enter.

"In you go, son," said Astronitus.

Sirien turned to his brother. "Let us go, brother."

"You go on ahead," said Percivine. "We'll Orb you when we are ready."

Sirien nodded and happily gazed at his brother. "I owe you my life, Percivine. You go on, Dad. I'll seal the portal."

Astronitus listened to his son, and the shape of their father had vanished beyond the veil of the portal.

"I didn't do anything," said Percivine.

"Yes, you did," said Sirien. "You were the one who helped me the night I stumbled into Headquarters bloodied up. You never gave up on me. With your heart and perseverance, I was able to make my return without death. You showed me that, with the help of others, many great things can be achieved. I now know that I don't always have to work alone when I have a brother that will be there for me through the worst of times, and to guide me whenever I seem to go astray."

"I—I did not know I made y-you feel that way, Sirien," said Percivine, his cheeks being highlighted by pink..

"You do."

"Faruin, Seleborn," said Sirien. "You two have been very fond of my brother since the day you met him, and I owe you my gratitude for that."

"It was no problem at all, Sirien," said Faruin. "We've found a friendship in your esteemed brother."

Sirien said no more, and vanished as well through the portal. The portal closed, and they remained at the Main Courtyard. They walked towards the burning carcasses of the Argoms, watching quietly as the fire burned the flesh from bone.

A gentle breeze played across their faces.

"Well…" said Percivine.

"Well," said Faruin and Seleborn.

"This has certainly been quite a day," said Percivine, as he gazed at the sun pushing up from the horizon. Daylight approached. "I couldn't have imagined anything like this happening five months ago. Such a short time for so much to unfold."

"Much to our surprise, too," said Seleborn.

"I had a word with Elwerth before we departed," said Percivine. "She's going to speak with the Triumvirate regarding your situation. It looks like you may be underway to getting the mark of 'murderer' removed from your record."

"How did you manage that?"

"Who cares?" said Seleborn at the grand news. "Are you not pleased?"

"I am," said Faruin. "But do you really think Ni'shorus is going to listen to Elwerth? They may think she's lost her head. They will not take kindly to her association with a 'murderer.' It will not do me justice, if that is the case."

"You're so cheerful at times, do you know that?" said Percivine.

They laughed and thought about the the dead soldiers who'd fought so bravely defending Nell and its government. Although they were complete strangers, Percivine found it troublesome not to grieve for them.

"They did not die in vain," said Seleborn. "Don't destroy yourself for that, Perci."

"I wish—I wish I could have done more," said Percivine.

"We did all we could do," said Seleborn.

"I have never seen so much death in my life," said Percivine. "When my mother died, I had hoped that would be all the death I ever needed to experience. I still can't fathom this."

"Death is a natural part of life, Perci," said Seleborn. "It is unpreventable. You would have eventually witnessed another death."

"I've seen enough death for one day," hissed Percivine.

"Are you ready to head back to Frodrir?" asked Faruin.

"Gods, yes," said Percivine. He looked to his new friends and could only stare at them, a delicate smile on his face.

"What is it, Perci?" said Seleborn.

"I—I was rather glad that I met you two," said Percivine softly.

"We are rather fond of you too, Perci," said Faruin.

Percivine recalled the day he met them both before stepping foot into the portal. He breathed deeply, and said, "This is going to be a great friendship."

Dunn came into their view, looking quite pale and completely beside himself. "Didn' see me cousin, did ye?"

"We thought you went into the portal?" said Percivine, alarmed.

"Nah, though' I'd look around a bit more," said Dunn. He looked dejected and distracted.

"I'm sorry, Dunn," said Seleborn. "I'm sure…Thiurwold will turn up soon enough."

Percivine pitied Dunn's somber appearance. What could he possibly say to cheer Dunn up? Perhaps Dunn had some similar inclination that Astronitus and Linaus had? Is this why he looks so glum?

Do you still have the parchment you retrieved from Bartholev's corpse?

Percivine's mind voice asked.

The aggression of battle had removed his remembrance of the parchment, prioritizing combat instead. Percivine used his index finger and thumb to pull out the bit of parchment.

"What've you got there, Perci?" asked Faruin, him and Seleborn gathering around Percivine.

Percivine unrolled the parchment, and the faint letters began to burn their mind.

Thiurwold, the island is where I shall meet you.
—U.B.

Their mouths hung agape while their eyes watched Dunn in horror.

"Wha' is it?" said Dunn, sensing an odd feeling in the pit of his stomach. He boldly pulled the parchment from Percivine's grip and examined it. Eyes watering and staring back at them, he said, "Oh no..."

EPILOGUE

THE CALL

Star's Swelter

Meanwhile, far, far away, on the distant lands of Argoth, a group of battered Argoms regrouped in a mountain cave, while heavy rain poured outside.

"My lord, the Orcs are preparing for our arrival," said Murgoy.

"Excellent," murmured Talus, who had suffered a wound to the lower part of his chest in his fight with the Solemn Hand.

"You're injured, my lord," said Murac. "Allow me to look at it—"

"*Get away!*" he snarled. How had they suffered such a humiliating defeat at the hands of lesser beings? "I am fine!"

He was not, of course. He did not want to admit it, but this defeat had set them back farther than he'd planned, especially for the next step. Now, however, he would have to pay the price for his failure from an upper hand.

"My lord," said Murgoy.

"*What is it?*"

"There is—there is someone here…"

Talus quickly removed his hand from his wound, then and turned to face the shadowy figure that had appeared at the opening to the cave, the leaves of the trees behind the stout figure being blown.

"*He* awaits," the figure's thick voice said.

"I don't care if Bel'zan waits, he is just an Orc," spat Talus.

"Not him…the Master," said Thiurwold Galon, removing his black cowl. "Veros has sent word to him of your recent…ah…failures. To make

matters worse for you, the Master will not be pleased to hear of Urian's…
unfortunate death. We had the necromancer where we wanted him, and
you let all that fail."

Talus the Dark clenched his darkened teeth and grunted something
unintelligible.

"Where is Veros?" he asked. "Has he passed through?"

"We've cleared out the Kinship of Eradell from the Fields of
Undiniuf, so he will wait for you at the Gates of Maracath."

"And you are not to come?"

"I don't see how that is any concern of yours, Talus, but if you must
know, I have another task to take care of."

"You've probably been found out by now," sad Talus, forming a
vengeful smirk. "Was it wise to have Bartholev carry that note?"
However, he was secretly pleased to know Thiurwold would not be
accompanying them to the Orcen capitol of Maracath.

"You've stalled long enough," said Thiurwold icily, "you must
depart."

"I will go when I'm ready!" snapped Talus furiously. "I will have no
Dwarf—or scum—give *me* orders!"

Thiurwold, in the last of his patience with Talus, walked slowly to
him. Murgoy and Murac got in his way and were thrown to the sides by
magic. He drew uncomfortably close to Talus, who glared at the Dwarf.

"What are—?" Talus the Dark froze and could not move. "Let go of
me, disgusting Dwarf!"

Thiurwold made no inclination to do so. He saw that Talus's wound
was at perfect height to him, hastily inserted three fingers into the
wound. Talus the Dark gave such a loud scream that all the wildlife in
the trees and in the surrounding areas hiding from the rain got so startled,
they scattered regardless of the pouring conditions.

Panting, Talus fell to the floor. He tried desperately to fight back,
who easily and calmly avoided each miserable icy bolt.

"Now get up," said Thiurwold. "Filthy Argom. And save your breath
for Veros, for I understand you two have quite a history with one another.
You two—pick him up! Now."

"You dare give orders to my Argoms!" spat Talus.

"I do dare, and will continue to do so at my own convenience, when
I see you are falling short of a proper command," Thiurwold said hotly.

"You will pay incredibly for your insults, Dwarf."

"Then so be it," said Thiurwold, unconcerned.

Slowly getting up and beginning to recover, Murgoy and Murac went to aid their weakened leader.

"Go," Thiurwold told them venomously, "it is time you answer the Master."

THE STORY CONTINUES IN BOOK II